MORE THAN

DIANE BARNES

Unlocking New Worlds

More Than
Red Adept Publishing, LLC
104 Bugenfield Court
Garner, NC 27529
http://RedAdeptPublishing.com/
First Print Edition: October 2019

Cover Art by Streetlight Graphics

This is a work of fiction. Names, characters, places, and incidents either are the product of the author's imagination or are used fictitiously, and any resemblance to locales, events, business establishments, or actual persons—living or dead—is entirely coincidental.

For Liza Fleissig. For believing in this story – and my writing.

Chapter 1

This is the day I start my diet, Peggy thinks when she wakes up. It's what she tells herself every morning, but today she means it.

Yesterday, her new physician, Dr. Richardson, pointed at her medical chart. "You are obese, Mrs. Moriarty."

Obese! At most, she needs to lose thirty to forty pounds. That does not make her obese. *Obese* is her old next-door neighbor, Lannie Fitzgerald, who had to have her clothes specially made and drove around the supermarket in one of those motorized carts. Peggy is a long way from that.

Her former physician, Dr. Sheridan, never would have told Peggy she was overweight. She was kind, always asking about Peggy's twins during the exam. Skinny Dr. Richardson, in contrast, made no small talk and didn't even address Peggy by her first name, making her feel old—and fat. Frankly, Peggy is stunned that Dr. Sheridan handed over her practice to such a rude, impersonal young thing. Peggy doesn't want a doctor who's insensitive and prone to exaggeration.

Maybe she should find a new doctor. Yes, that is exactly what she will do today.

Downstairs, footsteps cross the hardwood floor. Peggy glances at the clock. It's 7:17. She struggles to get out of bed, shuffles into the bathroom, and lumbers downstairs to say goodbye to Grace and Greg before they leave for school. As she reaches the last step, her

1

daughter's boyfriend, Julian, beeps his horn three times in quick succession.

Talk about rude. That boy has no manners. She has told him several times not to wake up the entire neighborhood when he comes to pick up the twins.

Peggy steps into the hall and almost trips over her son, who is bending over, picking up his book bag. It's in the exact same place where he dumped it yesterday afternoon. "Did you do your homework?"

"I've got it covered, Ma." He kisses her forehead. "See you tonight."

Got it covered. Peggy's not sure what that means and is about to ask for clarification when the horn blares again. Greg calls his sister's name, grabs his Hudson High letterman jacket off the bench, and opens the front door. He doesn't close it behind him, and Peggy can hear Julian's stereo. In fact, she's sure the entire neighborhood can hear Julian's music. Every morning, it's the same damn song, "Lose Yourself."

Peggy once asked Julian to turn it down, and he shook his head. "Eminem has to be played with the volume up, Mrs. M." *Mrs. M.* As if they have an amicable relationship.

Peggy pulls the door shut so she doesn't have to listen to the noise. She should write a letter to the entire neighborhood, apologizing for Julian's thoughtless behavior. Better yet, she should drag Julian in here by his completely inappropriate ponytail and have him write the letter.

If Patrick were still alive, he would have had a serious talk with Julian the first time the boy showed up to pick up Grace. Peggy imagines Patrick stepping much too close to Julian and speaking in a low, soft voice. "If my daughter ever has a problem with you, you're going to have a problem with me."

She can see Julian's smug look transforming to one of fear as he stutters one of the inane phrases he's overly fond of. "It's all good, sir." Yes, he would definitely address Patrick as *sir* and not as *Mr. M.*

In the kitchen, Grace leans into the refrigerator, studying its contents. She is wearing the outfit Peggy got her for her birthday last week—a high-waisted black skirt and short red cardigan that together accentuate her tiny waist. When she first saw them, Grace claimed the clothes were frumpy and would make her look middle-aged.

"That outfit looks great on you," Peggy says. She can't see Grace's expression, but she imagines it conveys disagreement. "What are you looking for?"

"Something healthy," Grace snaps. She shifts the carton of chocolate milk and then the two-liter bottle of Pepsi and pulls out a small cup of pudding from the back of the top shelf. "We have pudding but no yogurt?"

The horn blares again. If Peggy were dressed, she'd march outside and give Julian a piece of her mind. Grace leans down and pulls open the fruit drawer, where a lone apple rolls around. She grabs it and runs out the door, shouting a farewell to Peggy, who follows her daughter to the door and watches until Julian's black Mustang disappears down the street. With the kids gone, the house is quiet and still. Like every other morning after they leave, Peggy misses the commotion.

A moment later, her phone whistles with a text from Grace: *Greek yogurt, almonds, bananas, spinach for salad, cheese.*

Maybe after Peggy finds a new doctor, she will go grocery shopping. Yes, that's exactly what she will do. Now that Grace and Greg are older, she has a hard time filling her days and worries about what she'll do next year when they're away at college. Although she has been a stay-at-home mom since right before the twins were born, she never wanted to be one. It was Patrick's idea. When he died, Grace and Greg were only four, and Peggy thought it was important to be home with them—and lord knows, that was what Patrick would have wanted. It was one of the reasons his life insurance policy was so big. She can't imagine going back to work now. Not only are her skills outdated, but she also can't imagine who would hire a woman who's been out of the workforce for over eighteen years.

Pleased that she has two items on her agenda today, Peggy settles into her morning. She fires up her laptop and opens a package of brown-sugar Pop-Tarts. She pulls out two before she remembers she's supposed to start her diet, so she puts one back in the box and the other in the toaster. As she waits for the sugary pastry to heat, she makes a cup of coffee and adds a shot of vanilla caramel creamer. She sits at the counter with her breakfast and logs into her health plan's website to search for a new doctor. She would be fine with not having a doctor at all except that she will eventually run out of refills for her blood-pressure prescription.

Peggy wishes the provider directories included photographs of the physicians. She doesn't want a skinny young thing like Dr. Richardson. A doctor with some meat on her bones and gray at her roots would be just fine. Because there are no pictures on the website, Peggy uses first names to estimate age. She skips right over Dr. Courtney Callahan because no one her age is named Courtney. The same goes for Dr. Brittany Kaplan.

Dr. Nancy Levy. Yes, she sounds like she is right around Peggy's age, a few years short of the half-century mark. Maybe this Dr. Levy is even older. Peggy sees the Accepting New Patients icon and calls to make an appointment. The soonest they can get her in for a physical is June 16, four months from now. Peggy books it and cancels her appointment with Dr. Richardson for next month.

Now that she doesn't have to lose five pounds in the next few weeks, she toasts a second Pop-Tart and moves from the kitchen to the couch to catch up on her favorite show, *Messages from Beyond*. It's about a housewife in Tampa who claims that she can communicate with the dead. Peggy doesn't like watching it when the kids are home because they make fun of it and say the medium, Lynda McGarry, is a fraud. Maybe she is, but Peggy likes to think the woman is legit because it allows her to believe that someday, somehow, Patrick will be in touch, and more than anything, Peggy wants to talk to him. In Peggy's favorite episode, Lynda connected a widow from California with her husband, who'd been killed in an automobile crash. He spoke about the first time he'd ever told his wife he loved her, on their second date, at the top of a Ferris wheel. Through Lynda, he said he would love her forever and promised that someday they would be reunited.

More than once, Peggy has fantasized about being on the show and having Lynda reach Patrick. He would tell Peggy he loves her and to keep an eye on the kids. She can hear him clearly. *Head on a swivel, Pegsta. Can't be too careful. You got to watch them at all times.* If she listens closely, she can hear his Long Island accent.

She wanted to go with him on his trip to San Francisco, but he thought the kids were too young to leave with a sitter for a few nights and insisted she stay home. They fought about it for weeks. Thank God she wasn't on that plane with him. What would have become of her children? Since then, she's barely taken her eyes off them. Even when they don't know it, she's watching them. Today, after her show ends, she returns to the kitchen, pours another cup of coffee, toasts another Pop-Tart, and logs on to Instagram to search for their latest photos. It's her favorite part of her morning ritual. She scrolls through several shots before coming to one of Grace, posted forty-five minutes ago. In the picture, Grace is wearing a bright-blue skirt she most definitely did not leave the house in—a skirt Peggy has never seen before. It's so short that she's sure the principal will be calling or emailing to discuss it. Grace is also wearing a sweater with a plunging neckline revealing more cleavage than Peggy realized her daughter had. She's sitting on a table in the cafeteria with Julian, whose hand rests high on her exposed thigh.

As Peggy looks at the snapshot, rage gushes through her, and she accidentally bites her tongue while chewing her Pop-Tart. She gulps her coffee while thinking about how to handle this. The answer comes to her quickly. She edges off the stool and wobbles upstairs to get dressed.

Less than a half hour later, she's standing in the school office, demanding that the secretary page Grace. The secretary's high-pitched voice soon sounds over the PA system. "Grace Moriarty, please come to the office immediately. Grace Moriarty, to the office."

As Peggy waits for her daughter, she momentarily thinks that perhaps she should have waited until Grace got home from school to address this. Then Grace rushes through the door. The skirt is even shorter than Peggy thought.

Grace looks at the secretary. "What's going on?"

The secretary shrugs and points at Peggy, who is leaning against the wall on the other side of the room.

"Mom, is everything all right?"

"Where are the clothes you left the house in this morning?"

Grace squeezes her eyes shut and opens them wide. "What?"

"Where did you get that skirt?"

The phone in the office rings, but the secretary makes no move to answer it. Peggy shoots her a pointed look, and the secretary grabs the receiver. "Hudson High."

"I want you to go to the restroom and change back into what you were wearing when you left the house this morning." Peggy keeps her voice low.

Grace's eyes well up with tears. "Mom, you're embarrassing me. Just go home."

"Change, come back here, and hand me the outfit you're wearing."

The secretary finishes the phone call. She and Grace stare at Peggy with expressions of disbelief.

"It's the middle of English. I have to get back to class." Grace steps toward the door.

"I will follow you to your English class." Peggy means it. She imagines all the students looking up at her with their mouths gaping. Grace would never forgive her.

Grace freezes. *She's trying to figure out if I'm serious,* Peggy thinks. *Go ahead—test me.*

The office door squeaks open, and Julian appears. He does a double take when he sees Peggy and hurries to Grace's side. "Everything okay?"

"Everything's fine, Julian," Peggy answers.

The secretary smiles at Julian. Her big, goofy grin annoys Peggy because it's completely inappropriate for the situation.

"My mother's a psycho," Grace says to Julian, storming by Peggy and out the office door. Julian follows close behind her.

The secretary studies Peggy without saying anything.

"That wasn't what she was wearing when she left the house," Peggy says.

"I gathered that." The secretary straightens a pile of papers while continuing to watch Peggy as if she's thinking, *That's Grace and Greg's mom, overreacting again.*

More than one parent at this school has told her that she is too strict with the twins. "You need to give them space." That's what she often hears. But no, she doesn't. She knows how quickly life can change. She learned that thirteen years ago when Patrick boarded the plane for California.

The secretary clears her throat. "All the girls wear outfits like that. Really, I've seen a lot worse."

Peggy doesn't care what anyone else is wearing or what anyone else thinks. She doesn't want her daughter dressing in skimpy skirts and sweaters with plunging necklines. She wishes the secretary would stop staring at her. She's sick of the way people in this Massachusetts town look at her with their judgmental eyes. People in the Midwest, where she grew up, would never be so rude.

Peggy leaves the office to wait for Grace in the hallway. The bell rings, and soon, waves of laughing students stream by. Grace approaches from the other end of the hall in the black skirt and red sweater that Peggy bought her. She is almost running. "What are you doing out here? Why didn't you stay in the office? Haven't you embarrassed me enough?" Grace flings the plastic bag with the offending clothes at Peggy.

"Where did you get that outfit?"

"Oh my God, Mom. Just go home."

Some of the kids in the hallway slow down to watch Peggy and Grace. Peggy steps backward and leans against the lockers. "Not until you tell me where you got that outfit."

Grace folds her arms across her chest. "Carmen bought it for me. She took me shopping for my birthday."

Peggy knows all of Grace's and Greg's friends. She has never heard that name before. "Carmen?"

Grace sighs. "Julian's mother."

Peggy doesn't like her children being disrespectful. She taught them to call their friends' parents *Mr.* and *Mrs.* "Don't refer to her by her first name, Grace. To you, she is Mrs. Tavarez."

Grace throws up her hands. "She's the one who told me to call her Carmen. She said Mrs. Tavarez is Julian's grandmother."

Of course, Julian's mother is that *mother.*

As Peggy leaves the school, she runs into Greg's girlfriend, Allison Parker. "Hi, Mrs. Moriarty." Allison beams. "What brings you here?"

Peggy notes Allison's friendly smile and cute preppie cloth-ing—a skirt that hits her knees and a blouse under a classic cardigan. "I had to see Grace."

"Did you find her? I think she has Spanish now."

"We spoke," Peggy says.

A bell rings. "I'd better get to class," Allison says. "Nice seeing you."

On the drive across town, Peggy can't help thinking how much easier her life would be if Allison were her daughter instead of Grace. She feels guilty for the thought, and when she gets home, she imme-diately toasts another Pop-Tart, her fourth on this first day of her di-et. She devours it while watching a second episode of *Messages from Beyond*.

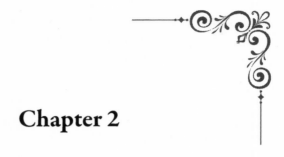

Chapter 2

Greg jumps up from the sofa and rushes to the living room door to help Peggy. "Thanks, Mom," he says, taking the tray of sandwiches.

She places the chips on the coffee table. Greg's friend Aidan reaches into the bowl for a handful. "You're the best, Mrs. Moriarty."

She winks at him. "What do you boys want to drink?"

Greg's best friend, Tyler, who doesn't take his eyes off the video game he's playing, responds, "Can you make some of those milkshakes you made last time we were here?"

Peggy was hoping they would not ask for milkshakes. Just this morning, she told Grace she would start her diet for real today, not like last week when she first tried, and there's no way she can resist a milkshake, especially a thick chocolate one. The year the kids started kindergarten, she drank so many of them that the man who worked at the Hudson Dairy Joy nicknamed her Mrs. Chocolate Milkshake. She started making them at home after that and became an expert. If she whips up the ice cream drinks for the boys now, she knows she will have one herself. Maybe she should refuse.

"Yeah, no one makes milkshakes like you, Mrs. Moriarty," Aidan adds.

Well, how can she say no now? She will be strong. She will practice self-restraint.

In the kitchen, she scoops eight heaping spoonfuls of chocolate ice cream into the blender. It's Friendly's, her favorite. Surely, one tiny bite won't hurt her diet. She stuffs an overflowing spoonful into her mouth. *So much for being strong.* She adds a little bit of milk and a few squirts of chocolate syrup into the mixer. Before pressing the on switch, she squeezes a few drops of the Hershey's syrup onto the spoon and licks it clean. She hears the boys laughing over the noise of the blender. The sound makes her smile. She loves that Greg and his friends congregate in her living room. Their deep voices, rapid-fire laughter, and playful roughhousing fill her house with life, a stark contrast to the painful silence that taints the place when Greg and Grace are at school.

She watches the contents of the blender swirl together, its color changing from tan to deep brown. She hits the off button and squeezes in more syrup and lets it mix for another few seconds. She switches off the machine, pours a small amount into a tall glass, and sips it. *Mmm, ecstasy in a glass.* She refills her cup, this time to the top. She can always start her diet tomorrow. She guzzles down the milkshake, pulling it away from her mouth only when the iciness of the drink rises to her temples, making her head feel like it's about to explode. Her hand shoots to her forehead, and she doubles over in pain. When the feeling subsides, she straightens herself and turns to get glasses for the boys. That's when she notices Grace. The dirty look her daughter gives her makes Peggy feel as if Grace caught her shooting a heroin-filled needle into her vein.

"Brain freeze," Peggy says, hoping Grace's sour expression means she's worried, not disgusted.

"Aren't you supposed to be on a diet?"

"Had to make sure it was good before I give it to the boys."

Grace folds her arms across her chest. Ever since she started dating Julian, she's become a nutrition Nazi. Peggy's not sure why. It's not as if Julian eats healthy. The boy stuffs himself with cookies and candy every time he visits.

"Mom, your blood pressure. You need to lose weight," Grace finally says.

Rude Dr. Richardson did say losing weight would help bring down Peggy's blood pressure, but the creamy goodness of ice cream makes her happy and helps her relax. Surely, that helps lower it as well. The doorbell rings, and Grace leaves the room without further comment.

A second later, Peggy hears Julian's voice and smells his overpowering leather-scented cologne. She asked him once if he knew he wasn't supposed to use the entire bottle in one application, and he laughed. "Good one, Mrs. M."

Grace, of course, defended him. "I love the way he smells." Peggy doesn't. To her, he smells like bad intentions.

Julian and Grace are talking in a hushed tone. Peggy slows her movements so that she can listen, but she can't make out their words. Finally, Julian says, with his normal volume, "Ask her." Then, suddenly, he is standing beside Peggy in the kitchen with his hand on her shoulder. "What you making, Mrs. M?" Instead of waiting for an answer, Julian reaches for one of the drinks Peggy poured and takes a sip. "Ahhh. Wish my mom cooked like you." He squeezes Peggy's shoulder.

She shakes his hand off, not liking how at ease he is with touching her. If he feels this comfortable with her, she can only imagine how he is with Grace. The thought causes her to shudder and quickly turn back to the task at hand. She pours another glass and attempts to carry all three into the living room.

"Let me help you, Mrs. M," Julian says, taking two cups from her.

As Peggy and Julian place the beverages on the coffee table in the living room, the boys all stand. Soon, they are slapping their palms with Julian in a gesture that is half handshake, half high five.

"What's up, men?" Julian asks. He is the same age as Greg, Aidan, and Tyler but somehow seems much older. Maybe it's because of the cologne. Greg and his buddies don't wear it, and this is one of the many reasons Peggy trusts them more than she trusts Julian Tavarez.

"We're just hanging," Greg answers. "Mom made us lunch." He points to the tray, where there is one sandwich left. Julian grabs it and plops down on the couch.

Peggy returns to the kitchen to clean up the mess. Grace is sitting at the counter, eating an apple. She grins at her mother. Peggy's antenna goes up because she knows all the ways Grace tries to manipulate her and is sure her daughter is about to ask for something Peggy will not want to grant. She plays along with Grace and returns the smile while grabbing the blender to bring to the sink.

Grace waits until Peggy's back is to her before speaking. "Carmen invite—" She stops and starts over. "Mrs. Tavarez invited me to go skiing with them at Sunday River next weekend."

Peggy fills the blender with hot water. "That's awfully far to go for the day."

"We're leaving Friday after school and coming back Sunday night."

Peggy yanks the faucet off and turns toward her daughter. "You're asking to go away with Julian for the weekend?"

"With Julian's family." Grace bites into her apple and crunches loudly.

"No." Peggy's voice is sharp. The look she gives her daughter is sharper.

Grace stands and stomps across the room toward her mother. The way her daughter's green eyes flash reminds Peggy so much of Patrick when he was angry that she has to grab hold of the counter to steady herself. Other than the blond hair that she inherited from Peggy, Grace's features are all her father's. Sometimes it hurts Peggy to look at her.

Grace has at least two inches on Peggy and stares down at her as she spits out her words. "I knew you'd say no. You never want me to have fun. You want me to be as miserable as you are." She flings her apple core into the trash.

No one could be as miserable as I am. The thought startles Peggy, and she wonders where it came from. "You're much too young to go away with your boyfriend for the weekend."

"His parents will be there."

Peggy turns back to the sink. She shakes her head, thinking about Carmen Tavarez, the woman who bought Grace that slutty outfit, chaperoning her daughter and her touchy-feely son for the weekend. *No way!*

"I'm plenty old enough. I'm leaving for college soon."

"I said no."

Julian enters the kitchen, carrying the empty plates and glasses. "Everything okay in here?"

"I told you she wouldn't let me go." Grace stalks out of the room.

"My parents will be there." Julian's words are punctuated by the sound of the front door slamming. "Think about it at least." He squeezes Peggy's shoulder again before leaving to catch up with Grace.

TWO DAYS LATER, WHEN Peggy logs on to Facebook, she notices a friend request. She excitedly clicks on it, wondering if one of her old high school or college friends in Chicago wants to get back in touch. Most of them stopped calling shortly after Patrick died. Peggy doesn't blame them. The conversations were awkward, with Peggy either breaking down in tears or acting much too cheerful. But the request is not from an old classmate. It's from Carmen Tavarez. The photo on her profile is of Julian holding a small girl's hand.

Why would Julian's mother want to be Peggy's Facebook friend? Well, clearly, a woman who lets her son's seventeen-year-old girl-friend call her by her first name and takes her shopping for inappropriate clothing is desperate for friends.

Carmen has written a short message with the request. "The kids are spending so much time together that I thought it would be nice for us to get to know each other. Perhaps we could meet for coffee?"

Ha! Peggy is certain Grace put Carmen up to this. She imagines Julian and Grace sulking in a living room with Mrs. Tavarez, who in Peggy's head looks like a younger, ugly version of Rita Moreno. *My mother is such a bitch*, imaginary Grace says. *She won't let me come skiing. Maybe you could talk to her.*

Peggy pictures Mrs. Tavarez nodding. *Leave it to me.*

Well, Peggy has no intention of letting Grace go skiing, but she is curious about Julian's mother and would like to meet the woman. She might even ask Mrs. Tavarez to speak to Julian about the horn blowing and loud music. Should she mention the cologne?

Peggy accepts the friend request and tells Carmen that she would be thrilled to meet her. Via Facebook messages, they arrange to get together the following day at Holy Grounds, a coffee shop on Main Street next to Our Lady of Fatima and across the street from the hair salon where Carmen works.

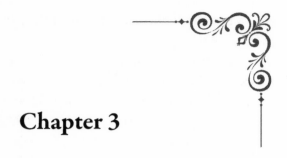

Chapter 3

Peggy arrives at the coffee shop fifteen minutes early, which is ridiculous, considering it's only a few miles from her house. When she pushes the door open, a bell rings, and the man behind the counter looks over at her. Peggy nods. His eyes travel up and down her body, and his mouth twists to a snarl before he turns away. *Well, who was he expecting, Angelina Jolie?*

She glances around the room, looking for Carmen. There is only one other customer, a hefty middle-aged man wearing a grimy Red Sox cap. As Peggy walks by him, he pushes his seat back and stands, bumping her. "My bad," he says, patting her shoulder and grinning.

She bristles and scowls at him. It was bad enough that he accidentally bumped her. Did he have to intentionally touch her too? He grabs his coat off the back of the chair and flees, going out into the arctic air without putting it on. She chooses the table next to the one he abandoned and watches through the window as he pauses on the sidewalk to slip into his jacket. He must feel her looking at him, because he turns toward the window and waves then sets off.

Well, now she feels guilty she wasn't nicer.

Peggy doesn't want to interact with the barista after the dirty look he gave her, but she hasn't had any coffee this morning and knows she'll need some to get her through this meeting with Julian's mother. She feels the waistband of her jeans cutting into her gut as she approaches the counter. Greg tried to help out by doing laundry and put her pants in the dryer, where Peggy is certain they shrank.

She'll have to get new ones. She arrives at the cash register and studies the menu board.

The barista approaches. "Can I help you?"

His voice is high and nasally. Peggy wonders if his wire-rimmed glasses are pinching the bridge of his nose, causing it to sound that way. She orders a large caramel macchiato. As he turns away to fill her order, Peggy notices he's wearing skinny jeans. She didn't realize they made those for men. *Why would a man want to showcase that he has thin legs and not bulky, muscular ones?* She herself would never wear those kinds of jeans because they would show how big her legs are. Well, that, and they would never fit her.

While she waits for her coffee, she studies the pastries in the display case. Her stomach growls and her mouth waters as she looks at the blueberry muffins, apple turnovers, and chocolate chip cookies. She spots cream-cheese brownies in the bottom right-hand corner. They are her absolute favorite. Greg loves them too. Maybe she'll get one for him. The barista returns with her drink, and she adds a brownie to her order for Greg. As she waits for her change, she imagines herself watching Greg eat his treat and desperately wanting a bite, which he reluctantly offers because he feels obligated. Why go through all that when she can get her own?

"Excuse me."

The barista turns from the cash register.

"I'll actually take two of those," she says, thinking of the gooey chocolate and smooth cream cheese warmly melting in her mouth.

As he tosses another brownie into the bag, he chuckles to himself.

"What?" Peggy asks.

"Enjoy."

As Peggy returns to the table, a young Latina woman wearing jeans tucked into stylish tall black leather boots rushes through the door. She's wearing a black version of the ski coat that Grace and all her friends have in bright colors. She smiles, walking toward Peggy. When she reaches the table, she stops. "Peggy?"

"Yes?" Peggy wonders if this is one of the kids' friends that she doesn't recognize.

The woman extends her hand. "Carmen Tavarez. So nice to meet you."

There's no way this twenty-five-year-old woman is Julian's mother. His sister, maybe, but mother? Not a chance. Wondering what trick Grace and Julian might be trying to pull, Peggy picks up her drink. As she tilts the cup toward her mouth, a stream of coffee trickles from under the lid and spills onto her sweatshirt and the table. The barista must not have put the cover on correctly. The woman claiming to be Carmen rushes to the counter to grab a bunch of napkins. When she returns, she hands some of them to Peggy and wipes the table with the rest. Peggy studies her carefully. There is not a wrinkle on her face or a strand of gray in her long, wavy dark hair. Her waist and hips are so small that there is no way she could have pushed out a baby. Surely, Grace and Julian are playing her, but why? Do they really think this girl will convince her to let Grace go away for the weekend with Julian? Peggy has no intention of saying yes to that, but she decides to play along anyway.

"Do you mind if I ask how old you are?" she asks when they are both seated again. Ordinarily, she would never ask someone—especially a female—her age, but in this case, she feels the question is warranted.

"I get that a lot," Carmen says. "I had Julian when I was very young."

"How young?"

Carmen exhales deliberately and folds her hands on the table. She looks Peggy in the eye. The women stare at each other without speaking for several seconds. "How old do you think I am?" she finally asks.

"Twenty-eight. Maybe younger."

Carmen laughs. "So I had Julian when I was ten?"

"Exactly," Peggy says. "Look, I don't know who you are or what Grace and Julian are up to but—"

Carmen interrupts. "Thirty-five."

Peggy does the math. "You had Julian when you were seventeen?"

Carmen nods. "It worked out fine. Julian is a great kid, and Antonio and I are still together."

Peggy stares at Carmen but doesn't say anything.

"You don't believe me?" Carmen reaches into her pocketbook and pulls out her wallet. She flips it open so her license is showing and hands it to Peggy, who studies the birth date. Sure enough, Carmen is telling the truth.

Peggy closes the wallet and hands it back. "I'm sorry. You look much younger than thirty-five. I was sure the kids were playing some type of trick on me."

"Why would they do that?"

Peggy stares at her, surprised. "They're teenagers." She thinks back to the summer, when Grace told her she was going to a movie with her girlfriends but instead went to a concert that Peggy had forbidden her to attend. Peggy learned about the lie when she was doing the laundry and found the ticket stub in the pocket of Grace's jeans.

Carmen stands. "Excuse me. I need some water." She makes her way to the counter. The hipster barista dude greets her with a cheerful "Good morning" and a huge grin.

Based on the way he treated Peggy, she would have sworn he didn't know how to smile. She reaches into the pastry bag and breaks off a corner of the brownie. She greedily swallows the bite and returns her hand to the bag. This time, she pulls out the whole brownie and places it on a napkin.

Carmen returns with her water and looks pointedly at Peggy's snack. "Would you like a piece?" Peggy asks.

Carmen shakes her head. "Looks good, but too much sugar for me."

Of course this super-fit woman doesn't eat cream-cheese brownies. A thought comes to Peggy. "Grace has been eating a lot healthier since she started dating Julian."

Carmen cocks her head. "That's a good thing, isn't it?"

Peggy breaks off another piece. "I suppose."

"Grace is a wonderful girl. I think the world of her. She's so good for Julian, and she's great with Sophia too."

Peggy stares blankly, so Carmen adds, "My daughter. She's three."

The two sit in awkward silence. Carmen sips her water while Peggy chews. Peggy should say something nice back. The problem is, she can't think of anything good to say about Julian.

"Grace is going through a stage," she finally says. "She's been very temperamental lately."

Carmen laughs. "Well, she's a teenage girl. Weren't we all like that at one point?"

No. Peggy was never rude to her mother. *That*, she is sure of. Her sister, Mary, on the other hand, gave her mother ulcers—sneaking out the bedroom window to meet her friends late at night, missing curfew, getting caught with a fake ID so she could buy alcohol. "You're my good one, Peggy," her mother always told her. Peggy has never told Greg he is her good one, but she has certainly thought it on several occasions.

"I think she hates me," Peggy confesses. "I mean, really hates me. We used to talk. We don't anymore. Not since she started dating Julian." That came out more accusatory than Peggy meant. Carmen returns her water bottle to the table with a thud. "I didn't mean..."

"I think it's natural for a young woman to pull away from her mother, especially when she's in love."

Peggy shifts in her seat and folds her arms across her chest. "I don't think she's in love. She's seventeen. She doesn't know what love is."

"I was certain I loved Antonio when I was seventeen."

Yeah, and he knocked you up. Peggy's face flushes. She looks down and breaks off another piece of her brownie.

"You know, Peggy, I realize it's probably hard for you to think of Grace as a grown woman, but she is."

"She's a teenager, a high school kid, hardly an adult."

The bell announcing someone has entered the coffee shop rings, and a loud male voice shouts, "Get them to come down on price, and don't call me back until you do." Peggy glances toward the door, and Carmen looks over her shoulder. A man dressed in a business suit but no winter jacket has entered the café.

Carmen shakes her head and turns back to Peggy. "People have no manners when it comes to those devices."

This is the first thing that Carmen has said that Peggy agrees with, so she smiles. For the next few minutes, the two women talk amicably, but then Carmen ruins the cordial conversation. "So Grace tells me that you didn't like the outfit I gave her."

Peggy's worst suspicions are confirmed—Grace talks to Carmen about her. "Look," she says, "I know you were trying to be nice, but in the future, I'd appreciate it if you didn't buy clothing for her."

Carmen leans forward. "The skirt was a little short but nothing outrageous." Peggy says nothing, and Carmen continues. "Perhaps the problem is you still think of Grace as your little girl instead of the lovely young woman she's become."

"She'll always be my little girl," Peggy says. An image of Grace as a sweet toddler flashes through her mind, but then she sees the snarling teenager her daughter is today—always with Julian by her side—and begins to feel uneasy. Her brownie is gone, and she seriously considers reaching into the bag for Greg's.

"When I was her age, I already had Julian," Carmen says—as if that's what Peggy would want to hear from the mother of the boy dating her daughter. Peggy wonders if Carmen is trying to goad her. She concentrates on not choking on her coffee.

Carmen repeatedly twists the cap on her water bottle. "What I'm trying to say is perhaps the reins are too tight. You have to start letting go. Grace will be leaving for college in the fall."

Peggy clears her throat. "I don't need your advice. You know nothing about raising a teenage girl. Boys are much easier." She thinks of Greg with his quick smile and even temperament.

"Ah, yes, Grace mentioned you are not as tough on her brother."

"Greg is a good kid," Peggy says.

"And so is Grace."

Peggy has had just about enough of Carmen Tavarez. Meeting was not a good idea. "I should get going," she says, even though she has nothing else to do today.

"We would really like to take Grace skiing with us. Not only would Julian be thrilled, but so would Sophia."

"I'm afraid that's not going to happen." Peggy reaches for her coat. Carmen stands. It's impossible not to notice how tall and lean she is. Peggy feels like Humpty Dumpty standing next to her. "Goodbye." She takes a step away from the table.

Carmen reaches for her arm. "Will you at least consider it?"

Peggy smiles brightly. "Nope."

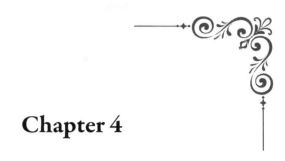

Chapter 4

The identical bulky envelopes with the return address from Saint Michael's College in Vermont both arrive on the same day. One is for Grace, the other for Greg. Peggy considers shoving them back in the mailbox or tearing them into tiny pieces. She knows exactly what the letters will say and what they mean. Her twins, her babies, will be abandoning her in the fall, moving more than two hundred miles away, and leaving her alone in this split-level ranch that is much too big for three people, never mind one.

Peggy holds the envelopes tentatively by her fingertips, as if she is afraid of being contaminated by them, and slowly walks back up the icy driveway. Maybe she should drop them, kick a pile of snow over them. She imagines Grace and Greg finding the soggy letters weeks from now after the monstrous snowbanks melt. "I don't know how they could have ended up there," Peggy will say.

Her eyes tear up as she inches toward the house. She tells herself they are watering because of the glare from the sun reflecting off the snow. She should be happy that her kids are staying in New England and that the two of them will be together, but there are so many schools in the Boston area that they could have chosen. They picked Saint Michael's because it's Patrick's alma mater. He would be thrilled by their choice. A few days after Greg sent his application, he found one of Patrick's old St. Michael's Purple Knights sweatshirts in the basement and has been wearing it on weekends ever since. Peggy is certain Patrick led Greg to it. Why, just last night, she watched an episode of *Messages from Beyond* in which a woman found her deceased mother's engagement ring in an old coffee can filled with loose coins. Up until then, the woman had been certain her sister-in-law had stolen it and had even accused her. Of course, the situation caused a rift in the family. Lynda McGarry said the dead mother helped the woman find the ring so that the family would reconcile. She said ghosts did those sorts of things often.

Peggy's face heats up as she thinks about Lynda's remark. *Shouldn't Patrick do something to help with Grace?* If Patrick could read her thoughts, he would be exasperated. She pictures the slight twitch in his cheek as he says, *I'm dead, Pegsta. You're gonna have to handle this on your own.*

Back inside the house, Peggy tosses the envelopes onto the kitchen counter, where Greg is certain to see them. Grace might not. Usually, when she gets home, she rushes straight to her bedroom and slams her door. She's been extra surly over the past few weeks since Peggy met with Carmen and said Grace couldn't go skiing.

"Even Carmen said you're unreasonable!" Grace cried, causing Peggy to begrudge the woman even more.

Peggy fired off an email to Carmen. *Please don't speak disparagingly about me to my daughter.*

Carmen promptly replied with a single question mark.

Peggy's fingers flew across the keyboard as she typed a response, but then common sense prevailed, and she closed her laptop without sending the message. If she runs into Carmen, though, she will give her a piece of her mind. She's even looking forward to the confrontation.

PEGGY IS FOLDING LAUNDRY on the couch when she hears tires crackling on snow and an engine running. She knows it's Grace because Greg is at hockey practice. Several minutes later, when her daughter still hasn't entered the house, Peggy gets up and goes to the living room window. She pushes the curtain back just far enough to see Julian's car in the driveway. He and Grace are talking in the front seat. Julian glances at the house and waves at Peggy, who lets go of the curtain and steps out of sight.

Well, now she's done it. Grace will accuse her of spying. Peggy sighs, grabs the empty bag of chips off the table, and makes her way to the kitchen to start dinner. She is kneeling on the floor, pulling a frying pan out of a lower cabinet, when the front door bangs shut. Grace doesn't call out "Hello," but Peggy can hear her stomping up the stairs and the loud bang of her bedroom door slamming.

Enough! With one hand, Peggy grips the countertop and uses it for leverage to lift herself off the floor, feeling an ache in her lower back. Once on her feet, she spins toward the stove and deposits the frying pan on the front burner with a thud. As she makes her way out of the kitchen toward the stairway, music suddenly blares from Grace's room—well, Grace and Greg would call it music, but to Peggy, it's audio diarrhea. She grips the railing tightly as she climbs the stairs. When she reaches Grace's door, she pauses to catch her breath before knocking. Grace does not respond, so Peggy, assuming Grace can't hear over her stereo, pushes the door open.

"Get out! Shut the door!" Grace screams. Peggy freezes, stunned to see her daughter wearing a sexy red matching underwear-and-bra set. Grace, who is standing in front of her bureau, pulls a sweatshirt from a drawer and drapes it in front of herself. She turns to face Peggy. "Get out!"

"Sorry," Peggy mutters, backing out of the room and closing the door behind her. Peggy, who does Grace's laundry, has never seen that lacy bra or those panties. *A thong, for crying out loud.* Her first thought is that Carmen purchased them for her daughter, but she realizes even Carmen would have better sense than that. Grace bought them, or maybe Julian gave them to her as a gift. The sour-cream-and-onion chips churn in Peggy's stomach.

She pounds on the door again. The music stops, and Grace says, "What?"

"Get dressed, and come downstairs."

Twenty-five minutes later, Grace saunters into the kitchen, which smells like the ground beef Peggy is browning. "Mom, you can't barge in my room anytime you want."

"I knocked." Peggy sprinkles taco seasoning into the pan and mixes the contents with a wooden spoon.

"What did you want?" Grace asks over the sound of the sizzling meat.

Peggy turns to see her daughter standing with her hands on her hips, staring at her through narrowed eyes. Pointing at Grace with the wooden spoon, Peggy snaps, "I don't like your attitude. You'd better change it quick, or you and I are going to have a big problem."

"Whatever." Grace steps toward the door.

"Grace!"

Grace sighs and faces Peggy again.

Peggy clears her throat. "Are you...?" She stops and looks at the floor. "Are you sleeping with Julian?"

"Oh. My. God! I can't believe you just asked me that."

Peggy can't believe it either, but she needs to know. She lifts her head and meets her daughter's eyes. "I hope you're not, but if you are, we need to talk about birth control."

Grace closes her mouth and bites down on her lip. After several seconds, she speaks. "We don't have to talk about birth control."

As Grace stares at her mother defiantly, a list of follow-up questions runs through Peggy's mind like credits at the end of a movie. *We don't have to talk about it because you're not sleeping with him? Because you're already pregnant? Because you already have birth control? Because you'd rather talk to Carmen?*

She's deciding what to ask when Grace breaks the silence. "Are we done? Can I go back to my room?"

Realizing she won't get any information out of Grace no matter what she asks, Peggy turns her attention back to the stove.

You did a fine job of handling that, Pegsta, she imagines Patrick saying in the sarcastic tone she found funny as long as he wasn't using it on her.

"Well, what would you do?" she asks out loud as some of the meat flies over the side of the pan and onto the granite countertop. She loosens her grip on the spoon and slows her stirring motion.

BALANCING A PLATE ON her lap, Peggy sits on the couch, watching *Messages from Beyond.* Even though she has seen this episode before, she doesn't change the channel, because seeing Lynda McGarry make contact with the deceased comforts Peggy in a way not much else does. She is certain that if she went to Florida to watch the show in person, Lynda would relay a message from Patrick. She has often thought about calling for tickets, but who would she go with, and how would she get to Florida? She hasn't been on a plane since before Patrick died.

In the show that's on now, Lynda connects parents in Texas with their son Mark, a soldier killed in Iraq. He joined the military as a way to pay for his college education because his parents refused to foot the bill. The worst part is that they had more than enough money to pay his tuition. Mark's message to his parents is that they should forgive themselves.

"But does he forgive us?" his distraught mother wants to know.

"There's nothing to forgive." Lynda answers so quickly that Peggy suspects the words are her own and not the dead son's.

The show breaks for a commercial, and at the same time, Peggy's front door swings open. She hears it bounce against the doorstop and then Greg's voice saying, "I'm starving." She shuts off the television as he steps into the living room and drops his hockey bag at the entrance. He sniffs loudly. "Tacos?"

Peggy nods while she finishes chewing. A dollop of sour cream drips out of the shell onto her black sweatpants. She swipes it up with her finger and licks it off. "I made you a plate. It's on the stove."

Greg returns a few seconds later with the two envelopes, one opened, the other still sealed. "I got in!" He rushes to the couch to hand Peggy his letter. "Gracie!" Greg screams at the stairway. "Your letter from St. Mike's is here."

Holding the stationery, Peggy feels her heart pounding as she reads. *Dear Mr. Moriarty, I am delighted to inform you...* Beads of perspiration collect above her upper lip. The words on the page blur. She tries to swallow, but her throat is too dry. She drops the letter and grabs her soda. She downs the cola in two quick gulps. *This is really happening. They're leaving me. I'm going to be all alone in this house.*

"Gracie!" This time, Greg walks to the stairway and yells up.

Grace's door clicks open, and she glides down the stairs. Greg hands her the envelope. Grace doesn't look at her mother as she tears it open and pulls out the letter. Peggy could swear her daughter's eyes are glowing as they move across the page.

"Yes!" Grace looks directly at Peggy and waves the letter high above her head. "My ticket out of here!"

Peggy flinches as if she's been slapped. Grace hugs her brother and runs back to her room, probably to call Julian or Carmen.

Greg returns to the couch and sits next to Peggy. "You okay, Mom? You don't look so good."

Peggy's eyes well up. *Ridiculous. They're not leaving for another six months.*

"I'm going to miss my kids," she says.

Greg wraps his arm around his mother's shoulders. "We're not going that far. We're just a car ride away."

"Maybe I'll move to Vermont."

Greg laughs. Peggy wonders if he would think it were funny if he knew how many online searches for homes in Vermont she has done over the past few months.

Chapter 5

Cars line both sides of Orchard Avenue, so Peggy has to park the next block over. The heat from earlier in the day has not let up, and sweat drips down her back as she huffs and puffs her way down the street. She can't believe it's already the end of May and Grace and Greg's senior year is coming to an end. Tonight, they are attending their senior prom. She has been invited to the before party at Julian's house so she can see all the kids in their gowns and tuxedos. She wishes the twins had taken pictures at her house so that she didn't have to come here. She'd much rather be home on the couch in her air-conditioned living room, watching the two new episodes of *Messages from Beyond* that are waiting for her on the DVR.

She is several houses away from the party when the strap on one of her sandals breaks, making it unwearable. Peggy curses under her breath and thinks about returning home to change shoes but decides instead to ask Carmen for tape or a safety pin to hold the strap in place. Barefoot, she resumes walking.

As she approaches Julian's driveway, the song echoing through the neighborhood becomes louder. She pauses by his Mustang to take in the house. She never would have guessed that a boy with a hipster ponytail and a tattoo on his shoulder, with a mother who dresses and acts like a teenager, lives in this classic colonial with a two-car garage and beautiful landscaping. She pictured him in one of the town's triple-deckers or tiny bungalows.

She follows the noise around the side of the house and pauses by the open fence gate to take in the scene. The backyard is decorated in Hudson High colors, red and gold. A sign taped to the fence reads Welcome Seniors. Helium balloons tied to the backs of folding chairs dance high in the air. Plastic tablecloths cover small round tables. Teenage girls dressed in long colorful gowns, some of which have sequins, stand talking to boys in tuxedos with cummerbunds and bowties. A few feet from them, groups of adults, more casually dressed, ooh and aah over the teenagers.

By a flower bed to the right, a photographer snaps pictures of a boy and girl Peggy doesn't recognize. She searches the crowd for Grace and Greg but doesn't see them. She wants to find them fast so that she can get home to watch Lynda McGarry connect spirits with their living loved ones. Peggy straightens her shoulders and inhales deeply. With her shoes still in her hand, she advances through the gate and makes her way into the crowded backyard.

"Peggy!" a voice calls over the music.

She looks up to see Carmen leaning over the railing of a deck. Before Peggy can respond, Carmen races down the stairs. Seconds later, she is standing in front of Peggy. She wraps her arms around Peggy's shoulders. Peggy keeps her hands stiffly by her sides, tightening the grip on her shoes.

Carmen takes a small step back and smiles brightly. "I'm so glad you made it."

Peggy nods, taking in Carmen's red sleeveless dress with the plunging neckline, and wonders if Carmen knows that the prom is for the kids and not the parents. Then again, she wouldn't be surprised if Aidan, Tyler, or another of Greg's friends asked Carmen to the prom. Just last week, she overheard them talking about Julian's mother.

"She is smoking hot," Aidan said.

"I'd definitely do her," Tyler agreed.

"A little Mrs. Robinson action," Greg added.

"Who's Mrs. Robinson, dude?" Tyler and Aidan both asked.

"*The Graduate*." That information was met with silence. "Never mind. Anyway, you shouldn't be talking about Julian's mother like that, even if she is a MILF." He laughed while his friends high-fived him. Later, Peggy googled the term and was horrified by what she read.

Now she looks down at her shapeless sundress and back at Carmen's curve-hugging dress and ridiculous cleavage. *No wonder the boys talk about her that way.* "Where are Grace and Greg?"

"They're around somewhere." Carmen glances toward a group of teenagers congregating by a table with bowls of chips and salsa, trays of sliced fruit, plates of crackers and cheese, and bottles of water. A man in Ray Ban sunglasses walks from the food toward Carmen and Peggy. The first four buttons of his shirt are undone, revealing a heavy gold chain nestled in thick dark chest hair. He's wearing a matching chain on his right wrist and a bulky gold ring with a red stone on his finger. "Well, look at you," he says, placing an arm around Carmen's waist and giving her a kiss that lands on the corner of her mouth as she turns her head away. "You look more beautiful than all these girls dressed for prom." His hand settles on Carmen's backside.

She shoots Peggy a look of disgust while stepping away from his touch. Peggy's amazed by how quickly Carmen creates distance between herself and the man and figures Julian's mother has plenty of experience dealing with unwanted attention. Peggy thinks about when she was younger and thinner and the focus of the same type of attention. She can't remember the last time a man looked at her that way. This man hasn't even glanced at her. She wonders if Patrick would still find her attractive.

"Do you know Peggy?" Carmen asks.

He tears his eyes off Carmen and glances at Peggy. "Nope."

"This is Jonathan. Alex Monroe's dad," Carmen says, touching Peggy's arm and turning back to the man. "Peggy is Grace and Greg's mom."

Jonathan looks at Peggy again. He lifts his sunglasses into his hair. His eyes meet Peggy's and slowly travel down her body and back up to her face. "Grace is your daughter?"

"Why is that so surprising?" Peggy imagines throwing her shoes at him or maybe beating him over the head with one.

"Grace is gorgeous," Jonathan says.

Every muscle in Peggy's body tenses. She has the distinct impression that this jerk just called her ugly, but that's not what gets her goat. No, it unnerves her to think about creeps like this guy leering at her daughter. "She's a little young for you, slick."

Although there is nothing in Peggy's tone that would suggest she is joking, Carmen and Jonathan both laugh. Carmen puts her hand on Peggy's back and pushes her lightly. "Come. Let's get you a drink." She leads Peggy up the porch steps to a long card table with various bottles of alcohol on it. A tall, muscular Latino man stands behind it. "This is Peggy, Grace's mom," Carmen says to the man. "Peggy, my husband, Antonio."

He comes out from behind the table and embraces Peggy.

So this is who taught Julian how to put on cologne.

"Such a pleasure to meet you. We love Grace and think of her as part of the family," he says.

"Thank you." Peggy struggles to free herself from his hug while wondering if Tavarez means *touch others* in Portuguese.

"Make her something special," Carmen says before disappearing to greet other guests.

Antonio resumes his position behind the table. "What will it be?"

Peggy, who can't remember the last time she had a drink, shrugs.

Antonio winks. "I'll take care of you." He pours a generous amount of tequila into a stainless-steel cocktail shaker and adds green liquid from a glass bottle. He lifts the container above his head and rigorously shakes it. He pours the concoction into a red plastic cup filled with ice and hands it to Peggy. The strong taste instantly takes her back to her honeymoon in Aruba. She and Patrick stayed at an all-inclusive resort and drank margaritas like they were water. At the end of the vacation, Patrick's brother, Sean, picked them up at the airport.

"How was it?" he asked.

"The new Mrs. Moriarty got quite intimate with Jose Cuervo," Patrick answered, kissing his wife on the top of her head.

Peggy gulps the drink down, wishing she could be transported back to that time in her life or that Patrick were here with her now.

"I guess you like it." Antonio reaches for Peggy's glass and fills it again.

Twenty minutes later, she is done with her second drink and back down on the patio with one hand resting on the food table to help keep her balance. She still hasn't seen the twins, and somewhere along the way, she misplaced her shoes. Behind her, she hears her son's distinctive machine-gun-like laugh, and she turns in time to see him, Allison, Julian, and Grace descending the porch stairs. In this moment, Peggy sees the twins exactly as they are—a handsome young man and beautiful young lady. All traces of the kids they once were are gone. Every day without Patrick has seemed like a century, yet the years have gone by in a blur. Just yesterday, she was lying on the living room floor while they pushed Hot Wheels across her back and walked Little People down her legs, and now they are standing here, all grown up. She blinks away the tears that are forming in the corners of her eyes, knowing Grace will kill her if she breaks down crying at the perfect Carmen's house.

Greg catches Peggy's eye and waves. He says something to the others, and they all turn their heads toward her. A dark expression flashes across Grace's face, but she quickly recovers and smiles. It's the no-teeth-showing version of Grace's smile, so Peggy knows it's not real, but still, she is pleased that her daughter is at least pretending to be happy to see her.

The two couples make their way across the patio to Peggy. She breathes in Julian's overpowering leather-scented cologne as he leans in to hug her. Allison and Greg also embrace her, but Grace stands with her arms folded across her chest, staring at Peggy's feet. "Mom, where are your shoes?"

Peggy shrugs. "The strap broke, so I took them off." For some reason, this strikes her as funny, so she giggles. She looks down, and a memory of the Mother Goose rhyme comes to her. She points at her toes. "This little piggy went to the market. This little piggy..."

Grace looks over her shoulder, surveying the people within earshot. "Mom, what's wrong with you?"

"Absolutely nothing." Peggy laughs as she removes a small digital camera from her purse. "The four of you line up."

Grace mumbles something. The only words Peggy understands are "so embarrassing."

"Everyone say cheese," Peggy says, causing herself to laugh harder.

Grace shoots Julian and Greg a worried look.

"My dad's known to be heavy-handed behind the bar," Julian says.

"How much have you had to drink?" Grace asks.

"Oh, for crying out loud. I'm fine. Now, all of you, pose."

Peggy looks through her camera while stepping backward, bumping the table so hard that water bottles tumble off and a bowl of chips smashes to the ground. Conversations stop as people turn to stare. A man in a yellow golf shirt bends to clean up the mess.

"Oh dear," Peggy says.

"Mom, why don't you find a place to sit," Greg says, taking Peggy by the elbow.

She shakes free of his hold. "I'll leave after I take a few pictures."

"Carmen hired a photographer. She'll be sure you get some," Grace says.

"I want some of my own."

"Come on, Grace," Greg says. He, Allison, and Julian pose while Grace remains where she is, staring at Peggy. Julian grabs Grace's hand and pulls her into the shot.

Peggy takes pictures of the four of them, of each couple, and then one of Grace and Greg. As she's taking the last shot, Carmen approaches with a woman holding a camera with a heavy-duty lens.

"Barbara," Carmen says to the woman, "please get a picture of Peggy and her kids."

"Oh God, no," Peggy says.

Carmen dismisses Peggy's response with a wave of her hand. "How many pictures do you have of you and the kids together?"

The only pictures Peggy has with her and the twins are the ones that Patrick took almost fourteen years ago. "No recent ones."

"That's what I thought. Come." Carmen points to a spot on the patio and directs Grace and Greg to stand on each side of Peggy. Greg immediately goes to his spot, but Grace doesn't move.

"Grace," Carmen says, "stand on the other side of your mother."

"This is ridiculous," Grace mumbles, moving in slow motion. Peggy knows if Carmen weren't here, Grace wouldn't agree to this at all.

Barbara snaps a dozen or so pictures of Peggy and both kids and then some of Peggy and Greg. The photographer points at Grace. "Now you and your mother."

"I don't want a prom picture with my mother."

Peggy reaches for Grace's hand. "Well, I would like one. And for just one picture, pretend you like me." *It's true,* she thinks. *My daughter doesn't like me.* To stop herself from crying, Peggy fake laughs.

Grace lets out a deep breath and stands next to her mother. Peggy glances up and sees her daughter smiling without showing her teeth.

Barbara takes three different pictures and is about to put her camera away when Grace grabs Carmen's hand. "Will you take a picture of the two of us?"

The two stand side by side with an arm around each other's waists while Barbara clicks away. Grace smiles widely with her teeth all showing. Peggy's buzz fades a little more each time the camera's shutter opens and closes. She imagines the framed picture of Carmen and Grace on Grace's desk at college.

That's my mother, Grace will tell anyone who looks at the photograph.

But she's Latina, her friends will say.

Yeah, I was adopted, Grace will lie.

Chapter 6

The smell of pot roast and fresh-baked bread floats through the house. Music blasts from Grace's room. Greg races back and forth from his bedroom to the driveway, carrying boxes and suitcases on the way out and loading them into the CRV. Peggy sits motionless on the couch. Tomorrow morning, she is taking the kids to Vermont for their freshman year at Saint Michael's College. She remembers clearly the first time the kindergarten bus stopped at the end of the driveway and the door swung open. Greg marched straight up the stairs and into the bus without looking back, but Grace grabbed hold of her mother's leg and screamed. Peggy had to carry her onto the bus and place her in her seat. As Peggy walked back up the aisle, Grace jumped up and chased after her, latching onto her leg again. Peggy picked up Grace for a second time and deposited her back in the seat. This time, she slid her over on the bench so as to place her on the side closest to the window. Then she persuaded Greg to move from his seat to Grace's so that he was blocking her in.

"It's okay, Gracie," he said. "We're going to school. We're big kids now."

Peggy can still see Grace's tear-streaked face staring out the window as the bus rolled away. It's hard to believe she's the same girl who now has an insulting countdown on the bulletin board in her bedroom that reads, *One day until freedom.*

The screen door bangs closed as Greg comes inside, wiping sweat from his brow. "Get your sister. It's time for dinner," Peggy says. She's not sure he hears her because he runs upstairs without saying anything.

While waiting for the kids, Peggy collects the magazines and mail spread over the table, stacks them in a neat pile, and brings them to the living room, where she deposits them on the arm of the sofa so that she can sort through them later. Back in the kitchen, she sets the table. Above her, feet pound across the floor, and drawers squeak open and slam shut.

As Peggy lifts the lid off the Crock-Pot, the condensation drips onto the counter. She scoops out a carrot and potato with trails of steam coming off them. She brings the spoon to her lips and blows on the vegetables before sliding them into her mouth. They are so soft they practically melt when they touch her tongue. She transfers the meat and vegetables into a large serving bowl, carries it to the table, and goes to the bottom of the stairway. As she calls up to the kids, she realizes they can't hear her over the loud music. She doesn't have the energy to climb the stairs, so she returns to the kitchen, grabs her cell phone off the counter, and texts them both.

A few minutes later, the twins join her at the table. Grace takes her usual seat to Peggy's right while Greg sits to her left. The seat across from Peggy, which she will always think of as Patrick's, remains empty.

"Smells delicious," Greg says.

Grace pokes at her phone as Peggy fills the twins' plates.

"Put that away," Peggy says, fighting the urge to rip the device out of her daughter's hands.

"In a minute. Just telling Julian to come by at seven."

Peggy sighs loudly. "Now."

"Done." Grace slides the phone into her pocket and smiles at her mother. "So, I'm excited to meet Nikki tomorrow," she says, talking about the roommate she chose online.

"I'm dreading meeting Chuck," Greg says. "Even his name is gross."

Peggy slices the bread. "Greg, you need to give him a chance."

Greg uses the serving spoon to scoop more potatoes out of the bowl. "He lives in Vermont. That's all I need to know about him."

"As of tomorrow, we'll be living in Vermont too," Grace says.

"Yeah, but he lives on a farm. With cows and pigs."

"His clothes will probably smell," Grace jokes. She and Greg laugh. Peggy wishes she could press a pause button and prevent this meal from ever ending. Better yet, she'd like to be able to rewind right back to the morning Patrick left for San Francisco.

She pours herself a glass of soda and refills Greg's glass.

"Hey, Mom," he says, "you okay?"

Peggy musters a smile. "My babies are leaving. What will I do without you two?"

Grace picks up the serving spoon and scoops more carrots and potatoes onto her plate. She never has seconds. Peggy wonders if she is nervous about tomorrow.

Grace looks at her mother. "Oh, you're glad I'm going."

"I'm not."

Grace smiles. "Tell the truth, Mother."

"Not even a little," Peggy says.

"Such a liar."

Grace and Greg laugh. Peggy wants to record the sound so she can listen to it repeatedly after they are gone. Grace's phone rings. She pulls it from her pocket and glances down.

"It's Carmen," she announces while standing. "Hello." She leaves the kitchen and jogs back upstairs to her room.

Peggy butters another piece of bread. Greg gets up to load his and Grace's plates into the dishwasher, while Peggy thinks about how her archnemesis Carmen Tavarez has ruined her last dinner with the twins.

"Hey," she calls to Greg as he leaves the kitchen. "I made dessert."

"Be right back."

Peggy finishes eating and clears the rest of the table. Upstairs, Grace gives a belly laugh. Why in the world is that woman calling her daughter? Can't she just leave them alone?

Peggy opens the refrigerator and pulls out the chocolate cream pie she made this afternoon. It's Grace's favorite and hers as well. It may be the one thing they agree on. She carries the pie to the table and cuts three large slices. By the time she hears footsteps on the stairs, she's on her second piece. Greg enters the kitchen first. Grace trails a few steps behind him with her hands clutched behind her back.

"What did she want?" Peggy asks.

"Carmen? To say goodbye. Wish me luck." Grace speaks in the same giddy tone she always uses when talking about Julian's mother.

"How nice," Peggy says, reaching for more pie.

"Yeah, it was," Grace says, clearly missing the sarcasm in Peggy's voice. "We got you something." She brings a small gift bag out from behind her back and places it in front of her mother.

Well, Peggy was not expecting this. Her anger dissipates, and the tears that she's been fighting for the whole day—for months really—fall freely. "You shouldn't have."

"Just open it," Grace instructs, digging into her dessert.

Peggy reaches through the tissue paper and pulls out a hinged double frame. The years streak by as she studies the pictures of her and the twins. The one on the left was taken by Patrick when the kids were three. Grace is wearing a green plaid dress that matches the vest Greg is wearing. Patrick hated it when Peggy dressed them alike because he was afraid it would stunt their individuality. It was one of many child-rearing opinions they disagreed about. After Patrick's death, Peggy never bought them matching outfits again. The photograph on the right is the one Carmen insisted on taking at the pre-prom party, the twins' distinct personalities perfectly captured by Grace's sneer and Greg's smile. Maybe if Peggy had kept dressing them alike, Greg's sunny disposition would have burned through the stormy clouds darkening his sister's personality.

"It's lovely," Peggy says, though she wishes she weren't in the pictures.

"There's more," Grace says.

Peggy reaches back into the bag and pulls out an envelope with an image of a treadmill's belt winding through a heavily wooded area, the words RailTrail Fitness under it. *What is this?* She tears the envelope open, afraid to see what the kids have done. Inside is a bright-orange flyer with a green headline that reads, NO MORE EXCUSES. The text under it describes a boot-camp-style exercise class starting in September. Along with the flyer is a gift certificate good for one twelve-week session.

Peggy has never belonged to a gym. She's never had her toenails ripped out either, but she imagines the two experiences are equally torturous. "Is this a joke?"

"No," Grace and Greg say in unison.

"I won't use this. I hope you can get your money back." She looks directly at Grace as she says it because she has no doubt that this horrible gift was her daughter's idea.

"It's nonrefundable," Grace answers. "Mom, you should do this. You need to do this."

"Why do I need to do it?" Peggy shoves the offending gift back in the bag and flings it to the floor.

Grace slides the picture frame so that it's between her and her mother. She points to young Peggy. "You don't even look like the same person."

Peggy stares down at the photo. She doesn't feel like the same person either. She used to have so much energy, and she was social. She enjoyed connecting with her friends and meeting new people.

These days, all she wants to do is curl up on the couch, watching *Messages from Beyond*. She can't remember the last time she socialized at an event that wasn't related to one of the kids' extracurricular activities.

"You've changed so much that I bet Dad wouldn't even recognize you now," Grace says. She may as well have ripped out Peggy's big toenail.

Greg gasps. "Grace."

The kitchen light flickers. Grace looks up at it. "I'm sorry, but he wouldn't."

Determined not to let Grace see how hurt she is, Peggy forces a smile. "You and Greg don't look the same either."

Grace rolls her eyes. "Don't you want to look like that again?"

"Grace, I would need a time machine, not a gym membership."

"Mom," Greg says, "we were trying to do something nice for you."

"Something nice? It's clear that since you two met Julian's mom, you've been embarrassed by my appearance. I have news for you both—most mothers don't look like Carmen Tavarez." The woman's name tastes bitter in Peggy's mouth, so she takes another bite of pie.

Greg slouches in his chair. Grace looks pointedly at her mother, who scrapes her dish with her fork. "You need to lose weight," Grace says. "We're afraid if you don't, you won't be around to see us finish college. We'll be orphans."

Peggy licks her utensil. "Stop being so dramatic."

"I'm not being dramatic. You breathe hard when you climb stairs. Your face gets bright red when you have to walk a short distance. You sweat walking from the garage to the living room. You have high blood pressure. We're afraid you're going to have a heart attack." Grace's voice cracks, on the verge of tears.

Peggy turns to Greg. His eyes dart toward his sister.

"I'm fine." As Peggy says the words, she hears the dreadful Dr. Richardson's voice. *You are obese, Mrs. Moriarty. You need to get your blood pressure under control. Even a slight weight loss can help lower it.*

"Mom, this would be really good for you. It will give you something to do, and you'll meet people," Greg says.

"Not to mention you'll lose weight," Grace adds.

Barking floats into the kitchen through the screen door. An unleashed dog must have wandered off the bike path and is probably crapping in her backyard now. Earlier today, Peggy stepped in a mess near the bottom of the porch stairs.

"Grace, all women my age need to lose weight. In ten years, you'll be telling Carmen that she should diet." Peggy offers up a silent prayer that Carmen will be out of all their lives long before then.

"You need to exercise," Grace says.

Greg cuts another piece of pie. "At least think about it."

Peggy doesn't want to fight with her kids on their last night home. "How about this. I'll start walking on the bike path. As soon as I get back from Vermont." Surely she can manage that.

"That's a start," Greg says.

"Promise?" Grace asks.

"I do."

Out front, there's music, first soft then louder and louder until it abruptly ends. A car door slams, and Julian's voice calls, "Hello" as the screen door squeaks open and bangs shut.

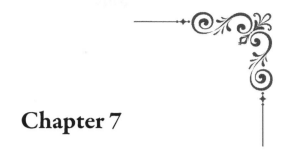

Chapter 7

Peggy and the twins climb into the CRV at ten the next morning. The kids used to argue about who would ride shotgun. Not anymore. Greg sits in the front passenger seat, and Grace slides into the spot behind him and puts her headphones on before they pull out of the driveway. Greg opens a package of brown-sugar Pop-Tarts and hands one to Peggy. Before biting into it, she glances into the rearview mirror, expecting to see a judgmental expression on her daughter's face, but Grace is busy typing into her phone.

Peggy hears a soda can snap open and turns to look at Greg, who is guzzling Red Bull. He didn't get in until two thirty last night, and Peggy is pretty sure he tripped on the staircase on the way up to his room. She heard a bang, and then he cried out in pain. When she got up to check on him, his eyes were red, and he smelled like alcohol.

"Have you been drinking?"

"Give me a break, Ma. It's the last night with my high school friends."

"Sleep it off. We're leaving early tomorrow."

In fact, they were supposed to be on the road at eight, but Greg couldn't get out of bed, and Grace was sluggish.

"Greg," Peggy says as they drive, "I hope you'll make better choices at school than you did last night." She has read horrible stories about hazing rituals in which kids drink themselves to death on college campuses. It's something else she'll have to worry about now.

"Last night was a special occasion. It was the night before I leave for college."

"A special occasion is no excuse for getting drunk."

"Don't worry. I'll be fine." He turns the radio on and tunes it to a station that plays music Peggy can't stand. Like, right now, some guy is singing about being the man. She lowers the volume from the steering wheel. Greg uses the knob on the stereo to turn it back up. He grins at Peggy while singing along.

She playfully slugs his shoulder. "Are you nervous?"

"Nah." He twists in his seat to look at his mother. "You going to be all right here alone?"

"Sure," Peggy lies, flipping on her blinker to turn onto the highway.

"What will you do?" He bites into his Pop-Tart.

"I'm not sure yet."

"How about visiting Aunt Mary or Uncle Sean?"

"I don't think so." Peggy's sister lives clear across the country in Tucson. They see each other every other year when Mary visits for a week in the summer to escape the desert heat. As far as Peggy's concerned, the visits are too often. The two sisters have never been especially close, probably because of their seven-year age difference. Mary never bothered to make time for her little sister and resented the love Peggy's parents showered on the baby of the house. As for Patrick's brother, his contact with Peggy and the twins has dwindled since he left his wife, Kelly, for that Hannah person who's half his age.

"Well, you could go to that boot-camp class," Greg says.

"Don't start with that again," Peggy warns.

Greg raises his hands in mock surrender. Done with his drink and pastry, he reclines in his seat and closes his eyes. Within minutes, he's asleep. Peggy glances in the rearview mirror. Grace is sleeping with her head propped up against the window. A teary-eyed Julian showed up at seven thirty this morning to say goodbye, and Grace has been melancholy ever since. Even Peggy had a lump in her throat as she watched the black Mustang back out of the driveway, its radio—for once—inaudible.

Another song she can't stand comes on, so she changes the station to one that plays older music. "Won't Get Fooled Again" is playing. Patrick loved the Who. Peggy sings along softly, thinking about the day they drove home from the hospital with the twins. Patrick, sitting upright in the driver's seat, clutched the steering wheel with both hands and kept the car in the right lane, never going more than fifty-five miles per hour. Usually, Peggy had to plead with him to slow down as he tailgated the car in front of him before recklessly changing lanes. Peggy sat in the back between the twins' car seats. They slept for most of the ride, but on the curvy exit off the Mass Pike onto Interstate 495, they both woke up wailing. Grace was louder, so she tried to soothe her first. Having no success, she attempted to comfort Greg. Her efforts made him crankier. Their screams were ear piercing. They were crying in stereo. Peggy wanted to cover her ears with her hands and shout with them. She didn't know a thing about babies. How could she take care of two?

Patrick's eyes met hers in the mirror. "Keep calm, Pegsta. Babies cry. It's what they do. We'll figure it out. Together."

And they did figure it out. They had everything running smoothly until Patrick was asked to take that business trip to San Francisco.

UNLOADING THE CAR AT the college takes no time at all because as soon as Peggy parks, a group of upperclassmen approaches the CRV to welcome the Moriarty family to Saint Michael's. Some of the students bring Greg's belongings to Joyce Hall while the others carry Grace's boxes up to the third floor of Ryan. After two trips to Greg's dorm, Peggy takes an armful of Grace's clothes and traipses to

Ryan Hall. The stairway smells like stale beer, and her shoes stick to the rubber-coated flooring.

A man and woman her age descend the stairs as she climbs them. The man has his arm around the woman. "Honey, she'll be fine," he says.

Peggy stops and leans against the railing to rest, wishing there was someone who could comfort her. The woman brushes Peggy's shoulder as she passes, but neither she nor the man acknowledges Peggy, making her feel more alone than ever. Come to think of it, she hasn't seen another single parent. Her lips tremble, and her eyes fill with tears. *Poor Grace and Greg. They lost out on so much.*

When Peggy arrives in Grace's room, her daughter is talking to a dark-haired girl with piercing blue eyes. A man, woman, and smaller girl sit on an already-made twin bed. The woman appears to be at least fifteen years younger than the man.

"Mom, this is my roommate, Nikki," Grace says, taking the clothes from Peggy's hands and carrying them to the closet on the right.

Nikki extends a hand to Peggy. "Nice to meet you, Mrs. Moriarty." She points to the people on the bed. "My dad, sister, and step-mother." She makes the last word sound like a vulgarity.

The man stands. "Frank Mazzone." He points to the woman, who also stands. She towers over her husband. Peggy glances down and notices the woman's spiked heels. She wonders why any sane person would wear those shoes on move-in day. "My wife, Stacey, and my daughter Samantha."

Peggy's mouth goes dry as she hears his Long Island accent. He sounded like Patrick when he said "daughter." *Oh God, Patrick should be here.* She wonders what he would think if he could see the twins moving into his alma mater. Would he be proud of them? Would he be proud of her for the job she did raising them? She imagines him standing behind her, rubbing her shoulders. *You done good, Pegsta. I knew you would.*

Frank says something to her, but she has no idea what.

"Excuse me?"

"Where do you live?" he asks.

She's having a hard time keeping her balance, as if the floor below her is moving. "Hudson. Massachusetts. You?" She needs to sit.

"Clifton Park."

She knew that. Grace told her. So why is she hearing Long Island in his accent? She steps toward the empty bed and stumbles.

Frank catches her, saving her from falling. "Are you all right?"

Grace rushes to Peggy's side.

"I'm a little dizzy. I need to sit."

Frank helps her to the unmade bed.

"It's an emotional day," Peggy says. "Grace is a twin, and I'm leaving her brother here as well."

"Tell me about it. I can't believe I'm the father of a college kid. Unbelievable."

I'm a father, Pegsta. Father of twins. Unbelievable. Patrick was holding Grace while the doctor handed her Greg. Other than his mother's funeral, it was the only time she ever saw Patrick cry.

"Are you sure you're all right?" Frank asks.

"I'll get you some water," Grace says, rushing out of the room.

"Long Island," Peggy whispers. "I hear it in your accent."

He nods. "Right. Lived in East Hampton for the first thirty-two years of my life."

Peggy doesn't respond. Patrick's hometown was Montauk. Grace is back with the water. Her daughter's usually pale complexion is red. Peggy's not sure if it's because Grace is worried about her or embarrassed by her.

"Maybe you should lie down," Grace says as she hands Peggy a plastic cup.

"I'm fine."

"We'll give you some space. Let you get unpacked." Frank motions for his family to head out the door. "Nice meeting you. And, Grace, I'm sure we'll be seeing a lot more of you."

After they're gone, Grace sits in the desk chair. "Going up and down the stairs all those times was probably too much for you."

"He sounded like your father. Had the same accent anyway." Peggy can't hold back her tears, so she lifts her hands to cover her face.

Grace moves so she's next to her mother. She wraps an arm around Peggy's shoulder. "Greg's living in his old room. He called Uncle Sean to find out Dad's old room and then asked for the same one."

Peggy looks up at her daughter. "Why didn't he tell me?"

"I guess he didn't want to make you sad."

Peggy is about to say that it wouldn't have made her sad, but she probably wouldn't be convincing with the tears rolling down her cheeks. So instead, she takes Grace's hand, and the two sit quietly.

PEGGY SPENDS THE AFTERNOON with the twins, exploring Burlington. The day passes much too quickly, and by nighttime, she is back on campus, dropping off her children. She parks the CRV and steps out onto the sidewalk. Though the day was warm, the temperature plummeted twenty degrees after the sun went down, and the air has that crisp fall feel. She wraps her arms around herself.

Dressed in shorts and a tank top, Grace shivers. Greg stands beside her with his hands stuffed into his jeans pockets, bouncing from one foot onto the other. The glow from the streetlamp shines down on them like a spotlight. Peggy studies their faces. Greg has a five-o'clock shadow. Grace's mascara has smeared under her left eye. Peggy wishes he weren't old enough to shave and Grace too young to wear makeup. She wishes they were all home and she were tucking them in and reading a bedtime story.

Laughter breaks out in the distance as a group of students cuts across the grass. Peggy watches them until they disappear into a dormitory. She turns her attention back to her children. "So, this is it." Even as she tells herself not to let the kids see her cry again, tears stream down her cheeks.

"Hey, hey," Greg says, stepping toward his mother. "We'll see you Parents' Weekend." He pulls her into an embrace. She doesn't say anything, just clings to him tightly. Finally, he pulls away. "I love you, Mom."

"Love you more."

He kisses her forehead then turns to Grace. "Let's go. It's freezing out here."

Peggy looks at her daughter, who stares back. Peggy can't believe it—Grace's eyes are moist. "My contact is bothering me," Grace says, raising her hand to wipe away a tear.

"Of course." Peggy smiles at Grace. They both laugh. "Come here." Peggy opens her arms wide. Grace rushes into them. They hug without speaking for a few seconds, and then Grace ends the embrace.

"Are you going to be okay?" Grace asks.

Peggy sniffs loudly. "I'll be fine."

"Take care of yourself, Mom. Remember the walks you promised to take."

"I will."

Peggy steps away from the twins and climbs back into the CRV. They stand on the sidewalk, waving, as she backs out and drives off. Peggy glances at them in the rearview mirror as they walk to their dorms. She's tempted to stop the car, run back to them, scoop them up, and carry them into the vehicle. Instead, she drives faster.

THE BRIGHT-RED HAIR of the woman entering the hotel in front of Peggy looks familiar. Peggy remembers her from campus. The woman steers her oversized suitcase into a pole.

"Could you help me with this, Joe?" she yells.

A man in a Patriots cap, with a small gym bag flung over his shoulder, looks back. "Why the hell did you bring so much for an overnight trip?"

"Just shut up and take it." The redhead stops suddenly, causing Peggy to slam into her.

"Excuse me," Peggy mutters.

"For Christ's sake, Audrey. Get out of people's way!" the man yells.

"Make sure you get a room with two beds," the woman answers.

Peggy scoots around them to the counter. As she checks in, they continue to bicker behind her. Maybe it's not so bad to be by herself after all. When she enters the elevator and pushes the button for the fourth floor, that thought disappears. Even though no one else is in there with her, she feels self-conscious. She has never been to a hotel by herself before. Patrick or the children were always with her.

Inside her room, she turns on the television so that she can hear other voices. *Law and Order* is on. She and Patrick used to watch that together. It was his favorite show. She wonders if it being on the television is a sign that he is here with her now. *Yes,* she decides, *it is.*

After changing into her pajamas, Peggy thumbs through the room-service menu. She took the kids to dinner, and they all had dessert at Ben & Jerry's, but the description of chocolate cake with salted caramel frosting makes Peggy's mouth water. She picks up the phone. Fifteen minutes later, she's tipping the bellboy.

At quarter past ten, she texts the kids to say good night and spends the next several minutes staring at her phone, waiting for a response that never comes. She finally places the phone on the night-stand, turns off the television and lights, and climbs into bed.

Later, she wakes to the sound of a headboard rhythmically hitting the wall. She covers her head with a pillow as a woman moans. What feels like several hours later, the moaning, grunting, and pounding are still going on, so Peggy reaches for the TV remote and presses the power button.

She wonders how she and Patrick would have survived the years together. Would they have been like that couple, unable to get enough of each other? That was certainly what they were like before the twins. Once they had children, Peggy was so exhausted all the time that she would fall asleep as soon as she climbed into bed. Maybe they would have ended up like the couple who checked in behind her, unable to be civil to one another. She thinks about Patrick's brother and Grace's roommate's father and stepmother. Would Patrick have traded her in for a younger, prettier second wife? Would that have hurt more or less than his death?

She remembers Patrick's memorial services. Even in her dazed condition, Peggy clearly heard her sister asking, "Who is that?" Mary pointed to an attractive, fit blonde at the back of the church who was calling attention to herself with her loud sobbing.

The woman Mary was talking to answered, "Patrick's secretary."

Mary's face took on a judgmental expression as she murmured, "Hmmm," through pursed lips.

The secretary was new. *Carly*, Peggy thinks her name was. To this day, Peggy hates her—not because of Mary's implication but because Carly was the one who booked Patrick's flight to San Francisco.

PEGGY WAKES TO THE sound of heavy footsteps above and slamming doors in the hallway outside her room. She glances at the clock. It's eight forty-five. The twins' orientation started at eight thirty. She wonders how they're doing and how their first night in their dorm rooms went. She checks her phone for messages from them, but there are none.

She takes her time showering and getting dressed. Finally, a few minutes before eleven, she checks out.

"I hope you'll come back and stay with us again soon," the woman at the front desk says.

Peggy resists telling her that she would like to take a room permanently or at least for the next four years. Once in her car, she thinks about driving to the campus to see the kids one last time before heading home. She imagines them waiting on the same sidewalk where they said goodbye last night, suitcases beside them.

"Thank God you came back," Grace will say. "We can't stand it here. We want to go home with you."

Before getting on Interstate 89 for the long drive back to Hudson, she stops at a McDonald's drive-through and orders two Egg McMuffins and a coffee. The voice coming through the speaker informs her that breakfast is over, so she changes her order to a Big Mac, fries, and a chocolate shake. She eats the food in the parking lot, and before leaving, she hits the drive-through one last time for a large soda.

Once on the highway, she turns on the radio. She flips through the stations and stops on the song Greg was singing on the ride up about being the man. This time, she sings along.

Chapter 8

Even though she has the queen-sized bed to herself, Peggy sleeps on the left side, confining her entire body to a narrow strip on the edge. She often imagines what Patrick would say about this. *You barely gave me enough room for one butt cheek, and now that it doesn't matter, you've learned to sleep on your side of the bed. Unbelievable, Pegsta.* She pictures him throwing his hands in the air.

Fourteen years after losing him, she still reaches for him sometimes in the fog of first waking up. When her arms collide with his empty side of the bed, cramps rip through her abdomen as if she's hearing about the plane crash all over again. Sometimes just seeing a contrail has that effect too.

Today, on this first day of waking up in the house alone, she feels Patrick's absence more than usual because Grace and Greg aren't here to soften it. She lies in bed, listening to the creaks of the house, sounds she never heard when the kids were here. She wonders how they are adjusting and thinks about calling them. She pictures Grace seeing the word *Mom* flash across her screen and hitting the ignore button.

As she struggles to get out of bed, a sharp pain streaks down the back of her left leg. *Great.* All that time in the car has triggered her sciatica. That walk on the bike path she promised to take will have to wait. She limps down the hall, pauses in front of Greg's open door, and steps in. She'd never know he was gone. The room smells like his sweaty clothes. Hockey trophies line the bureau. His comforter and sheets hang off the unmade bed, and a half-empty bottle of soda sits on his nightstand next to a dish with dried-up remnants of cookies-and-cream ice cream. Papers, pens, and wrappers from protein bars litter his desk. There's also a framed picture of him and Allison at the prom. Allison must have given it to him. Peggy picks it up, wondering why Greg didn't take it with him to school. She'll ask him if he wants her to mail it. As she returns the photograph to the desk, she notices spots of a brown gooey substance on it and on the hardwood floor. The room needs to be sanitized. After breakfast, she will clean it. She feels good about having something on her agenda for today.

Back in the hallway, she stops in front of Grace's partially closed door. She pushes it open, expecting to hear Grace admonishing her for not knocking. The stripped-down space that greets her is worse. Grace took almost everything with her as if she has no intention of ever coming home. Hoping to feel something of her daughter, Peggy steps into the room. All the posters and pictures have been removed from the walls, and in their place are rectangles and squares that are a darker shade of green than the rest of the room. Only the bulletin board remains hanging in its usual spot across from the bed, but it, too, has been cleared of its contents—all but the cut-out piece of poster board that has been pinned to the center since March with the word FREEDOM written in large red letters. Even the Post-it Notes with the ever-decreasing number are gone.

Maybe Peggy will start her own countdown marking off the days until Parents' Weekend. *Forty-one.* She figured it out yesterday on the drive home. What will she do with all that time to herself? She sighs and leaves Grace's room, shutting the door behind her. The closed door will make it easier to pretend that her daughter is home.

Downstairs, she flips on the light. The kitchen brightens, but immediately, there is a buzzing sound. The light flickers, and the room darkens. The bulb has blown. Her first thought is that she will have Greg replace it when he wakes up, but then she remembers Greg is gone. She will have to change it herself. She makes her way to the door leading to the basement and pulls it open. As she steps down, her toe catches on the frayed carpet, and she stumbles. She grabs hold of the railing to steady herself and stares down the staircase. In the seventeen-plus years she has lived in this house, she has been up and down this staircase thousands of times and never once given it a second thought. Today, the steep decline frightens her. What if she falls? She imagines herself lying unconscious on the cement floor, a puddle of blood by her head. Then she realizes it would be worse if she were awake and in pain and unable to get back upstairs. No one would find her for months. She'd be stuck down there with the spiders crawling all over her body, winding webs through her fingers and toes. She climbs back up to the doorway and retreats to the gloomy kitchen. She lifts the shade covering the window of the door leading from the kitchen to the outside deck. Sunlight pours through, illuminating the room. She opens the door and steps onto the deck. A smattering of leaves on the trees separating her backyard from the bike path have changed from green to orange and bright red. Muffled voices and the sound of heavy footsteps pounding pavement float into the yard. Through the branches, Peggy notices streaks of motion as bikers race by.

The rail trail wasn't there when she and Patrick bought the house. She voted against building it, not wanting the pedestrian traffic running through the back of her property. She was on the losing side of the battle, and construction began when the kids were in fourth grade. By the time they reached middle school, the old railroad tracks behind her house were paved. Through the years, Peggy couldn't have been happier the trail was there. Until recently, Grace and Greg used it regularly for rollerblading, running, and biking, which was much better than playing in the streets with all the traffic. She was sorry she ever fought it.

Back inside the kitchen, Peggy notices the flyer and gift certificate for boot camp posted to the refrigerator. Grace must have put them there. Peggy will call the gym later today to see if she can get a refund. In the meantime, she opens the refrigerator, takes out the remaining pie, and heads to the living room to watch back-to-back episodes of *Messages from Beyond*. In the second one, Lynda connects a grieving bride-to-be with her deceased mother. The mother lets the daughter know she wholeheartedly approves of the fiancé and that she will be at the wedding, although her daughter will not be able to see her. A warmth spreads through Peggy's chest as she imagines Patrick's spirit attending the key celebrations of the twins' lives.

Eight hours later, Peggy is still dressed in the black sweatpants and Hudson High T-shirt that she slept in. The empty pie tin sits on the coffee table along with two empty soda cans and a half-eaten family-sized bag of potato chips. She should make herself something for dinner but doesn't feel like cooking, so she picks up the phone to order a pizza.

"CJ's Pizzeria. Pick-up or delivery?" a man's voice booms. Peggy opens her mouth to speak, but no sound comes out. "Hello...?"

Peggy clears her throat. "Delivery." It is six thirty in the evening, and she realizes it's the first word she's spoken all day.

As she waits for the pizza, she flips through the channels and finds *An Officer and a Gentleman* playing on one of the old movie stations. Peggy remembers going to the theater in Chicago with her mother to see this movie. They shared a bucket of popcorn while drooling over Richard Gere. They always agreed on what movie stars were handsome. Peggy is certain that if her mother had ever met Patrick, she would have winked at Peggy and whispered, "He's a looker." Peggy can even see Patrick's cheeks turning crimson. Her mother's whisper was loud.

Peggy has often imagined her mother meeting Patrick in heaven. Sometimes, the introduction takes place on a fluffy white cloud in the middle of a bright-blue sky. Other times, it takes place in heaven's version of the kitchen in the house Peggy grew up in. Patrick brings her mom sunflowers, and she serves him her famous lasagna.

"It's not right that an Irish woman makes such a good Italian dish." His smile widens, and he adds in that sarcastic tone of his, "Too bad you didn't give Pegsta the recipe."

Her imaginary mom laughs but lightly touches Patrick on the shoulder. "Now, Patrick, Peggy is a fine cook. I saw you go back for seconds more often than not."

Peggy is convinced her mother is the one who brought Patrick into her life. She met him a few weeks after her mother's death. It was a sweltering-hot night, and Peggy and her friend Tina had just had dinner together on Chicago's Upper East Side. Peggy was walking back to her apartment across town when the skies opened up, soaking the turquoise sundress that exactly matched her eyes, making it clingier than it already was. She popped into the first place she could find to get out of the rain, O'Grady's Pub. Ordinarily, she would never go to a bar by herself. The place was packed. Peggy stood by the door, looking outside at the rain. She planned to leave as soon as it let up.

As she pulled her long wet blond hair into a ponytail, a voice next to her said, "It's not supposed to end anytime soon. You may as well have a drink." His accent was definitely not Midwestern. She guessed he was from the East Coast, not Chicago. She turned. The first thing she noticed was Patrick's eye color. Emerald green. She had never seen eyes that shade before and wondered if he were wearing colored contacts. He was also sporting a Yankees cap, confirming her suspicion about where he was from. "I'm on my way to the bar. What can I get you?"

"Nothing. I'm fine. But thank you."

He shrugged. "Suit yourself." He turned away from her and made his way through the mob to the bar. Most people had to push and fight their way through the room, but the crowd seemed to magically part for him. A few minutes later, he was back, a bottle of Heineken in one hand and a glass of white wine in the other. He handed her the wine as if she hadn't just declined his offer.

"Why did you get me wine?"

"In case you want it later. You're gonna be here for a while." He tilted his head toward the window. The rain was coming down in sheets, and water was collecting in the street.

"But why wine?"

He shrugged. "I figure a girl like you doesn't drink beer."

It wasn't true. Peggy loved beer and had chugged down two Rolling Rocks at dinner. Her mother had hated that she drank beer and pitched a fit whenever she saw Peggy with it. "A lady doesn't drink beer, Peggy," she'd always said.

PEGGY WAKES TO THE sound of rain the next morning. Even with the window shade pulled up, the kitchen is still dark, so armed with her cell phone, she ventures down the basement stairs for a light bulb, feeling ridiculous that she was afraid to go there yesterday. Still, she grips the banister tightly and makes sure she has both feet securely planted on the same step before advancing to the next.

The cement feels cool on her bare feet as she crosses the basement floor to the back corner of the room. When she gets there, she reaches above her head and pulls on a long white string attached to a fluorescent light. The space brightens so that Peggy can make out the contents on the metal shelves. The first thing she sees is a stack of board games—Apples to Apples, Battleship, Connect Four, Scrabble, Trouble, Life, and on the very top, Monopoly. *God,* how she hated playing that. Grace and Greg would fight about who got to be the dog, and Peggy would have to intervene by saying neither of them could be the dog. Greg was always the banker, and Grace would lose patience with how long it took him to make change when she bought a property. Grace would sulk when Greg refused to make one of the ridiculous trades she would propose. And the games would never end. The twins insisted they continue playing until someone won. For weeks, every night after dinner, they would gather in the living room. Decorated with little green plastic houses and red hotels, the board would remain on the coffee table, the colorful money strewn across the carpet below it. *God,* what Peggy would do for one of those never-ending Monopoly games now.

Back in the kitchen, Peggy stares at the light fixture in the ceiling and tries to figure out how to reach it. She sighs as she pulls a chair away from the table and into the center of the room. *No.* She does not want to stand on it. That's definitely not safe. *Oh, for God's sake.* She wonders when she became such a wimp. But then again, the chair swivels. It's definitely not a good idea for her to climb up on it. She needs something more stable. She returns to the basement to look for the small ladder but can't find it. Back upstairs, she texts Greg to ask him where it is.

His reply is instant: *What do you need it for?*

Peggy answers: *To change the kitchen lightbulb.*

Greg does not respond to this message. The kitchen remains dark.

Later that day, Peggy is lying on the couch, trying to decide what to have for dinner. Once again, she doesn't feel like cooking. Popcorn, she decides. She turns the lights on in the surrounding rooms to illuminate the kitchen so she can search the cabinets for her Pop Secret. She finds what she's looking for and places a bag in the microwave.

It has just started to pop when the doorbell rings, startling her. *Who could possibly be here?* She doesn't want to leave the kitchen because she doesn't want the popcorn to burn, but whoever is at the door is pressing the doorbell over and over again. She mutters about the ringing as she makes her way down the hall. Julian stares into the window by the door. Well, she should have known by the rude doorbell pressing. *What in the world could he want?*

As she reaches the foyer, she can hear the popcorn still popping quickly. She pulls open the door. Julian is holding the missing ladder. Before she has a chance to ask him why he has it, he answers. "Borrowed it to decorate for the pre-prom party."

"That was three months ago," she says, holding open the screen door so that he can enter. The time between pops is getting longer. She has to get back to the kitchen. "Just leave it there." She points to a spot in the foyer.

She watches his ponytail bob from side to side as he shakes his head. She wants to get a pair of scissors and clip it off. She wonders why Carmen doesn't cut her son's hair. *The woman's a hairdresser, for crying out loud.*

Julian moves past Peggy toward the kitchen. In addition to the ladder, he's holding a package of light bulbs. The popping has stopped, and the scent of burnt popcorn now wafts through the air. Peggy rushes past him to stop the microwave.

He follows behind her and sets up the ladder under the light fixture. She wants to protest that she doesn't need his help, but she wants to climb that ladder even less. As he changes the bulb, she pours her burnt dinner into a bowl. When Julian is done, he grabs a handful and stuffs it into his mouth. He carries the ladder downstairs without her asking.

While he's in the basement, she tastes the popcorn. It's charred. She'll have to throw it away and make a new bag or figure out something else to have for supper. When Julian returns to the kitchen, he immediately reaches for more overcooked popcorn.

"Are you hungry?" Peggy asks.

"Starving," he answers with his mouth full.

Peggy hates cooking for just herself, the popcorn is ruined, and he did help with the kitchen light. "Sit. I'll make BLTs."

"You're the best, Mrs. M." Julian takes Grace's seat.

While Peggy fries the bacon and toasts the bread, he tells her about the orientation he attended yesterday at his college in nearby Worcester. Peggy can't help but think how lucky Carmen is. Not only does she still have a young daughter at home, but her son is enrolled in a college just twenty minutes away as well. "I get to build my own robot this year," Julian says. "It's going to be killer."

As they eat, he tells her about all the different things robots are used for. "There's even cuddly robots to help kids with autism." She can tell by how fast he's talking and how much he's using his hands that he's excited. She wonders how she didn't know until tonight that he wants to be an engineer. She assumed he'd take over his father's gas station.

They finish their sandwiches, and Julian gets up to leave. Peggy walks him to the door. "I'll be coming back to Hudson all the time to work for my dad, so call or text if you need anything."

"Thanks, Julian," Peggy says, but she can't imagine that she would ever call him.

"You have my number, right?"

She nods.

"Okay, then." He hugs her quickly before leaving.

Minutes later, sitting on the couch by herself, Peggy wishes she had challenged Julian to a game of Monopoly, one that lasted for days.

Chapter 9

Peggy jerks awake to a high-pitched voice blaring from the television. She rolls her head back and forth, trying to work out a crick in her neck, as the woman on TV blabbers on about the secret to getting rid of saggy arms and shoulders. Peggy lifts herself to a sitting position and glances at the commercial. The woman is quickly rubbing her hands up and down a... Peggy gasps. *What is that?* Did she roll over the remote and accidentally change the channel to an adult station? She leans toward the TV for a better look, but she still can't tell what's in the woman's hand. It's a long, thick cylindrical object with some sort of explosive ball at the end of it.

"Order the Shake Weight now," the announcer says, "and shake yourself into shape."

The commercial is for some sort of fitness device. Peggy laughs, wishing there was someone she could talk to about the absurdity of this ad—or about anything, really.

She glances at the clock. It's three in the morning. Every night since dropping the kids off at school, she has fallen asleep on the couch. She looks around for the remote but can't find it in the mess of candy wrappers and empty chip bags that clutter the area around the sofa. She struggles to her feet, turns off the television, and lumbers upstairs. Tomorrow, she promises herself, she will get dressed and clean the house.

WEARING HER FAVORITE black sweatpants and new St. Michael's College sweatshirt, Peggy attacks the living room with more energy than she has had in the past few days. One by one, she tosses empty chip bags and candy wrappers into a small grocery sack. When she's done, the bag overflows. Peggy stares in disbelief as she ties it shut by the handles. When she was eating all that food, it soothed her, but now she realizes how much she ate. She feels sick. She can't stand to look at the bag, so she trudges out to the garage and buries the evidence deep in the barrel.

Back inside, she gathers the magazines and books spread over the coffee table. Hidden under a pile in the far corner is her wedding album. She took it out before the kids left because Grace asked to see it, probably looking for a picture to fit in the frame. Peggy sinks onto the couch and opens it to the first page. She doesn't remember being the woman staring back at her. Was her hair ever that long or blond? Well, of course she stopped dying it when she was pregnant, and when Grace and Greg were babies, she cut it so it would be easier to take care of. Peggy reaches for a strand of hair and stretches it forward in front of her face so that she can see it. It's certainly not blond. It's not brown either. How would she describe it? *Hmm.* She thinks for several seconds before it comes to her. It's the color of dirty dishwater. She wonders if Crayola makes a crayon for that.

Peggy studies the face of the young bride while running her fingers over her pudgy middle-aged face. The girl in the picture has well-defined cheekbones. What happened to those? Well, apparently she traded them in for an extra chin or two, she thinks as she feels the skin above her neck wobble.

She looks into the bride's bright-blue eyes and marvels at how large they are. Is it possible that over the years her eyes have shrunk while every other part of her has expanded? Her wedding gown was a size 6, and it had to be taken in because it was big in the hips. The last time she went shopping, she had to buy size 16 jeans, the same pants that now cut off circulation around her waist. She looks down her torso and counts three well-defined rolls bulging from under her sweatshirt. *How did this happen?*

Studying the pictures causes a most uncomfortable realization. Her face suddenly feels like it's on fire, her throat contracts, and her breathing becomes fast and shallow. Grace is right—Patrick would not recognize the woman she's become. She can hear him saying, *What the hell happened to you, Pegsta? You auditioning to be the Stay Puft Marshmallow Man's wife?* He loved making references to *Ghostbusters.*

Peggy sighs and turns the page. Patrick stares back at her. She gently runs her index finger over his image while softly speaking his name. With his jet-black hair and bright-green eyes, he looks just as handsome in the picture as she remembers him being. She slams the photo album shut and returns it to the coffee table with a bang. She has always wondered if in the afterlife, people look like they did at the time of their deaths. If you die a child, are you a kid for eternity? Patrick was in the prime of his life when he died.

She remembers what Grace said when she gave her that awful gift certificate for the gym—that she and Greg were worried Peggy was going to have a heart attack. What if she did, and she died today? Would she look like this for eternity? *God*, she hopes not. She doesn't want to spend forever in this oversized body. In fact, she doesn't want to spend another minute in it.

Slowly, she gets to her feet and shuffles to the kitchen. The bright-orange flyer for boot camp hangs on the refrigerator exactly where Grace placed it. Peggy pushes away the magnets holding it in place, takes it down, and reads it for the first time.

The list of exercises may as well be written in Greek. Calisthenics? TRX? Medicine balls, battling ropes? She imagines herself doing jumping jacks. *Surely that's what calisthenics are, right?* Her chest tightens, and a bead of sweat forms on her forehead just thinking about it. Who is she kidding? She can't do this. She leaves the flyer on the counter, grabs a bag of chips and a large glass of soda, and returns to the living room, where she queues up another episode of *Messages from Beyond*.

In this show, Lynda McGarry makes contact with a spirit who offers forgiveness to a loved one. Peggy crunches on a chip and tastes the salt. She remembers fighting with Patrick in the weeks before he died. She wanted to go with him to California because she desperately needed time away from her four-year-old twins.

"What kind of mother wants to be away from her young children for a week?" Patrick asked.

He didn't understand that she needed time to herself. It felt like she hadn't had a moment's rest or any adult time since they were born. She'd been pregnant when she gave up the PR job she loved in Chicago and moved to Boston with him for his career. She planned to go back to work after the kids were born, but he wanted her to wait until they were in school, so she reluctantly agreed to be a stay-at-home mom. For four years, she hadn't been away from them for more than a few hours at a time. Didn't she deserve a break? He didn't think so, and they fought. She screamed and sulked, even pretending to be sleeping when he left that morning because she was too angry to kiss him goodbye.

If she could talk to him now, she would tell him she's sorry. Would he tell her he forgives her? No, Patrick would never say those words. He would say something like, *See? I was right. It's a good thing you didn't come with me.* She imagines him grinning as he says it. If only they could have the opportunity to clear the air.

On TV, the music for the closing credits starts. As it does at the conclusion of every episode, a phone number scrolls across the bottom of the screen. Lynda looks into the camera. "If you would like to be part of our live studio audience, call 800-777-7777. Who knows? Maybe I'll make contact with one of your loved ones."

I'm going to do it, but first, I'm going to get ready for it. I don't want him seeing me like this. She rises from the couch and marches to the kitchen. Her hand shakes as she punches in the phone number.

"RailTrail Fitness," a young female voice answers.

Peggy hangs up. Should she do it? Can she do it? She raised two kids by herself. Of course she can do it. She dials the number again.

"RailTrail Fitness." This time the voice is less enthusiastic.

Peggy clears her throat. "I'm calling about the boot camp."

"Would you like to register?"

Peggy holds the phone without speaking for several seconds.

"Hello, are you still there?"

"I would like—" Peggy stops. "Can I try a class before registering?"

"There's a sample class Saturday morning at nine o'clock."

"I'll be there." Peggy hangs up, wondering if there will be a Shake Weight in class. She hopes there is.

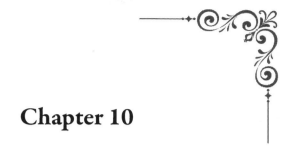

Chapter 10

Peggy reaches into the bag of peanut M&M's she bought this afternoon and pulls out a handful of the oval-shaped candies. She pops a brown one in her mouth and then a yellow. She puts the bright-blue ones in a Ziploc bag on the coffee table in front of her. She's been saving those for Greg since he was five because he insists they taste the best. She will send him a care package with blue M&M's and the cream-cheese brownies she baked earlier this afternoon.

She hasn't come up with anything to send Grace, though she briefly fantasized about bagging the pile of dog poop she found at the bottom of her porch stairs. Her muscles tense as she thinks about her encounter with Carmen Tavarez in the grocery store earlier today. She had to hear how Grace likes school from that woman of all people. *Outrageous.*

"I was with Julian when she called, so naturally, I talked to her," Carmen boasted.

Peggy wanted to shout that there was nothing natural about it. She pictures Carmen standing in the frozen food aisle in her short black shorts and sleeveless blue blouse with a plunging neckline that calls attention to her perky breasts.

Peggy zipped her own hooded sweatshirt higher as Carmen continued. "She seems to be flourishing up there, and that accounting professor sounds like a hottie." Laughing, Carmen touched Peggy on the shoulder, and Peggy fought an overpowering urge to rip the woman's arm out of its socket.

Since she returned home from shopping, Peggy has been envisioning Grace stretched out on her dorm-room bed, lying on top of the green comforter they bought at Bed Bath and Beyond. One hand holds the phone while the other twists her blond hair around a finger. "He's so hot," Grace blurts in that high voice she uses when she's talking to her friends about something that excites her. Imagining Grace using that voice when speaking to Carmen makes Peggy's stomach burn. She tries to remember when Grace last used the high pitch when talking to her. Before Julian, for sure.

Peggy picks up her cell phone and tries her daughter's number but has the same result as the last six times she's called: seven rings and voice mail. "Call me." Peggy hangs up fast, hoping Grace won't be able to hear the tears in her voice.

As always, Peggy receives a text a few minutes later: *Can't talk. Studying. Am fine.*

Peggy forgoes her usual *Miss you* response and instead writes: *Just wanted you to know I'm going to boot camp.* Even as she's typing the words, though, she's having second thoughts about trying Saturday's sample class.

As Peggy puts her phone back on the table, it rings, and her daughter's face flashes across the screen. "I'm so proud of you!" Grace squeals.

Is it Peggy's imagination, or did Grace just use her excited voice?

"When's your first class?" Grace continues.

"I'm going to a sample class Saturday." Peggy says it like she means it, and maybe she really will go. It's only one class, after all.

"Great, so you'll know what to expect when the real session starts."

Peggy doesn't want to lie to her daughter, but this is one of the few amicable conversations they have had in months. "Right. A warm-up class. Got to break in gradually."

"Oh, Mom, this will be so good for you." Yup, Grace is definitely talking in the high-pitched voice. "Make sure you follow the nutrition advice too."

"Planning on it." Peggy feels a tad bit guilty about that lie as she glances at the enormous bag of M&M's.

"What time is the class?" Grace asks.

"Starts at nine."

"Call me after. I want to hear all about it."

Peggy pumps her fist. Her daughter actually wants her to call. "How are classes?"

"A lot of work." Grace has returned to the clipped tone Peggy knows all too well. "Should be working on a paper right now. Talk to you Saturday."

PEGGY HAS BEEN LYING in bed, staring at the clock for the past two hours. It's eight fifteen. If she wants to get to the sample boot-camp class on time, she needs to get up now. She pulls the covers up higher and closes her eyes, wondering if she could fake her way through a conversation with Grace. She tries to remember what the flyer says and pictures herself speaking to Grace the way she bets Carmen does. "TRX was so hard, but I rocked the jumping jacks." What if Grace asks what TRX is? Peggy will google it when she gets up.

Just as she is finally drifting off, a loud crack wakes her. She has no idea what it is. Ever since the kids left, she has noticed that her house makes all kinds of noises. Sometimes, she lets herself believe the sounds are Patrick's ghost floating around from room to room. Every now and then, he smashes into a wall. He was a bit clumsy in life.

God, what would Patrick think about her planning to lie to their daughter? If Grace found out, she'd never forgive Peggy. Then Peggy remembers that she's supposed to be getting herself in shape to make contact with Patrick. She opens her eyes and pushes the covers off. Slowly, she swings her legs over the side of the bed and, with one hand on the headboard, pushes herself to a standing position. *Jeez, getting out of bed is enough of a workout these days.*

That's why you have to do this, Mom, she imagines Grace saying.

On the way to the gym, Peggy passes two Dunkin' Donuts. Both times, she flips on her blinker, steers to the right, and veers back into her lane at the last second. There's nothing she wants more than a chocolate cruller right now, but she will wait until class is over and treat herself to one as a reward.

In the distance, she sees the sign for RailTrail Fitness. Her hands feel sweaty on the steering wheel. She lowers the window to get some fresh air. As the sign gets closer, she taps the brake. The blinker on the sedan in front of her flashes, and the driver turns into the gym. Peggy steps on the gas and races by the vehicle on the left. She can't do this.

As she continues down the road, her cell phone whistles with a text. Even though she knows she shouldn't, she reads the message. It's from Greg. "Grace told me you're going to the gym. Go, Mom!" She tosses the phone back into the passenger seat. She's at the rotary now, and she drives around it, reversing her direction. She told Grace she would do this, so she will.

Peggy circles the gym parking lot a few times, looking for an empty spot near the door, but all the open spaces are at the back of the lot, at least the length of a football field from the entrance. *Who knew so many people exercise?* she thinks as she backs her car in front of a No Parking sign mere feet from the door. For a few minutes, she sits in her Honda, watching people walk in and out. They all look thin, like they should be going to an all-you-can-eat buffet to fatten up and not to the gym to get thinner. There should be a special gym for fatties. Then Peggy wouldn't feel so intimidated. She notices people on the way into the building racing by her with determined expressions, but those on the way out stagger, almost looking lost as they meander back to their vehicles with their sweaty clothes and beet-red faces.

The clock on the dashboard reads 8:57. *Time to do this.* Peggy kills the ignition and pushes her door open. As she steps onto the pavement, her stomach growls. In one hour, she'll be done with this class and can have that donut.

As she gets to the door, someone calls her name. She turns and sees Carmen rushing through the parking lot toward her. *What is she doing here?* Carmen reaches Peggy and drapes an arm around her shoulder. Peggy shakes Carmen's hand off her.

"Grace told me you were coming today. She's so proud of you."

Every muscle in Peggy's body tenses. "When did you speak with my daughter?"

"She emailed me this morning," Carmen says, pulling the door open and waiting for Peggy to enter.

Great. Grace has time to email her boyfriend's mother but not the woman who gave her life.

The girl at the front desk smiles at Carmen. "Good morning." She looks at Peggy. "May I help you?"

"She's with me." Carmen wraps her arm around Peggy again. "We're taking the sample class." The woman opens a drawer and pulls out a stack of papers. Carmen pushes Peggy forward. "Keep moving," she whispers, "or she'll have you here all morning filling out paperwork."

Carmen directs Peggy to a large room in the back right-hand corner of the gym. A group of about ten women huddle together near the front, talking loudly and laughing. Some of them wave at Carmen, who waves back, walking toward them. Peggy retreats to a corner by herself, silently studying the group of women. *Well, apparently people get dressed up to go to the gym,* she thinks, noticing their coordinated outfits, perfectly coiffed hair, and makeup. Peggy didn't even wash her face or brush her hair this morning. As for her clothes, she's wearing the black sweats she lives in and a maroon Hudson Hawks T-shirt Greg gave her for Christmas last year. She looks across the room at the group of women again and then down at herself. *One of these things is not like the other.*

Carmen steps away from the group and toward a wall of cubbyholes with coats and sweatshirts thrown in each one. She removes her jacket, revealing a yellow spandex tank top with greenish piping that is the exact color of her yoga pants. Except for the straps that crisscross below her neck and a thin band above her waist, the tank top is wide-open in the back. *She even has sexy gym clothes. Unbelievable.*

A tall black woman wearing a headset enters the room, and by the way the conversation and laughter suddenly taper off, it's like she has pressed a mute button. All eyes are on her as she climbs the stairs to the raised platform at the front of the room. She smiles brightly. "Good morning, everyone. I'm Shauna Williams. I lead this class, and I'm excited to see so many of you here. Today, we'll do an abbreviated version of the workouts we'll be doing in my boot-camp class starting on Monday." She pauses and points to each woman as she counts the number of people in attendance. "Spread out across the room in three rows of five."

Peggy hides at the far end of the last row, as far away from the instructor as possible and where no one will be able to watch her from behind. To her surprise, Carmen sets up in the spot next to her.

"We're beginning with a brief warm-up. Jumping jacks for sixty seconds," Shauna says.

She fires up music that Peggy doesn't recognize and blows her whistle, indicating that everyone should start. As Peggy does her first jumping jack, her stomach jiggles, and her fat rolls bounce all over.

Three jumping jacks in, she is breathing hard. *How much time has passed?* She glances at the clock. Surely, a minute has gone by.

"Fifteen seconds," Shauna announces.

Fifteen seconds? That's it? Peggy's heart races. Her chest is about to explode. She will die right here in boot camp. Death by jumping jacks. Grace and Greg will feel awful they gave her that gift certificate. Grace will feel awful she wasn't nicer to her mother. Peggy cannot die at the gym. The kids would be ruined.

"Thirty seconds in. You're all doing great," Shauna yells.

Peggy has relaxed her pace. Jumping jacks in slow motion—that's what she's doing. She glances at Carmen, whose jumping jacks look like a video on fast-forward. Carmen catches Peggy staring at her. She smiles brightly. "Doing great, Peg. Doing great."

"Forty-five seconds in."

Sweat drips down Peggy's face. Carmen is not perspiring. Carmen is not human, Peggy decides. Peggy stops moving, puts her hands on her knees and bends at the waist, gasping.

"Time!" Shauna blows the whistle.

Carmen pats Peggy on the back. "You okay?"

Peggy is too winded to speak.

"In ten seconds, we're starting sixty seconds of high knees," Shauna announces.

Peggy has no idea what high knees are. Shauna continues speaking, but Peggy isn't listening. She's trying to find an escape route. She shouldn't have picked this spot so far away from the door. Everyone will see her leave. She imagines these well-dressed exercising women, who are not breathing hard or sweating, pointing and laughing as she makes her exit. *Your mother only lasted sixty seconds,* she pictures Carmen telling Grace.

Shauna blows the whistle. Peggy looks up. Women all around her are running in place, lifting each knee to their chests. She stands completely still watching them. Well, they are all at least half her age and half her size. No wonder they have no problems doing this.

"You, in the Hudson Hawks shirt," Shauna yells. Peggy glances over at her. "Lift each knee to your chest. Move at your own pace, but move." Shauna says the last two words in an unnaturally deep voice that compels Peggy into action.

Next Shauna instructs the group to do push-ups, but she comes off the platform and leads Peggy to a wall to show her how to do vertical push-ups against it. Shauna modifies the remaining exercises for Peggy as well, and somehow, Peggy makes it through the rest of the class. Sure, she stops many times for water breaks and makes one trip to the restroom, taking her sweet time, but she stays at the gym for the entire hour.

"Grace is going to be so proud of you," Carmen says as the two leave the gym.

"I'm sure you'll tell her all about it."

Carmen shakes her head. "No. I think she'd rather hear about it from you." They reach Peggy's car. A piece of paper sticks out from under the windshield wiper. "See you Monday," Carmen says as Peggy grabs the paper.

Peggy doesn't answer because she's reading the note: *Next time, please park in a designated spot.*

Next time, indeed.

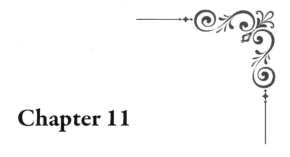

Chapter 11

The day after Peggy attends the boot-camp sample class, she wakes up stiff all over but feeling more refreshed than she has in decades. She actually slept through the night. That hasn't happened since before she was pregnant with the twins. She has so much energy that she varies her morning routine, showering and dressing before going downstairs to eat.

In the kitchen, she makes herself a cup of coffee and toasts two Pop-Tarts. Instead of eating them on the sofa while watching *Messages from Beyond*, she relaxes at the table on the deck. It's warmer than she anticipated, so she takes off her St. Michael's sweatshirt and drapes it over the back of the chair. Although the weather is nice today, she knows by the smattering of orange and yellow leaves that cooler temperatures are right around the corner. As she eats her breakfast, voices from the bike path drift into the backyard. She has yet to go for the daily walk that she told Grace she would take. She briefly considers going today, but when she reaches for her mug, she is reminded of how sore she is.

Something rustles in the bushes separating her property from the bike path, and she turns her head in that direction. A black lab scampers into her backyard. *So this is the little bugger that's been using my lawn for its morning constitutional.* She leaps to her feet as the dog races toward the porch stairs and crouches.

"Don't you dare," Peggy hisses.

"Wally," a male voice calls. "Get back here." An enormous man wearing a Red Sox cap barrels into the backyard as the dog charges up the steps and jumps on Peggy. The animal's paws rest on her chest as it licks her face. She stumbles backward, trying to push it off.

"Wally!" The man storms up the stairs and grabs the dog by its collar. He pauses to catch his breath. "He got away from me," he says to Peggy as he hooks a leash on his pet.

"If you can't control him, he shouldn't be loose," Peggy snaps, wiping the animal's slobber off her face with the back of her hand.

Wagging his tail, the dog strains on his leash, trying to get closer to Peggy.

"He usually stays right next to me," the man says.

"Looks like it." The guy looks familiar, but she can't figure out how she knows him.

"He saw a rabbit and started cha..." The man stops talking, watching Peggy as she steps behind the chair so that it's between her and the dog. "Are you afraid of him? He's harmless." He pats the dog's head. "You're a friendly boy, aren't you, aren't you?"

Peggy can't believe this oversized man is using a baby voice to talk to a dog. He's giving her a headache. "I don't want him jumping on me again."

"That means he likes you. Doesn't it, Wally?"

Still wagging his tail, the dog barks. Peggy glares at the man.

"He's saying hello." The man pulls Wally back toward him with the leash.

"I don't appreciate the poop bombs he's been leaving in my yard all summer either," Peggy says.

"I always clean up after him." He pulls a plastic bag from the pocket of his wind pants.

"I'd be more likely to believe you if the bag weren't empty," Peggy says.

A slow smile spreads across the man's face. "You're the woman from the coffee shop."

Now Peggy remembers. He's the guy who bumped into her at Holy Grounds. *Jeez.* First he touched her. Now he's standing on her deck. What's next? She'd better get rid of him fast.

"Make sure he doesn't go on my lawn." She turns her back on the man and dog and rushes inside to wash her face.

DESPITE THE RAIN LATER that afternoon, Peggy has an itch to get out of the house. She decides to go shopping. Maybe she'll find something she can send to Grace and Greg. She drives to the mall and parks near the Bertucci's. She didn't bring an umbrella, and by the time she has made her way across the parking lot to the entrance, her hair and clothes are wet. Inside the mall, the smell of pizza makes her stomach grumble, but she walks by the restaurant without stopping. A group of preteens loiters outside the drugstore. All the girls are made up with shiny lip gloss, eye liner, and heavy mascara. Peggy frowns as she passes them. They're much too young for makeup. Grace wasn't allowed to wear it until her junior year. Even then, Peggy thought it was too soon. Besides, Grace didn't need makeup. She still doesn't. She's pretty enough without it.

On the right is a store window with mannequins dressed in fancy exercise clothes similar to the outfits most of the women in the boot camp were wearing. Although Peggy hasn't decided if she will return to the class, she enters the store. The girl at the counter looks up at her and back down at her phone. Peggy peruses the racks. She finds a pair of yoga pants that she likes and pulls a size extra large off the rack for a closer look. *Even Barbie would have trouble fitting into these. They must be mislabeled.* She puts them back and continues looking around. She spots a navy blue T-shirt that she likes and searches the shelf until she finds an extra large. She pulls it out and unfolds it. She doesn't have to try it on. There's no way she could squeeze herself into it. As she refolds it, she wonders if maybe this is a kids' store and that's why the clothing is so small. Gymboree, the gym-clothes version. She leaves the store, wondering if yoga for toddlers is a new fad she knows nothing about.

As she makes her way through the mall, a woman with incredibly long two-toned red hair and a shiny face steps in front of her. "Can I ask you a question?" the stranger asks.

"You just did." Peggy pushes past her.

"Do you like your hair?" the woman calls out. "Do you wish it were longer?"

Peggy stops and looks back over her shoulder. The woman has moved back to the center of the aisle by a kiosk with what looks like animal tails in various shades of black, brown, red, and blond hanging from it. "Our extensions blend so well with your real hair that no one will know you're wearing one." She beckons Peggy toward her.

Peggy touches her own hair, which barely reaches her shoulders. She remembers the day she cut it, Patrick biting his lip when he first saw it and folding his arms across his chest.

"The babies are always pulling on it," she explained. "It hurt."

"What did you ask for—the harried mother's special?"

She threw her keys at him and stomped out of the room. He caught her from behind and pulled her into his arms. "Hey, you're beautiful." He kissed her until she stopped crying and then added, "Even with a dude's haircut."

The woman stationed at the kiosk approaches Peggy again. She takes Peggy by the arm and leads her back to the tail-like hair products. Peggy smells cinnamon gum and feels the woman's fingers grazing her scalp as she fastens the contraption to Peggy's head.

"Fabulous," the saleswoman murmurs. "Absolutely fabulous." She hands Peggy a mirror.

Peggy doesn't have to look in the mirror to know the extension will look ridiculous, but she does anyway. In Peggy's magnified reflection, the piece doesn't blend into her hair at all, but that's not what catches Peggy's attention. No, it's her face that causes her to pull the mirror closer. She examines the triple chin and round cheeks that swallow her eyes. Patrick certainly wouldn't think she was beautiful now. She can't stand looking at herself. She thrusts the mirror back at the woman and pulls the extension from her head.

"I'll find a better color," the woman says, but Peggy is already walking away, hustling toward the exercise clothing at JCPenney.

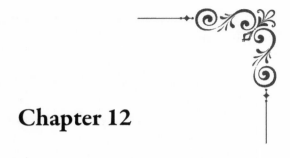

Chapter 12

It's almost six. Peggy has been awake since three. Nine past three to be exact. She's dreading this day, the official start of boot camp. Twelve weeks of exercise, three times a week. Thirty-six classes in which she will be required to run, jump, lift weights, and do sit-ups, push-ups, and God knows what else. What has she gotten herself into? She had to fill out a mound of paperwork and sign a statement saying she was healthy enough to participate. She thinks she is, but she doesn't really know. She didn't bother to keep her appointment with the new doctor and hasn't seen rude Dr. Richardson since the young physician told her she was obese. Well, if it turns out she's not healthy enough, the gym will not be responsible. She signed away her right to hold them accountable should she injure herself. She also learned that the kids invested quite a bit of money for her to take this class.

The class starts at seven. Peggy wonders if she should get up and eat a hearty breakfast so that she'll have fuel to get through the first session. A stack of French toast. Maybe some bacon too. Yes, that's what she'll do.

As she mixes milk, eggs, and cinnamon together, she wonders if the twins are eating well. She's especially worried about Grace. That girl has no meat on her bones. Peggy hopes that adage about the freshman fifteen is still true today. She dunks a slice of bread into the bowl and transfers it to a frying pan coated in butter. As it sizzles,

Peggy imagines a chunky Grace returning at Thanksgiving to find a svelte Peggy. Wouldn't that be something?

I'M REALLY DOING THIS. That's what Peggy thinks when she walks into the back room of the gym where the boot camp takes place. She pauses by the entrance and scans the small group gathered by the bottom of the raised platform where the instructor, Shauna, stands with a clipboard and a tape measure. *A tape measure!* Everyone over there is half Peggy's size. She most definitely does not belong here. She should leave before someone notices her. Yes, that's what she'll do. She steps backward toward the door and collides with someone behind her. As she turns to see who it is, a large man in a Red Sox cap rushes by her.

"Excuse me," Peggy calls out to him in the sarcastic tone she learned from Patrick.

He looks back over his shoulder. *Oh God.* It's that idiot with the dog that craps all over her yard, the guy from the coffee shop.

"I always seem to be in your way," he says.

Peggy steps toward him. "When you bump into someone, it's customary to apologize."

He crosses his arms and smiles, revealing a small gap between his two front teeth. "Well, then, go on."

"What?"

"You walked into me."

Just then, Shauna shouts, "Peggy!" She looks down at her clipboard. "You must be Henry."

He nods.

"We're ready to get started."

Great. Thanks to this fool, it's too late for Peggy to leave. Well, at least with him here, she won't be the largest person in the boot camp. She joins the ten or so class members on the other side of the room.

Oh boy. Because she was determined to get as far from the guy in the baseball cap as she could, she failed to notice Carmen, and now she is standing right next to her.

"I'm so glad you're doing this class," Carmen says, hugging Peggy, who almost gags on the woman's strong floral scent.

Who puts on perfume to go to the gym? Peggy frees herself from Carmen's embrace.

Shauna claps three times. "Good morning, everyone!" When no one returns her greeting, she repeats it louder.

"Good morning," the class says in unison, though not enthusiastically.

"I'm Shauna Williams, the instructor, and I'm telling you that you're going to need more energy than what you're showing me right now to get through the next twelve weeks. So show me what you got."

She raises her sculpted dark arms with her palms up. Peggy stares at them, remembering how her high school Spanish teacher's flabby arm jiggled every time the woman wrote on the chalkboard. Boy, that grossed out Peggy. Her own arms, no doubt, jiggle more than her teacher's ever did.

"Good morning, everyone!" Shauna yells.

Everyone around Peggy screams, "Good morning, Shauna!"

Peggy keeps her mouth closed and looks down. Less than three seconds into the class, she's already annoyed. Someone behind her snickers. Peggy turns to see a woman with shoulder-length curly black hair who is closer in stature to Peggy than to Carmen. The woman rolls her eyes. Peggy smiles at her. There's at least one person in this class she will like.

"Roni Cheevers," the woman says.

"Peggy Moriarty."

Peggy can't hear what Roni says next because Shauna has clipped a microphone to the neckline of her No Excuses T-shirt and is yelling into it while climbing the stairs to the platform. "Today, I'm measuring and weighing you, and then we're heading outside to run a timed mile." She points to racks of dumbbells and bright-colored large balls in the back corner of the room. "There are jump ropes over there. Stretch, and use them until it's your turn up here. Nick, I'm starting with you."

A tall dark-haired man with huge biceps approaches Shauna. Roni grabs Peggy's wrist while staring at Nick. "Oh. My. God!"

Peggy, who rarely notices men, concurs. Who wouldn't? She twists a strand of her hair around her finger. It's like having a Chippendale in the class. Nick has a broad chest, perfect cheekbones, and a cleft square chin. She and Roni watch Shauna place the tape measure high on the inside of his bulging right thigh. Peggy gulps.

"Oh my," Roni whispers. With their mouths hanging open, they watch Shauna wrap the tape measure around his leg and bend her head toward his crotch. Her long black braids brush his abdomen.

"What's she doing?" Roni squeezes Peggy's arm so tightly that Peggy is certain the blood inside it has stopped flowing.

Shauna places her hand on Nick's butt as she lifts her head. She glances toward Peggy and Roni and smiles, revealing perfect white teeth. The grin disappears in a flash as she looks down at the clipboard and jots something. When she raises her head again, her expression is stern. "You two should be stretching and jump roping. Get to it."

As if on cue, Carmen appears with jump ropes for all of them. Peggy hasn't used one of these since elementary school, and even then, she wasn't coordinated enough to be much good at it. She swings the rope over her head and down her torso. When it reaches her feet, she steps over it. Carmen, of course, moves effortlessly over hers. Roni holds hers, still staring at Nick on the platform. The only noise in the room is the rhythmic sound of feet jumping up and down on the wooden floor.

Shauna calls, "Christine," and a thirtyish woman with long black hair climbs the steps to be measured. Peggy squints at the woman's shoulder, trying to make out her tattoo. It's the number sixty-nine!

Why would a woman brand herself with that? What a ho! Peggy leans toward Roni. "Look at her tattoo."

Roni glances at it and shrugs. Before Peggy can say anything else, deafening music blasts from the platform, where Nick is fiddling with a stereo. He fumbles with the controls, trying to turn it down. "Sorry," he says, flashing a sexy smile at Shauna and Sixty-Nine.

"Why aren't you two jump roping?" Shauna calls down to Roni and Peggy.

Peggy immediately swings the rope over her head.

"I'm not coordinated enough," Roni answers.

"You're not even trying," Shauna says as Peggy stumbles while trying to jump. Shauna rolls her eyes and points to the other room. "Both of you, hop on a treadmill. I'll come get you when it's your turn for measurements." She pauses and looks at Roni. "I hope you're coordinated enough to walk."

Twenty minutes later, Shauna collects Peggy for her measurements. As they cross the wooden gym floor, Peggy keeps her head down, sure everyone around is watching her and wondering how much the fat woman weighs. She was up to two hundred fourteen seven months ago when rude Dr. Richardson told her she was obese, but she hasn't weighed herself since. She doesn't even own a scale.

Peggy stops in front of the stairs to the platform. Does she have to be measured up on stage?

Shauna pushes her. "There's no elevator. Climb right on up."

Once on the platform, Peggy surveys the room. Everyone is too busy jump roping to pay her any attention except the big guy, who is watching her with sweat dripping down his face. He's wearing mismatched socks, a white one and a gray one. He must feel Peggy staring at them because he looks down at his calves. His face reddens.

Well, now Peggy feels bad that she embarrassed him, so she smiles. He beams back at her so brightly it flusters her. She quickly turns away.

"Okay," Shauna says. "We'll start with your hips." She winds the tape measure around Peggy and bends toward her for a closer look. "Fifty-one and a quarter."

Clearly, Shauna does not know how to use a ruler. There's no way the distance around her hips is more than fifty inches. That's obscene. "That can't be right. Do it again."

"It's what it says." Shauna puts her finger on the spot where the two sides of the tape measure came together and shows it to Peggy.

"You must have done it wrong."

"Nope." Shauna winds the tape measure around Peggy's waist. "Is it over your belly button?"

Peggy adjusts it so that it is.

"Forty-six and a half."

Peggy wants to cry. She remembers buying Patrick pants with a thirty-four waist. She's over a foot wider than he was. "Maybe that thing's marked wrong."

Shauna frowns. She records the remaining numbers for thighs, chest, and arms without reciting them to Peggy.

"We're almost done," Shauna says. "Step up on the scale."

Peggy hesitates. She really doesn't want to do this and is about to say so when Shauna pushes her and, in an annoyed voice, says, "Let's go. We still have a lot to do this morning."

Peggy takes a deep breath and climbs onto the scale. Her heart pounds as she watches the red digital numbers flash across the display. The flashing stops. The number on the display reads 219.

Peggy gulps, certain the scale is wrong. She can't possibly weigh that much. She's only five foot five. She glances at Shauna, but the instructor is writing on the clipboard, paying no attention to her. *Oh God*, she's writing that number down. What if someone sees it? Peggy's embarrassed that Shauna saw it. Does anyone in the class weigh more than she does? Well, probably that dopey big guy.

"Do the work in class and in the kitchen, and you'll be surprised by how much those numbers come down by the end of the twelve weeks," Shauna says.

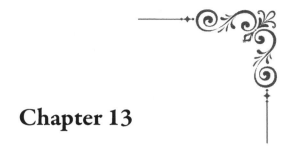

Chapter 13

The class is gathered on the rail trail across the road from the gym. Next to them, commuters stop at a red light on Main Street. A few honk their horns and wave at the group. Peggy looks up at the gray sky and wonders if they'll go back inside if it starts raining. She silently prays for a downpour, with thunder and lightning to boot.

Standing on a large rock on the side of the trail, Shauna addresses the group. "We're doing a timed mile." She tells the class there is a stop sign on the path about a half mile away. When they reach it, they should turn around and head back. "Not all of you will be able to run the entire way, so walk when you have to." She pauses. "But see that rail car?" She points to a section of a train on the grass separating the rail trail from the road. Peggy knows it well. It's a concession stand that sells the best pretzels she has ever tasted. During the summer, she and Greg came here often for the salty snack and ice-cold lemonade. Shauna looks directly at Peggy as she speaks. "The rule is you have to run at least until you get to the car on the way out, and from there back to here on the way in. No exceptions. It's not that far, and I know you can all make that short distance."

Clearly, Shauna has trouble with spatial relationships. The car is not a short distance away. Peggy estimates it to be a quarter of a mile at least. She can't imagine that she will make it all that way without walking or stopping to rest. She can't imagine she will complete the entire mile without dying. Roni is apparently thinking the same thing because she raises an eyebrow at Peggy while shaking her head.

Shauna pulls a stopwatch from the pocket of her Boston University sweatshirt. "Ready, set, go."

The class takes off. Carmen leads the group with Nick at her heels. Peggy and Roni follow well behind the rest of the group. Peggy tries to remember the last time she ran. Probably junior year in high school, the spring she played women's tennis because Bryan Morgan, her crush, was on the men's team, and the two teams traveled together. Her plotting paid off. Bryan took her to the junior prom. *God*, she hasn't thought about him in ages.

The trail is littered with acorns, twigs, and leaves, so Peggy keeps her head down to make sure she doesn't trip. Her hair falls over her face. She swipes it away from her eyes. Her breasts and stomach jiggle each time her foot strikes the pavement. Good. Maybe some of the fat rolls will come loose and fall off. She imagines gobs of fat stuck to the black tar behind her. She'll come back from this mile run weighing less than two hundred pounds. Maybe by the end of the twelve weeks, she'll look like her high school self.

A motorcycle zooms by, and Peggy lifts her head to watch it. She feels like she's been running forever, but the rail cart is still at least one hundred yards away. Roni is about ten steps in front of her, and Peggy can't see anyone else because they have all turned a corner. Her breathing is hard and fast. Just listening to it exhausts her. She slows her pace. It was already snaillike, but now she swears she can see ants passing her down on the path. Her legs feel like they are encased in concrete. She can't run another step. She stops pumping her arms.

Behind her, Shauna yells, "Keep running until you reach the car." Peggy fights the urge to turn around and give Shauna the finger. She has about fifty yards to go. "You're almost there." Shauna's voice booms over the passing traffic.

Just a few more steps, Peggy tells herself. Roni turns the corner and is out of sight. Peggy has less than twenty yards until she reaches the cart. The nausea from earlier is back, which is strange because Carmen and her flowery perfume are nowhere near her.

"Great job!" Shauna yells. Peggy has made it to the car. *Halle-freaking-lujah.* She stops and bends at the waist, praying the nausea will pass.

"Keep moving!" Shauna yells.

Bite me, Peggy thinks. Then she remembers that number on the scale. She weighs well over two hundred pounds. She has to lose weight if she's going to go on *Messages from Beyond* to make contact with Patrick. She straightens herself and walks briskly.

"Good, good!" Shauna calls behind her.

Peggy pumps her fist in the air as she turns the corner, where she spots Roni sitting on a bench a few feet ahead. "What are you doing?"

"Join me." Roni slides over. Peggy remains standing. "We'll wait until the others pass us on their way back, and then we'll jump in at the end of the line. Shauna will never know."

Brilliant, Peggy thinks, taking a seat next to Roni, who tilts her head in the direction of her classmates, who are a blurry image down the path.

"Fools," Roni says.

"Why did you sign up for this class?" Peggy asks. Now that she's sitting, she feels much better.

"My thirtieth reunion is in November. I'm divorced, and so is my high school boyfriend." She winks at Peggy. "You never know what might happen," she says, and Peggy laughs. "Why are you here?"

"My kids signed me up. They're under the impression that all women should look like Carmen." *Oh God. Carmen will tell Grace that I cheated.*

"Pfft. She's half plastic."

Peggy can't have her kids thinking she's a cheater. She stands. "Let's finish this mile."

"No way, but be my guest."

Peggy lets out a deep breath and takes off. She runs faster than before, trying to make up for the time she was sitting. Down the path, she can see some of her classmates sprinting toward her. Good-looking Nick is in the lead now. A young girl wearing a Julliard T-shirt is at his heels. Peggy tells herself she will run until they are by her. They pass her. Nick doesn't even look at her, but the young girl says, "You're doing great." She holds her arm out so Peggy can slap her five.

Well, that was fun, Peggy thinks as she stops running and walks.

In the distance, another figure comes toward her. Peggy glimpses a flash of yellow and realizes it's Carmen's sweatshirt. She doesn't want Carmen to see her walking, so she runs again. By the time they are close enough to see each other's faces, Peggy's heart is pounding so hard that she is certain it's going to break a hole right through her chest, fall out, and land on the pavement. Carmen will have to chase after it, catch it, and slam it back into Peggy's body.

She is even with Carmen now. Carmen doesn't look winded. It's not normal. "Go, Peg, go!"

Peggy wants to trip her. She imagines Carmen lying on the sidewalk. Then she imagines Nick sprinting back here and giving Carmen mouth-to-mouth resuscitation on the path. The resuscitation turns into a passionate kiss. Peggy sighs and looks over her shoulder, waiting till Carmen turns the corner out of sight before she starts walking again. *Finally!*

A little way down the path, a line of classmates passes her, running the opposite direction. The big guy trails along at the end. His face is fire-engine red, and his shirt is soaked. Peggy hopes someone in the group knows CPR.

She finally makes it to the stop sign. She turns and walks back as far as the corner. Once she reaches it, she starts running again because she doesn't want the entire class to see her walking. In the distance, she hears Shauna yelling out numbers, "Fifteen thirty-two, fifteen thirty-four." Peggy stops a few yards in front of the rail cart. She shouldn't have run that far. She does not feel well. Her stomach hurts, and she's been burping up French toast and syrup for the last several yards. She hears people calling her name and clapping.

"You need to run when you hit the car," Shauna yells.

Peggy can't run another step. She's not sure she can even walk another step. She bends at the waist, gasping. Nick and Carmen jog toward her. Maybe they will carry her back.

Nick reaches her first. "Shauna sent us out to escort you in. You know the rules—no walking once you reach the car." They are standing in front of the car. Well, Nick is standing. Peggy is staggering, trying to keep her balance. "Run!" Nick screams. Peggy wants to rip his tongue out of his mouth.

Carmen makes it to them and glares at Nick. "Just a little farther, Peg. We'll do it together." She places a hand on Peggy's lower back and gently pushes her forward. Peggy starts a slow jog. Nick zips ahead. Carmen keeps guiding Peggy with her hand. "Doing great, Peg. Almost there."

More French toast bubbles back up into Peggy's mouth. She's afraid she might throw up. *Mom, you puked on Carmen. How could you?* she hears Grace say. She has to get away from Carmen. She quickens her pace.

"That's right. Finish strong," Shauna yells.

Carmen is still by her side. "Don't overdo it."

Peggy's classmates crowd the finish line, clapping and cheering wildly. Sharp pains rip through her abdomen. The French toast lurches up toward her mouth. *Oh no.* Never mind Carmen—Peggy is going to drench the entire class in vomit. She has to make it past them. She gives it everything she has left and sprints by them and directly to a flowerbed several feet down the path. She collapses to her knees, hangs her head over a bush, and throws up her breakfast.

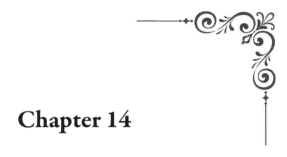

Chapter 14

Throwing up in class. Peggy has not been this embarrassed since... well, ever really. There's no way she can go back on Wednesday. She can't face those people again, especially that guy Nick, who screamed, "Oh my God, she's puking!" She's certain that motorists passing by heard him and stopped to look at her. Never mind the gym—she can't show her face in this town again. She'll have to move. Well, at least now she has a reason to relocate to Vermont.

Shauna didn't seem surprised that Peggy got sick. She hung back on the trail with Peggy as everyone else crossed the street and headed inside the gym. "What did you eat this morning?"

Peggy, who was wearing her regurgitated breakfast on her new shirt, wanted Shauna to go away and forget she'd ever met her. "French toast."

Shauna frowned. "Okay, so no French toast before class again. In fact, no French toast for the next twelve weeks. Just a little protein in the morning, a hardboiled egg, a piece of chicken. Okay?"

Peggy agreed, even though she found the suggestion of eating chicken for breakfast ridiculous.

The light was green, and a stream of fast-moving cars made it impossible to cross the street. "We'll go over diet next class. You are coming back?" Shauna asked.

The light turned red, and the traffic stopped. Peggy stepped onto the road. Shauna grabbed her elbow. "Someone throws up every session. You weren't the first. You won't be the last. It's nothing to be embarrassed about. What would be embarrassing is not coming back because of it." They made it across the street. Shauna rushed inside, but Peggy had her keys in her pocket and stumbled to her car.

It's two hours later, and she's sitting on her porch, sipping water and resting. She keeps looking at her phone on the arm of her chair, expecting a message from Grace. *OMG Mom! How could you embarrass me in front of Carmen like that?* Yes, Carmen definitely called Grace to tell her what happened—Peggy is sure of it. She'd even bet Carmen told Grace before leaving the gym's parking lot.

Waiting for Grace to admonish her is too stressful. Peggy decides to get it over with and calls her daughter, expecting voice mail followed by a short text. Instead, Grace answers on the first ring. "How did it go this morning?" Grace's voice is high, and her speech is fast.

"You don't know?"

"How would I know? Did you like it? Was it hard?"

A bird lands on the railing on the other side of the deck. Peggy notices the bright-red spot on its wing. She decides to tell Grace before Carmen does. "It was hard. So hard that I threw up."

After a beat of silence, Grace says, "Seriously? You threw up?"

The bird hops along the banister toward Peggy. "Yup!"

"Utterly fantastic, Mom. You exercised until you puked. That's so hard-core."

Hard-core? Peggy? "It was during a mile run. Carmen and I were sprinting at the end."

"You kept up with Carmen for a mile run?" The bird flies off.

"We crossed the finish line together." An image of Patrick pops into Peggy's mind. He's standing with his arms folded across his chest and shaking his head. *Knock it off,* she tells him. *Grace doesn't have to know that Carmen was escorting me.*

"Awesome, Mom. Hey, let's do the Thanksgiving Day 5K together. I'll sign us up."

Now Patrick buries his face in his hands.

"Oh, I don't know. A 5K is a lot longer than a mile."

"You have two months to get ready. Add a mile each month. You'll be fine."

"I don't think—"

"Time for accounting," Grace interrupts. "Gotta run."

A few hours later, Peggy receives an email forwarded by Grace, a confirmation for the Stow Gobbler on Thanksgiving morning.

Serves you right, Pegsta, she hears Patrick say.

LATER THAT NIGHT, PEGGY makes herself an omelet filled with smoked mozzarella cheese, bacon, red peppers, and onions and a side of home fries. She carries her plate to the couch and settles in for a new episode of *Messages from Beyond*. Just when Lynda makes contact with a spirit, Peggy's doorbell rings. *Son of a gun.* Peggy sighs and patters to the front door. She opens it, expecting to see Julian because who else could it be? She blinks fast when she sees Julian's mother standing there with a little girl. Carmen's holding a gym mat still wrapped in plastic.

"Can we come in for a minute?" Carmen asks through the screen.

Peggy pushes the door open, wondering what in the world Carmen is doing at her house. From the living room, she hears Lynda saying, "Do you understand what I'm saying? Does it mean anything to you?"

"Are we disturbing you?" Carmen asks.

"Just watching TV." Peggy bends so she is eye level with the toddler. "You must be Sophia!"

The girl stares at Peggy with big brown eyes. "You're Gracie's mom!"

Peggy returns to her full height. "Oh, she's precious. Come in."

"No, no, we can't stay," Carmen says. "I just wanted to give you this." She hands Peggy the red gym mat.

"What's this?"

"Those mats at the gym are disgusting," Carmen says.

"Disgusting," Sophia repeats. Peggy and Carmen both laugh.

"Who knows what kind of germs are on them. You should have your own."

Peggy can't figure out Carmen's motive. *Does she think I threw up because I caught a bug at the gym?* "Well, thank you. Let me pay you for this."

Carmen waves her hand. "Nonsense. I'll see you Wednesday morning. You'll be at class, right?"

Peggy looks down at the hardwood floor, wondering if Shauna has something to do with Carmen's visit.

"I'll pick you up on my way," Carmen says. "I'll be here at six forty-five."

"No!" Peggy says too loudly. "You don't have to do that."

"It's no trouble at all. I have to drive by your street on my way." Carmen pushes the door open. She and Sophia step onto the landing. Sophia waves goodbye.

"Make sure you don't beep," Peggy warns. "I don't want to wake the neighbors."

Chapter 15

The doorbell wakes Peggy from a fitful sleep. At first, she thinks the ringing is part of her dream, but it doesn't stop, and she realizes the sound is an actual noise and not something she's imagining. She rolls over to look at the clock. It reads 3:33, but the bright-blue numbers blink, meaning that at some point last night, the power went out. The doorbell rings again. Peggy lifts herself from the bed. On the way downstairs, she hears rain pounding on the roof and skylights.

At the front door, Carmen stands under a miniscule Minnie Mouse umbrella. Her Audi purrs in the driveway, with the lights on and wipers slashing across the windshield.

"I overslept," Peggy says. "The power went out. Go without me."

"Get ready. I'll wait in the car," Carmen says, and before Peggy can protest, she sprints down the stairs through the downpour back to her vehicle. All Peggy wants to do is climb back under the covers. Instead, she rushes to her bedroom and changes into her gym clothes.

Six minutes later, she slides into Carmen's passenger seat, new mat in tow. A Beyoncé song plays on the radio, and Carmen sings along while typing into her phone. She puts the phone in the center console and waits for Peggy to fasten her seat belt before backing out onto the street.

Peggy glances at the dashboard clock, which reads 6:58. "We're going to be late. I'm so sorry."

"No worries." Carmen sounds exactly like her son when she says it.

Peggy wonders what's happening to her life. How is she riding in a car with Julian's mother before seven in the morning on the way to the gym? Something has gone horribly wrong.

The rain falls faster. Carmen adjusts the windshield wipers, putting them on the fastest setting. When they arrive at the gym, she pulls up to the front door and instructs Peggy to jump out. "There's no sense in us both getting soaked."

Peggy protests, "No, I'll—"

"Go!"

Peggy scoots out of the car and hustles toward the door. Once she's inside, she hears Shauna's miked-up voice from the back room. "Everyone partner up."

Peggy removes her raincoat and glances into the parking lot, not sure whether to wait for Carmen. There's no sign of her. She heads for the boot-camp room and deposits her wet slicker in a cubby. When she turns, Shauna, who is squatting on the floor, motions her over. In front of Shauna, Nick lies on his back on a blue mat with his hands clasped behind his head. His legs are bent with his knees up and feet on the floor.

"You're Nick's partner now," Shauna says, rising. "Hold his feet."

Peggy kneels but makes no move to touch Nick. It all seems a little too intimate.

He glances up at her. "I don't have cooties."

She should have waited for Carmen. They could have been partners. She wraps her hands around Nick's ankles, making sure her fingers rest on his socks and not his bare skin.

Carmen enters the room with the big guy beside her. He runs his hand through his wet light-brown hair.

"You two partner up," Shauna yells. "We're doing sit-ups for two minutes. That's a long time, so take a break if you need to. The person holding the feet should be counting." Shauna waits for Carmen and the big guy to get positioned before starting. "Go!"

Nick lifts his head, chest, and abdomen to his knees and lowers himself to the mat again, with Peggy counting out loud. "One, two, three." Nick completes his fifth sit-up, and Peggy yells "Five."

Shauna taps her shoulder. "Count to yourself."

Nick moves at a freakishly fast pace, a determined expression on his face. On Monday, Peggy would have guessed he is in his early thirties. Today, she is close enough to notice the crow's-feet at the side of each eye and the gray mixed in with his dark hair, especially around his temples. *He's definitely in his forties.*

Roni, who is directly to Peggy's left holding Sixty-Nine's feet, catches Peggy's eye, looks pointedly at Nick, and winks. *Oh, please,* Peggy thinks, but she stifles a giggle and cranes her neck to catch a glimpse of his hand, which is clasped behind his head. He isn't wearing a wedding ring. Peggy doesn't wear one either, though she wishes she could. She had to take it off several years ago because it got so tight that it caused her finger to tingle. *Oh boy.* Why is she thinking about wedding rings and checking a man's hand for one?

"One minute in," Shauna yells.

Nick touches his knees with his elbows. As he leans back into the mat, his shirt slides up his stomach. Peggy catches a glimpse of his abdomen. *Holy cow!* A real six-pack ab. And did she imagine that narrow patch of dark hair under his belly button? She looks again. She did not imagine it. She flushes and feels her palms, now wrapped around Nick's lower calves, sweating.

"Fifteen seconds left," Shauna yells.

Nick's sit-ups have been smooth and steady, but he's frantic now, jerking up and down. His eyes are closed, and his breathing is fast and loud. When he reaches the top of the sit-up, he grunts. Peggy watches him descend. His shirt flies up again. His abs glisten with sweat. Peggy's entire body tingles. She wants to touch his stomach.

Lick it even. *Where did that come from?* Nick grunts louder. Peggy imagines running her tongue over his abdomen, moving right down to his...

"Time!" Shauna screams.

Peggy releases Nick's ankles and grabs her water bottle.

"So, how'd I do?" He wipes a towel across his forehead. Peggy is too embarrassed to look at him. "Hey!"

"How did you do?"

"You were counting, right?"

Uh-oh. "One hundred three." Peggy has no idea. She lost track the first time his shirt flew up.

Nick smiles. "Pretty impressive, huh?"

"Absolutely," Peggy says, fanning herself with her towel.

"What's your name again?" Nick asks as he and Peggy change positions.

"Peggy." She unrolls her mat and lies down on her back with her knees up.

Nick grabs hold of her ankles. His warm, rough hands on her skin send a chill up her spine. "Peggy," he repeats. "That should be easy to remember. Puking Peggy."

Peggy glares at him.

His mouth twists into a crooked grin. "I'm teasing, but, uh, make sure you don't toss your breakfast on me, okay?"

Shauna blows her whistle. Peggy's abdomen tightens as she does her first sit-up. *Puking Peggy.* She's never been so embarrassed. Well, not until she reaches sit-up number nine and farts on the way down. *Oh my God! Please don't let Nick have heard that.* She glances at him. *Yup, he not only heard it, but he smells it too.* He leans backward. Peggy stays at the bottom of her sit-up, staring up at the ceiling. She wonders what he'll call her now. Puking farting Peggy? Puking passing-gas Peggy?

"What are you doing, napping down there?" Nick asks. Peggy lets out a deep breath and looks up at him. "Let's go!"

She resumes the exercise. *Please don't fart again,* she tells herself.

"Forty-five seconds in!" Shauna yells.

Peggy has completed sixteen sit-ups, and her abdominal muscles burn. She doesn't think she can do another and stops to rest, watching her classmates next to her. On the mat to her right, the young girl rips off sit-up after sit-up. To her left, Roni protests, "That's twenty-eight, not eighteen."

Liar, Peggy thinks.

"Come on," Nick says. "Don't tell me that's all you've got."

She looks up at him. His skin is beautiful. Olive. A contrast to Patrick's light freckled complexion, which she also found attractive.

"You've got this, Peggy!" Nick says again. Her name sounds different coming from his mouth. "Use your arms to help you up. Wrap them around your legs and pull."

Okay, I can do this. She brings her elbows to her knees, struggles through two more sit-ups, and collapses back on the mat.

"One minute in," Shauna yells. "Halfway there."

"Let's get to twenty-five," Nick instructs.

Peggy moves her arms from the back of her head to her legs, determined to meet Nick's goal. She fights to pull herself up, ignoring the pain in her stomach. By the time she reaches number twenty-one, sweat drips down her back, and she gasps for breath.

"Almost there," Nick screams. After her twenty-second repetition, she collapses onto her mat. "No. Don't stop. Keep going!"

Peggy summons all her remaining energy and completes another. "Almost there!"

"Fifteen seconds to go," Shauna announces.

"Peggy!" Nick chants. "Come on, Peggy!" She uses all her might and makes it to twenty-four. "So close!"

Peggy falls back onto the mat. Nick leans forward, his head hovering above her knees. Peggy tries to pull herself up but has no more left.

Nick leans directly over her. His blue eyes pour into hers. "You can do this! You want this! I know you do!"

Peggy pulls her body forward. Her forehead grazes his on the way up, and he leans backward.

"Yes, yes, yes!" he says, catching her at the top of the sit-up and quickly hugging her.

When he lets go, she falls back to her mat and closes her eyes. Twenty-five sit-ups. Who would have ever thought?

THE ROOM REEKS OF BODY odor—or maybe it's not the room. Maybe it's Peggy. Her shirt is drenched, and so are her shorts, right through the crotch. She looks like she wet herself. If Nick notices, he'll call her peeing Peggy. She spreads her towel across her lap, hoping to hide the stain, and peeks at her classmates, who, like her, are all sitting on a mat, listening to Shauna lecture them on nutrition. They are all perspiring as much as Peggy, except for Carmen, who apparently doesn't have sweat glands and looks like she just stepped out of a beauty salon.

Shauna holds up her iPad, showing them an online food diary. "Starting today, I want you to track everything you eat and drink, even water. Throughout our twelve weeks, I'll randomly check your logs so I can see what you're putting in your mouths."

Roni catches Peggy's eye and frowns. Although the two women have known each other for just a few days, Peggy is certain that Roni's entries in the food journal will not be an honest representation of the foods she eats.

"If you don't do the work in the kitchen, it won't matter how hard you work here." Shauna looks directly at Peggy as she says this. "Your diet will determine eighty percent of your success."

Peggy wonders why the trainer addresses that warning to her. She has every intention of sticking to her diet. She can't possibly call for the tickets to *Messages from Beyond* until she loses weight. She wants Patrick to see her as she was when he was alive and not who she became after he died. Also, she has a score to settle with the rude young doctor who called her obese. When she loses the weight, she plans to march into the medical office. She pictures the shocked look on Dr. Richardson's face and imagines what the physician will say. Actually, once Peggy is thin, she thinks Dr. Richardson will be friendlier. "You're so skinny now, Peggy," the doctor will say, touching Peggy's arm the way Carmen always does. Maybe she'll even want to be Peggy's friend and invite her out for coffee.

Shauna is still talking, but Peggy hasn't been paying attention. She wishes she had been because tuning in now, she hears Shauna say something about potatoes and pasta, two of Peggy's favorite foods. She's not sure, but she thinks Shauna said to avoid them. Peggy must have heard her wrong. It's pasta and potatoes, for crying out loud, not ice cream and cake. Why would she need to avoid them? Potatoes are vegetables, aren't they?

"Stick to the outside aisles of the grocery store," Shauna says. "And avoid food that you order at a counter. Subs, burgers, pizza, donuts."

Peggy winces. Those are the exact type of foods she's been living on since the kids left. Roni leans closer to her and whispers, "We'll get it from the drive-through, then."

AS PEGGY PULLS HER raincoat out of the cube she stashed it in, Carmen and the big guy approach the shelves. Peggy looks up at him. "How's Wally?"

"Do you two already know each other?" Carmen asks.

"Yeah. He's the guy who doesn't put a leash on his dog." Peggy sticks one arm into her jacket.

"And she's the woman who's afraid of a friendly black lab," he says.

"Oh boy!" Carmen says. "Peggy, Henry. Henry, Peggy."

Peggy wants to warn him that his dog had better never poop in her yard again, but Henry grabs ahold of her jacket so that she can slip her other arm into it. The gesture distracts her. She can't remember the last time someone other than her son did that for her. "Well, thank you," she mutters. Her water bottle slips out of her hand and falls to the floor.

Henry bends over to pick it up.

"Thanks," she says again as he returns it to her. She's aware that Carmen is watching her with what can only be described as a twinkle in her eye.

"I would love a cup of coffee," Carmen says. "What do you say we all head over to Holy Grounds?"

Henry checks the Fitbit he's wearing around his wrist. "Another time. I have a conference call in twenty minutes."

The three walk to the door. The rain has stopped, but they have to dodge puddles as they make their way across the parking lot. "See you Friday," Carmen says to Henry when he stops in front of a dark-green Mini Cooper.

That can't be his car, Peggy thinks. There's a beep, and Henry walks toward the side of the vehicle. Carmen has unlocked her Audi, but Peggy makes no move to open the door. Fascinated, she watches Henry, wondering how in the world he's going to squeeze himself into that tiny automobile.

He stuffs himself behind the steering wheel. Peggy peeks at him as he backs out. His large body spills over the center console, and his left shoulder is crammed against the door. He toots the horn and waves as he passes. Peggy laughs as she slides into Carmen's passenger seat.

Carmen stares at her with that same twinkle in her eye. "Henry is a nice man."

"It's utterly ridiculous that such a big man drives such a small car."

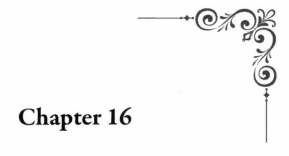

Chapter 16

Peggy wakes up Saturday morning, feeling euphoric. She made it through a week of boot camp, which is quite remarkable, considering she was ready to quit before the end of the warm-up in the sample class. Even better, she has plans today with Roni. During class, Roni mentioned she wanted to see a Julia Roberts movie, so they made arrangements to go together. Peggy added in the walk because she wants to eat a tub of popcorn with butter during the show. It's actually her favorite part of going to the movies. Anyway, she should be exercising on the weekend because the sooner she loses weight, the sooner she can call for her tickets to *Messages from Beyond*.

Three hours later, as she sits on her porch, waiting for Roni, a car door slams, and after a minute, Carmen climbs the stairs to the deck.

"What are you doing here?" *Darn*. Peggy didn't mean to be rude, but she's surprised to see Carmen.

"Roni invited me to walk with you."

"Oh." Although Carmen has been extra supportive at boot camp, Peggy frowns. She wishes she could be happy when she sees Carmen, but that seems more impossible than running a six-minute mile.

Carmen pauses on the top step. "Would you rather I leave?"

Well, now Peggy feels awful. "Of course not." She forces herself to smile. "I'm glad you're joining us."

Carmen sits in the lounge chair next to Peggy. "So Grace tells me you're running the Thanksgiving Day 5K."

Peggy frowns again. She wonders if Carmen is purposefully trying to annoy her by rubbing in the fact that she and Grace are in constant communication.

"You told her you kept up with me on the mile run." Carmen's voice rises on the last three words, so the sentence comes out like a question.

Peggy's face heats up, and she fiddles with the zipper of her sweatshirt. "I told her we crossed the finish line together."

Carmen pushes her sunglasses into her hair. The two women stare at each other for several seconds. Finally, Peggy looks away. "I might have forgotten to mention that you ran back out to escort me in."

Peggy laughs, and a second later, Carmen joins her. Relieved to hear Carmen's giggle, Peggy's face cools, and she stops fiddling with her zipper.

"I'll help you get ready for the race," Carmen says.

"You're running a 5K?" Roni has arrived without either Peggy or Carmen noticing. She's holding a paper cup with the Holy Grounds logo.

"And after that stunt you pulled on Monday, so are you," Carmen says. It turns out Shauna knew that Roni sat out most of the run on the first day of class. The instructor was so mad that when the class got back inside, she made everyone run sprints across the gym floor for the last few minutes of the session. When Peggy heard that, she thanked her lucky stars that, after getting sick all over the bushes, she'd left early.

"The hell I am." Roni plants herself at the bottom of Carmen's chair, causing the part that Carmen's sitting on to rise in the air like a seesaw.

"Whoa," Carmen screams, grabbing hold of Peggy's arm.

"Shit!" Roni jumps up, dropping her coffee in the process. The chair crashes to the floor with a loud thud.

"Are you all right?" Peggy asks.

"I'm okay," Carmen says.

All three women look at each other. Carmen laughs first, but a second later, Peggy and Roni join her. Peggy laughs so hard that tears streak down her face.

The three women walk single file down Peggy's porch step and carefully navigate their way around the dog turds scattered over her back lawn as they make their way to the rail trail. *Damn that Henry and his stupid mutt.*

"You're lucky this path is so close to you," Carmen tells Peggy.

Peggy doesn't answer, too embarrassed to confess that she's never taken advantage of it.

"Peggy," Roni says. "What was going on with you and Nick during sit-ups? Sounded like the two of you were having sex."

"Oh, stop." Peggy slugs Roni's arm.

Roni makes her voice lower than usual to imitate Nick's. "Yes, Peggy. Yes. Oh God, Peggy, so close. Yes."

Peggy's face heats up, and she's sure it has turned as red as the leaves on the tree they just passed. Carmen wraps an arm around her shoulder. "Nick was just excited Peggy did so well."

"On your left," comes a voice from behind. Peggy jumps as a man in a bright-green biking shirt and matching helmet rides past them.

"I farted." Peggy has no idea why she told them that.

"What?" Roni and Carmen ask in stereo.

"During the sit-ups. It slipped out," Peggy says, and the two other women exchange a look and laugh. "Also, he called me puking Peggy and warned me not to belch during the burpees, so I definitely don't think he was thinking about sex while holding my feet."

"Men are always thinking about sex." Roni pokes Peggy in the arm. "Admit it, you were too."

Peggy kicks one of the many acorns littering the trail and watches it skip across the black pavement. "More like trying to remember it." She has no idea what's wrong with her this afternoon or why she is saying these things to women she barely knows—admitting something like that to Carmen Tavarez of all people. What if Carmen tells Grace?

"How long ago did you and your ex split?" Roni asks.

Peggy stops walking. She hears Carmen's sharp intake of breath. So there's at least one person in this town who doesn't know what happened to Patrick. She hasn't had to say this in so long. She swallows hard. "My husband died in a plane crash fourteen years ago." All these years later, her voice still quivers. Carmen grabs Peggy's hand and squeezes it. And then as if it matters, Peggy adds, "He was flying to California for business."

"Oh, Peggy," Roni says. "I had no idea. I'm sorry."

The women walk in silence for several minutes. In the woods to the left, Peggy notices trees with broken branches surrounded by downed limbs. She wonders whether the damage is from Wednesday's storm or if it happened long ago and was never cleaned up.

Roni studies Peggy's profile. "So you haven't had sex in fourteen years?"

"Roni!" Carmen scolds.

"Well, I'm sorry," Roni says. "But we have to hook this girl up, pronto!"

"Oh God, no!" Peggy says. Even if she did let her imagination run wild about Nick during sit-ups, she can't imagine being with anyone other than Patrick. He's the only lover she's ever had. "I'm fine."

"What do you mean you're fine? Do you have a—"

"Roni! Enough!" Carmen interrupts.

Suddenly hot, Peggy removes her sweatshirt and ties it around her waist.

"No, really," Roni says. "You must be about to explode."

"Roni, knock it off. Now." Carmen touches Peggy's arm. "We have to get you ready for the 5K. Let's come up with a training plan."

"Sounds good." Peggy has never been more grateful for a change in subject or Carmen's presence.

"While Carmen comes up with a plan to get you ready for the race, I'll come up with a plan to get you laid," Roni says.

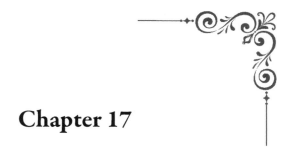

Chapter 17

"You won't believe how good you feel once you start exercising regularly." That was what Shauna told Peggy during the first boot-camp class. Good God, was she wrong. Three and a half weeks later, Peggy has never felt worse. Her entire body aches, even muscles she didn't know existed, like the ones in her toes. Are there muscles in toes? There must be, because hers ache.

She's splayed out on her couch with ice packs on each thigh. She has to go to the bathroom, but it hurts too much to move. She planned to go to the mall to buy new clothes for Parents' Weekend, which is a little over two weeks away—after almost a month of boot camp, she must have gone down a size, right?

She wonders if Grace and Greg will notice a change in her. *You look amazing, Mom!* she imagines Grace squealing while opening her closet filled with size 4 clothing. "Do you want to trade clothes?" Peggy chuckles because there's no way on God's green earth that she'll ever be a size 4 again, but maybe she can get to a 14 someday.

Because of how sore she is, Peggy doesn't want to walk through the mall. Instead, she decides to shop online. When she reaches for her laptop under the glass coffee table, her shoulder screams in protest. The overhead presses she did this morning with twelve-pound dumbbells are the cause of her shoulder pain. No doubt about it. Shauna had the class do five, which was fine. Peggy had no problem and was ready to move to the next exercise, but then Shauna said ten more. Peggy's arms were shaking by the seventh rep, but she persevered and made it to ten. She dropped her dumbbells to the floor, glad to be done with that stupid exercise—but no, Shauna made them do fifteen more. *Fifteen!* Peggy quickly did the math, calculating that she lifted more than seven hundred pounds over her head.

"How do you figure that?" Shauna asked.

"Thirty reps times twelve pounds, times two because I had weights in each hand," Peggy explained.

Shauna widened her stance, placing one hand on her hip. "It doesn't work that way." With her other hand, she pointed to Peggy's water bottle. "Take a sip, and get ready for squats."

The bloody squats are the reason for the ice packs on Peggy's thighs. They weren't regular squats. Of course not. Shauna made them extra torturous. The class had to hold each squat at the bottom until Shauna told them to rise. During the exercise, Shauna was fiddling with her iPad. Peggy swears the trainer forgot that the class members were holding their squats, waiting for her to yell, "Up!"

As Peggy sits up so that she can balance her computer on her legs, she feels a strain through her abdomen. Crunches, three rounds of twenty-five, are the culprit. One good thing about having a sore stomach is that it kills her desire to eat. She hasn't put a thing in her mouth since breakfast, six hours ago. She turns on her computer and navigates to the Macy's website. As she scrolls through several pairs of black pants, her need to pee grows more urgent. Dreading getting to her feet and walking down the hall, she jiggles her leg. Even if she makes it to the bathroom, she can't imagine lowering herself to the toilet seat. If she does manage to park her butt on the hopper, she's afraid she might get stuck on it. Shauna should have handed out adult diapers before today's class.

By the time Peggy finds and orders a pair of pants she likes, her bladder is about to burst. She has no choice. She forces herself to her feet, cursing Shauna with each painful step as she staggers to the restroom.

THE NEXT MORNING, PEGGY meets Carmen and Roni on the bike path behind her house to practice for the 5K. It's the second of a ten-week training plan that Carmen devised and calls for them to alternate between running and walking. Carmen somehow convinced Roni to register for the Thanksgiving Day race. Peggy would bet Carmen threatened to tell Shauna about Roni's cheating during class. Roni double counts each repetition of an exercise so that she does only half as much work as the rest of the class. Shauna hasn't caught on, but there will be hell to pay if she does. They are all a little terrified and in of awe of their trainer, who Roni has nicknamed the Goddess of Torture.

"How are you feeling, Peg?" Carmen asks with a bright smile.

Last night, Peggy called Carmen, trying to get out of running today because of her sore muscles. "Drink plenty of water and stretch," Carmen said. "You'll be fine." Peggy took Carmen's advice, sucking down three large bottles of Poland Spring before going to bed.

"Still achy," Peggy says. "And tired." She was up all night peeing.

"What the hell did Shauna do to us yesterday?" Roni asks. "My ass is killing me."

"Once we start running, you'll both feel better," Carmen promises. Roni and Peggy exchange skeptical looks, but Carmen doesn't notice because she's already jogging down the path. "Come on!"

The three women run in a tight vertical line, with Carmen at the front, setting the pace, and Peggy in the middle. Roni trails a few yards behind, uncharacteristically quiet. It seems the only time her mouth isn't running is when her legs are. Every once in a while, they pass walkers or are overtaken by a biker. As they wind their way down the trail, the neighborhood houses to the left and right fade from view, replaced by woods with rows of trees, exploding with vibrant red, yellow, and orange leaves. Although Peggy has lived in Massachusetts for eighteen years, she's still stunned by the beauty of fall in

New England. It's one of the reasons she'd never move back to the Midwest.

"You girls are doing great," Carmen yells over her shoulder.

Peggy doesn't feel great. Her breathing has turned to loud, deep gasps that she hears over her music, and there's a stabbing sensation under her ribcage that intensifies with each step she takes. "I need to rest," she whines.

"Hell, yes," Roni agrees.

"Just a little farther," Carmen says. It's the same exact thing she said five minutes ago when Peggy first complained. They turn a corner, and an incline comes into view. "We'll stop at the top."

Peggy focuses on the green wooden bench at the peak. Once she makes it there, she will sit down and rest. In front of her, Carmen pours on the speed, sprinting up the hill.

"Show-off," Roni yells. She's a yard or so behind Peggy.

Peggy pushes on, breathing in the scent of wet leaves from the surrounding woods. She powers her way up the hill and collapses on the bench. Moments later, Roni sinks to the spot next to her while Carmen jogs in place in front of them.

"Great job! You ran over a mile and a half in twenty-two minutes," Carmen says. "When you catch your breath, we'll head back."

Peggy figures she'll need two or three days to catch her breath. She imagines Carmen running down the trail, carrying a picnic basket, dropping off Peggy's meals as she races by. Two minutes pass, and neither Peggy nor Roni has made a move to get off the bench.

"Let's go," Carmen says.

Reluctantly, Peggy and Roni rise. They jog for five minutes and walk for one. They repeat the pattern until they reach Peggy's backyard. Carmen rushes home because she has to be at the salon, but Roni and Peggy remain seated on Peggy's porch, gulping from their water bottles.

"I'm starving," Roni whines.

"Do you want to come in, and I'll make us something to eat?" Peggy asks.

"Do you have anything good?"

"Oatmeal," Peggy answers. She has stopped buying Pop-Tarts.

Roni makes a face. "Let's go to Victor's."

Victor's is a small diner by the rotary. Peggy loves their pancakes, a stack of which will account for all her calories for the day. "We really shouldn't."

"It's fine," Roni says, taking the last sips from her water bottle. "We'll get egg-white omelets filled with vegetables, no cheese."

AS SOON AS THEY ENTER Victor's Diner, Peggy smells bacon, and her resolve begins to crack. *Darn.* Why did she agree to come here? As the hostess leads them to a booth, a waitress carrying a plate of pancakes bursting with blueberries passes them. Imagining the sweet taste of them, Peggy licks her lips. Once they're seated, both Peggy and Roni stare longingly as the man who ordered the blueberry pancakes drowns them with syrup.

Peggy sighs and turns back to Roni. "Our omelets will be just as good." She laughs after she says it because she's never been a good liar.

"The hell with omelets," Roni says. "We deserve a treat." Peggy stares at her without responding. "Come on. We ran half a 5K. A few weeks ago, we couldn't even run a quarter of a mile."

"No," Peggy says. "I'm getting an omelet."

Roni shrugs. The waitress comes to take their order. Peggy glances at the man at the next table, who is devouring his breakfast.

Roni's right, she thinks. She's worked hard. She deserves a treat. "Blueberry pancakes. A tall stack."

"That a girl," Roni says, ordering the same and adding sides of bacon and home fries for them to share.

Just over ten minutes later, the waitress drops off the side dishes and two plates of perfectly round fluffy pancakes. Peggy spreads melting butter on each of hers and pours a generous amount of real New England maple syrup over them. She and Roni eat in silence, savoring the sweet fruity taste of each bite until their plates are empty.

SITTING AT HER COUNTER, Peggy stares at the screen of her online food journal, debating whether she should record the blueberry pancakes she ate that morning. *Ate* is an understatement. She devoured them. If there were a speed flapjack-eating contest, she'd be world champion. No doubt about it. Roni would be a close second. *Roni.* She's the reason Peggy's considering lying about her breakfast.

"What we ate here today stays between us," Roni said before the waitress even cleared the plates away. Peggy took a sip of her coffee without responding. Roni persisted. "I mean it, Peggy. Don't even think about putting it in your food journal or mentioning to Carmen that we came here."

"What's the big deal?" Peggy asked.

"I don't want a lecture from the Goddess of Torture on what I should or shouldn't be eating, and I don't want to do burpees as punishment for having blueberry pancakes."

With her hands poised over the keyboard, Peggy realizes that she doesn't want a lecture from Shauna either. It would be embarrassing. She imagines the fitness guru calling her and Roni up on the platform and waving her iPad under their noses with the screen displaying nutritional information about their breakfast while Nick, Carmen, Sixty-Nine, and the young girl stare up at them.

Do you know how many calories are in blueberry pancakes? imaginary Shauna bellows.

The thought makes Peggy realize that she has no idea. Maybe they're not so bad. Blueberries are a fruit after all. She opens a browser window, navigates to Google, and types in *calories in blueberry pancakes*. Three blueberry pancakes with a diameter of four inches are only two hundred fifty calories. That's not so bad, though she has to admit that her pancakes were a lot bigger than four inches. Possibly double the size. She continues to read and learns that two tablespoons of real maple syrup add another hundred calories. Two tablespoons? That's ridiculous. It's nowhere near enough! She sighs as she does the math and realizes her pancakes were at least seven hundred calories. Add in the home fries and bacon, and breakfast was more than a thousand calories.

She picks up her phone and calls Roni. "What did you record in the food journal for breakfast?"

"An egg-white omelet, and you should write the same thing," Roni says. Peggy is silent. "It's not that much of a stretch. There are eggs in pancakes after all."

Peggy hangs up, thinking there are no eggs in pancakes, at least not in the kind she makes that only need water added to the mix.

She stares at the blank space in her food journal, thinking she won't fill in anything. *Oh, for crying out loud.* She's a grown woman. She wanted pancakes, so she had them. What's the big deal? She's been working hard for weeks. Doesn't she deserve a treat every now and then? Her fingers sink into the rubbery film protecting her keyboard as she types in the truth about her breakfast.

Chapter 18

At the end of class on Monday, Peggy is rolling up her mat when Shauna taps her on the shoulder. "We need to talk." Although Shauna says it quietly, she's wearing her microphone, so her words echo through the gym. Peggy's classmates' heads all turn toward her in what looks like a choreographed movement.

Embarrassed, Peggy looks down at the wooden floor while Shauna removes her headset. "I have to make a call, but meet me up there in five minutes," she says, pointing to the platform.

"What's that all about," Roni asks. "Are you in trouble?"

Peggy scratches her head. She has no idea why Shauna wants to talk to her. Roni's the one who cheated during burpees, doing only six reps instead of the twelve Shauna said to do.

"She probably wants to go over your food journal," Carmen says. "We all get a turn."

Roni waits with Peggy while Carmen heads to the cubbies. "You didn't document our breakfast at Victor's, did you?"

"I did," Peggy admits, wishing she had taken Roni's advice.

"You'd better keep me out of it," Roni warns before stomping off to get her coat.

Peggy climbs the platform steps and sits at the edge. Moments later, Shauna, armed with her iPad, joins her. Across the room, Roni and Carmen, the only other people remaining in the boot-camp space, laugh.

"What are you two still doing here?" Shauna yells down to them.

"Waiting for Peggy," Roni answers.

"Wait outside." Shauna points to the door and doesn't turn back to Peggy until Carmen and Roni leave. In a much gentler voice, she addresses Peggy. "I've been impressed by your effort in class. I can already see you're getting stronger."

It's a compliment from her fitness trainer, but it may as well be a standing ovation from a capacity crowd at the Boston Garden by the way it makes Peggy feel. She would even bow if she were on her feet. Instead, she smiles and says thanks.

"But," Shauna says, and just like that, the sold-out audience prepares to heave rotten tomatoes at Peggy. "You have to do the work in the kitchen if you want to see results."

If I want to see results? Of course she wants to see results. She needs to lose weight before making contact with Patrick. Peggy swings her legs back and forth so that her sneakers repeatedly bang off the side of the platform. What excuse can she give about her indulgent breakfast? Should she blame Roni? She glances toward the door to see if her friend is lurking nearby. All she sees is a man on a treadmill, mopping sweat off his face with a towel. "I know I shouldn't have eaten the blueberry pancakes, but..." She stops. *But what?* It's not as if Roni force-fed her. "It was a moment of weakness." As she says it, she glances at the entrance and swears she catches a glimpse of Roni peeking around the corner into the room.

"Were you out with friends, or did you make them at home?"

"At a restaurant." Peggy eyes the door then focuses on Shauna again. The trainer stares at her without saying anything. Peggy resumes swinging her legs. "With Roni," she blurts.

Shauna swipes at the iPad. "So you had pancakes, bacon, and home fries while Roni ate an egg-white omelet with broccoli, mushrooms, and peppers."

Peggy stares down at the gym floor.

"I appreciate you being honest in the journal because people who lie about what they eat are only cheating themselves."

Peggy thinks about lying for Roni. She imagines saying Roni really did have that, but she knows she wouldn't sound convincing.

Shauna clears her throat. "Anyway, I understand that was a one-time binge. I want to point out bad patterns I've noticed that need to change, like this here. It's doing you no favors."

Much to Peggy's surprise, Shauna points to Sunday's lunch entry, a salad. *What could be wrong with that? It's rabbit food, for crying out loud.*

"You're piling on the calories with all these add-ons. Cheddar cheese, croutons, candied pecans, ranch dressing. You don't need cheese on a salad. If you have to eat nuts, have them plain, not coated in sugar."

Well, of course Peggy knows plain nuts are better than candied nuts, but they don't taste nearly as good. Still, she nods.

"Use a low-fat Italian dressing or balsamic vinegar. And iceberg lettuce... sure, it's low in calories, but it has hardly any nutritional value. Make your salads out of spinach, kale, or arugula, okay?"

Peggy would rather eat grass than kale or arugula, but she nods again.

"And Oreos? I shouldn't have to mention these to you, but I see they're on here quite a few times."

"It's the hundred-calorie package."

"Yes, but when you have seven or eight of those packages a week, the calories add up. Have grapes or an apple or Greek yogurt as a snack."

"Fine," Peggy says. She's almost certain she saw Oreo yogurt in the grocery store.

"I don't want your diet sabotaging all the hard work you're doing in class." Shauna powers down the iPad. "Make these tweaks, and I promise, you'll see results."

Peggy leaves, thinking that she will make the adjustments. Parents' Weekend is only two weeks away. She wants the twins to notice a difference in her.

AT THE END OF BOOT camp the following Friday, Peggy's shirt is soaked in perspiration, and sweat runs down her arms and legs, dripping onto the gym floor. She bends down and uses her towel to wipe it up. When she arrives at the coat shelf, she gulps from her water bottle, emptying it. Carmen and Roni watch her drink without saying anything.

"Why are you looking at me like that?" Peggy asks.

"Just making sure you're okay," Carmen says.

"Why wouldn't I be?"

"You're bright red," Roni says. "We're wondering if we should call 911."

"I'm fine."

Nick and Sixty-Nine approach the coat cubbies. Sixty-nine has her hand on Nick's arm and laughs at something he says. Nick smiles at Peggy. "You killed it in there today, Peggy."

Peggy thinks about the six push-ups she did. They were from her knees, but a month ago, when she started this class, she had to do them against a wall. "Yeah, I did." She reaches for her jacket.

Nick and Sixty-Nine laugh as Peggy, Carmen, and Roni make their way to the door.

"What's gotten into you?" Roni asks. "You were a crazy person in there."

Peggy steps outside. The cool October breeze chills her damp skin, so she stops to put her coat on before stepping off the sidewalk. "I'm excited about seeing the twins next weekend. I'm hoping they notice a difference in me." She's been eating clean all week, making hard-boiled eggs for breakfast, salads with spinach for lunch, and chicken and vegetables for dinner. She discovered that Greek yogurt comes in flavors of salted caramel and chocolate, so she's been snacking on that.

"Oh, they will," Roni says, but Carmen frowns.

Peggy addresses Carmen. "You don't think they will?"

They've reached Carmen's car, and the three women pause by the trunk. "Are Grace and Greg supposed to come home next week?"

"I'm going to Vermont. Parents' Weekend." Peggy lowers her zipper. She can't stop sweating.

"Oh no," Carmen mutters.

"What?" Peggy asks. All around them, car doors slam, and engines start.

"Julian's driving up next weekend. He's surprising Grace with tickets to a concert in Montreal. He bought tickets for Greg and a friend too."

"Well, they can't go," Peggy says. "It's Parents' Weekend."

"Julian spent a lot of money on the tickets."

Tough luck, Peggy thinks, but she bites her tongue.

Shauna exits the building and walks toward them. "Great job in there today, Peggy. Make sure you eat some protein when you get home." She presses a button on her remote, and the car next to Carmen's beeps as the doors unlock.

Peggy waits until Shauna drives off. "I've been looking forward to Parents' Weekend since the kids left for school."

"You can always visit them another weekend," Roni suggests.

"I'm visiting them on Parents' Weekend," Peggy says before she storms off across the parking lot to her CRV.

AS PEGGY TOWEL DRIES her hair, her cell phone rings, and Grace's picture lights up the screen. She missed calls from both Greg and Grace while she was in the shower. She wraps the towel around her head and considers whether to pick up. If she ignores the twins all week, they won't be able to tell her she can't come up next weekend. Yes, that's what she'll do. The phone keeps ringing, and Peggy panics. *What if Grace isn't calling about Parents' Weekend? What if she hurt herself or is sick?*

"Hello," Peggy answers, carrying the phone from the steamy bathroom into her bedroom, where she sits on the unmade bed.

"How was boot camp today?" Grace asks. "Carmen told me you kicked butt."

"She called you?" Through the window, Peggy watches the garbage truck inching down the street.

"She texted," Grace says. Peggy clenches her fist, wondering exactly what Carmen said to her daughter. "I'm really proud of you, Mom."

Peggy's eyes fill with tears. It's absolutely ridiculous, especially when she knows Grace is only trying to butter her up before breaking her heart. "I can't believe how much I enjoy the class."

"Carmen says you guys have become friends."

"I don't know about that, but she's helping me train for the 5K."

"We're all going to have so much fun running together," Grace says.

Peggy wonders why it's taking Grace so long to get to the point and decides to help her. "I'll bring my running shoes next weekend."

Grace is silent. Outside, the garbage truck groans to a stop in front of Peggy's driveway. She watches as its mechanical arm picks up the barrel and dumps the contents into the back of the truck.

"About Parents' Weekend..." Grace finally says.

Chapter 19

Peggy looks at the empty pint in disgust. She can't believe she ate all of it. She doesn't even like Ben & Jerry's. The flavors all have too much going on. Like the kind she just devoured with chocolate and vanilla ice cream, fudge brownies, and cookie dough. Eating it is an assault on her taste buds. She wanted Friendly's—chocolate almond chip, to be exact—but it only comes in half-gallon containers, and she didn't want to eat that much.

She was hoping the ice cream would lift her spirits. Instead, it has sent her free-falling into a gaping abyss of despair. This was supposed to be a happy weekend. She should be in Vermont with the twins. Instead, she's been holed up in her lifeless house for almost forty-eight hours straight. She tried making plans, but Roni went to New Hampshire Friday night to visit her father and won't be back until late this evening, and Carmen said she had a crazy weekend doing the hair and makeup for three bridal parties. Peggy couldn't think of anyone else to call. The highlight of the past two days was when she ventured out to the grocery store for the ice cream. She drove to a supermarket three towns away so no one from boot camp would catch her buying the illicit item. That was only an hour ago, but now the ice cream is gone, and she has a raging case of heartburn. She pops two antacids and waits for them to kick in. They make the inside of her mouth feel like a chalkboard that someone has colored all over, so she downs a large glass of seltzer to wash the feeling away. Her heartburn worsens.

She checks her watch, hoping that she can go to bed soon and put an end to this dreadful weekend. It's not even five o'clock. The entire night looms in front of her. When the twins were home, Peggy's days flew by. Without them here, the hours drag. The only things she has to look forward to are boot camp and training for the 5K. Who would have thought? She needs to find a way to occupy her time and has considered applying for a job, but her skills are outdated. Maybe she should go back to school. She imagines sitting in a classroom with Grace and Greg at St. Michael's, the three of them lined up next to each other in the front row. The professor looks like George Clooney because, what the heck, it's Peggy's daydream. The mental picture makes her laugh because Grace would drop out before attending college with her mother.

Peggy checks her watch again. Only ten minutes have passed. *How is this my life?*

She remembers when she was the twins' age, studying advertising at the University of Illinois. She always pictured herself living in Chicago, working at one of the prestigious agencies such as Leo Burnett, and she was well on her way to that when she met Patrick. Okay, so maybe she was working at a small PR firm doing branding and not at a world-famous ad agency, but she loved her job, and it was in Chicago. Peggy gave it up for Patrick. She moved with him to Massachusetts, a state she had no desire to visit, never mind live in, and within four years, he was gone.

She pops another antacid and changes her train of thought, focusing on the positive. He left her with two beautiful children. Thinking about them makes her wonder if they had a good time at the concert, so she texts them.

So much fun! Grace responds.

Greg sends a thumbs-up emoji.

Peggy stares at the phone, waiting for one of them to inquire how she is or what she did all weekend. Neither of them does.

The burning in her chest intensifies. She worries that it's not indigestion and that she's actually having a heart attack. Sure enough, in addition to the fiery feeling, there's a tightness. Her heart is pounding and roaring. It's beating too fast. She's sweating so much that her T-shirt is soaked. *This is it. I'm going into cardiac arrest. Should I dial 911? Drive myself to the emergency room?* She decides to lie down on the couch, pull a blanket over herself, and plop her head on a throw pillow. She inhales deeply and lets out a long breath. Her heart slows. She closes her eyes and starts to drift off, wondering if she will die in her sleep. Who would find her? She realizes that her death wouldn't be discovered until Grace and Greg return for Thanksgiving. Will she be reunited with Patrick in heaven? Will he be happy to see her? She hears Grace's voice, from the night before the twins left for college, saying Patrick wouldn't even recognize her. *Oh, Grace, I don't even recognize myself.*

She wakes up hours later. Her heartburn, or whatever it was, has subsided, and it's finally time to go to bed. Only now she's wide-awake. She binge-watches old episodes of *Messages from Beyond* until three in the morning, starting with the one in which the husband reminds the wife about the first time he told her he loved her. In the last episode before Peggy goes to bed, Lynda contacts a poodle named Frosty. It's the only one that Peggy doesn't like and makes her wonder if sometimes Lynda makes things up.

THE NEXT MORNING, THE sound of the doorbell ringing wakes her. She glances at the clock. It's quarter after eight. Her first thought is that something awful has happened to Grace or Greg or both of them and the police are here to notify her. She races downstairs and yanks the door open.

"Why the hell didn't you come to class today?" Roni bellows, pulling open the storm door and bulldozing her way past Peggy into the foyer.

Carmen follows a few steps behind. "We called a few times and were worried when you didn't answer."

Peggy fights to swallow the lump that has swelled up in her throat. Someone would have found her body before Thanksgiving. "I forgot to set my alarm." She has an awful coppery taste in her mouth and is aware that her breath is atrocious.

"You picked a good class to miss," Roni says. Her curly dark hair is damp with sweat. Even Carmen looks a little off, with a few strands of long hair falling out of her ponytail.

"Have a seat in the kitchen, and I'll make coffee," Peggy says. While her classmates—no, her *friends*—head down the hall, she runs upstairs to brush her teeth and change out of her pajamas. When she joins them a few minutes later, Carmen has already started the coffee.

Roni points to the empty ice cream pint on the counter. "I'm taking a picture and sending it to Shauna. Payback for ratting me out on the blueberry pancakes." She pulls her phone from the pocket of her sweatshirt.

"Don't you dare!" Peggy grabs the container and deposits it in the trash can. She meant to bring it outside to the recycling bin last night but never got around to it.

"So how was your weekend?" Carmen asks as Peggy removes three mugs from a cabinet.

"Okay," Peggy lies. As she turns away from her friends to pour the coffee, she decides to be honest. After all, they came here to check on her. They deserve the truth. "Actually, it was miserable. I was looking forward to seeing the kids. I haven't seen them for forty-one days, and I won't see them for another forty-seven."

"You counted the days?" Roni asks.

Peggy looks down at the floor, embarrassed she shared that. When she lifts her head, her two friends are staring at her with expressions of sympathy. *God,* she hates that.

"Oh, Peggy, I'm sorry," Carmen says.

Seated between the two women at the breakfast bar now, Peggy feels ridiculous. It's not like her to feel sorry for herself. "Anyway, on to a new week." She takes a sip of coffee.

"My weekend was worse," Roni says. "Went to visit my father and ran into my ex-husband with his husband at the drugstore."

"Wait, what?" Peggy, jolted, spills coffee on the counter.

"Yup," Roni says. "My husband didn't cheat with my best friend. No, that's too cliché for him, trendsetter that he thinks he is." She balls both hands into tight fists. "He cheated with her husband. They got married last year. Fucking humiliating."

Peggy has no idea how to respond and waits for Carmen to say something comforting, but Carmen offers nothing.

"It's the first time I've seen him since I sent him my wedding gown with a note suggesting he wear it to his ceremony."

"Oh, Roni, you didn't," Carmen says.

"'Fraid so. He sent it back, saying it was too big. Bastard. He knows my weight is a sore spot." For a few seconds, the friends sit without speaking, the only sound in the room the hum of Peggy's refrigerator. "Cheer us up, Carmen," Roni finally says. "Tell us about your perfect weekend."

Carmen sighs. "Mine wasn't good either. Antonio's business has taken a hit because the bridge on Washington Street is out. No one drives by. To make up for it, I have to work more hours at the salon. I did the hair for bridal parties on both Saturday and Sunday. Lovely girls, but I would have rather spent the time with Sophia." She walks to the sink for a sponge to wipe up the coffee Peggy spilled. "And Rosalita let us know she's going to Brazil after Christmas until April, so I have to find daycare for Sophia. Frankly, I'd like to stay home with her, but we can't afford it right now, especially with Julian's tuition." She bites down on her lip.

Peggy takes a closer look at Carmen. Not only is her hair falling out of her ponytail, but it also is dull today rather than shiny. There are bags under her eyes, and the polish on her fingernails is chipped.

Peggy puts a reassuring hand on Carmen's shoulder, wishing there was something she could do to help. "Let's have a girls' night out this week. Do something fun together."

"Absolutely," Roni and Carmen say.

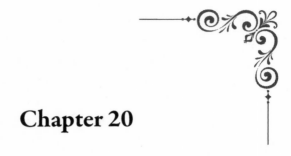

Chapter 20

The scent of freshly baked cinnamon buns wafts through Holy Grounds. Peggy eyes the man at the next table as he greedily eats his. Boy, does she want one of her own. If she hadn't already binged on ice cream this week, she'd get it. *Ha!* There's no use trying to fool herself. The only reason she hasn't ordered one is because Roni and Carmen are with her.

She watches Roni stride across the café to the table, sipping coffee as she advances. The brief display of vulnerability that Roni showed on Monday is long gone. "I've been thinking," Roni says as she slides into the chair next to Peggy. "Henry."

"What about him?"

"Any interest in him?"

Peggy swallows a sip of coffee before responding. "If you mean interest in dating, then, no."

A woman in a red raincoat walks by their table, carrying a cinnamon roll. Peggy summons every last ounce of her willpower to stop herself from storming the counter and demanding one for herself.

"Well," Roni says, "he's definitely got a thing for you."

"Henry? For me? He doesn't." Peggy isn't even all that nice to Henry, so there's no reason he would like her. During today's class, he caught her pushing his mat away because it was too close to hers. "You're dripping sweat on me," she said, and his beet-red face turned white.

Roni nods. "Oh yes, he does."

Peggy looks away from her friend's watchful gaze and toward the counter, where the usually scowling barista giggles at something Carmen says. Peggy tilts her head in their direction. "He doesn't, but frowny face over there sure has a thing for Carmen."

Carmen smiles at the barista as he hands her a pastry wrapped in wax paper. "Did she bat her eyes at him?" Roni asks.

Peggy nods, not at all surprised that Carmen is flirting with him but shocked that the woman who usually only gets bottled water here is having something to eat. "What do you think she ordered?"

Roni narrows her eyes but doesn't answer. Carmen winks at the barista and sashays toward their table. He doesn't take his eyes off her until she sits.

"Were you shaking your ass?" Roni asks. "You'll kill that poor boy."

The corners of Carmen's eyes crinkle. "He insisted on giving me a cinnamon bun." She tosses it onto the table. Groaning, Peggy eyes it hungrily. Now that it's right under her nose, her self-discipline is dissolving. Her stomach grumbles. Carmen glances at her and picks up the pastry. "This is for Antonio." She wraps the wax paper tightly around the pastry and deposits it into her canvas bag. "I have a better treat for you, Peggy." She pulls her iPad out of the bag.

The device reminds Peggy of Shauna's, and for a moment, she wonders if Carmen is about to log in to the food diary to review Peggy's diet, which still needs work. Carmen swipes at the screen before typing into it. Peggy's dread grows.

Carmen must see Peggy's worried expression because she says, "I promise you'll like this." She maneuvers the cover so that it acts as a stand, smiles at the tablet, and says something Peggy doesn't understand. A few seconds later, Carmen turns the iPad so that it faces Peggy.

Peggy can't believe what she sees—live images of Greg and Grace looking out of it, smiling. Tears fill Peggy's eyes. Her hand goes to her heart.

"Hey, Mom," Greg says. Sitting next to him, Grace waves.

"Oh my God!" Peggy squeals. The barista looks over but then turns away. "What is this? How is this happening?"

Grace rolls her eyes. Peggy studies her daughter's face. Grace's summer tan has faded, and two nasty pimples partially covered with caked-on concealer dot her chin, making Peggy wonder if she is stressed about her class work. Still, Peggy thinks Grace is more beautiful than when she left for school, even with the botched coverup of her blemishes.

"FaceTime, Mom." Greg sports at least three days of stubble, his lips are chapped, and small bags swell out from under each of his eyes.

"Are you getting enough sleep?" Peggy asks.

"Don't worry, Ma."

An ugly brown splotch stains the top right of his gray Patriots T-shirt. Peggy is about to remind him that he needs to do his laundry at least once a week when Greg leans closer to the camera. "Why are you so red and sweaty?"

Peggy wipes her forehead with the back of her hand. "I just finished boot camp. We're getting coffee."

"Who's *we*?" Greg asks.

"Well, I think you already saw Carmen." Peggy turns the iPad toward Roni. "And this is..."

"Shit, no," Roni yells, ducking away from the camera. "I'll meet them in person. When I'm showered." She turns the screen back toward Peggy.

"Who's that?" Greg asks.

"Roni. She's in boot camp with me."

"Your mom's a badass boot camper," Roni yells, causing the barista to look at them again.

"How's it going?" Grace asks. "Have you lost weight?"

Peggy thinks about the ice cream she ate. "Oh, you know..."

"Stand so we can see you," Grace urges.

Peggy feels the tension in her shoulders that often emerges when she's frustrated with Grace. *Why can't she be happy that I'm doing the boot camp and have made new friends? Why is my size the only thing she cares about?* "I don't think so," Peggy says, struggling to keep the frustration out of her voice so that she doesn't ruin this beautiful videoconference that Carmen has arranged.

"Come on, Mom," Grace whines.

"Your face looks thinner," Greg says. "Doesn't it, Grace?"

Grace scrunches her nose. "A little, I guess."

Carmen pulls the computer toward her. "Your mom's doing great. She's killing it running. You'll see when you come home for Thanksgiving."

Did Carmen just take Peggy's side over Grace's? Peggy stares at Carmen without blinking, thinking about all the times she was sure Carmen was plotting with Grace against her. Peggy cringes, remembering the accusatory email she sent Carmen last winter. It sure feels good to have Carmen stand up for her.

"Speaking of Thanksgiving," Peggy says, and Carmen turns the screen toward her again. "We should plan how you'll get home."

"We can hitch a ride with someone here," Greg says.

"Who?" Peggy asks, not sure she trusts a boy or girl she doesn't know to drive her kids all the way from Vermont to Massachusetts.

"Just this girl in my psych class," he says.

Maybe it's Greg's use of the word *just*, or maybe it's the way Grace struggles to keep her face neutral, but Peggy's sure there is a story that goes with this girl. "What's her name? Where does she live?" Peggy pulls the iPad closer and studies her son. *Oh my God, does he have a hickey?* "What's that on your neck?"

Grace smirks while Greg covers the incriminating evidence with his hand. "We gotta run. Time for US and the Twentieth Century," he says. "See you soon."

"Bye, Mom. Bye, Carmen," Grace says.

"Love ya," Greg throws out before the twins disappear from the screen. Peggy continues to stare at it, wishing she could jump through it and race after them.

Carmen gently slides the iPad away from her. "They'll be home sooner than you think, Peg."

"That was lovely. Thank you for arranging it."

"It was Julian's idea," Carmen answers. "He feels awful about ruining Parents' Weekend."

Peggy's eyes widen in surprise. She's not sure she believes Carmen. It would be easier to imagine that Greg suggested it. *Greg.* "My son, my baby, has a hickey."

"He's hardly a baby," Carmen says. Peggy is reminded of their first meeting, when Carmen tried to convince her to let Grace go away for the weekend with Julian.

"You expect your kids to be celibate because you are?" Roni asks.

"No," Peggy snaps, feeling ganged up on. "But his girlfriend is in California." She takes a sip of coffee. It's room temperature. She glances toward the barista, considering whether to ask him to heat it up, but when he looks at her with what can only be described as a snarl, she decides against it.

"He and Allison probably agreed to see other people," Carmen says.

Peggy hopes Carmen is right. She will talk to Greg about it in person when he's home for Thanksgiving. She imagines what advice Patrick would give their son. *Always treat the ladies with respect, Greggy.* Then she sees him look over his shoulder to be sure she isn't listening. *But if you're gonna two-time them, be smart enough not to get caught.* He slaps Greg on the back before turning to wink at Peggy, showing that he knew she was listening.

Chapter 21

As Peggy spreads her mat in her usual spot in the back row, a horrible scraping sound comes from across the room, where Shauna pushes a whiteboard on an easel to the front of the platform. The noise stops, and Shauna blows her whistle. The boot campers end their conversations and turn their attention to the instructor.

"Mid-session evaluations are today," she says. "While I take measurements, you should be doing this workout."

Peggy's eyes widen. "Mid-session evaluations? Did you know about this?" she asks Roni.

"She told us the first day."

Peggy doesn't think she would forget something like that.

"You left early," Carmen reminds her.

"I wish I had known," Peggy mutters.

Roni bends to tie her sneaker. "It's not like you could study for it."

No, but she might have fasted yesterday if she'd known. She has been trying to eat healthy, but sometimes she gets cravings. Yesterday, she desperately wanted something salty. She recalls what she ate. Tortilla chips and salsa. Better than potato chips, which she would have eaten in the past, but still she's probably retaining water because of them. *Great.*

"Carmen, I'm starting with you," Shauna says. "The rest of you, get going on the workout. Do it at your own pace, but don't leave until it's done. All of it." She glares at Roni. During the last class, Shauna stood behind Roni during some of the exercises, counting to make sure Roni did the specified amount of repetitions.

The boot campers in front of Peggy moan as they read the board. "What's it say?" Roni asks.

Peggy squints, trying to read it. It's no use. Stepping over and around mats, she and Roni make their way to the front of the room. "Ten reps of burpees, squats, lunges, and push-ups."

"That will take all week," Roni gripes, looking at Shauna. "You're out of your mind."

"Stop whining, and get to it," Shauna says.

Peggy hates all these exercises—truthfully, there isn't an exercise she likes—but this workout seems no worse than all the others they've done. She doesn't know why Roni and all her classmates are so upset. "Ten reps isn't so bad," Peggy says.

"It's not ten. It's a hundred," Roni says, pointing to a cryptic mark at the bottom of the board that Peggy now realizes says *x 10*.

"One hundred?" Peggy repeats. It may as well be one million. Roni's right. Shauna's crazy. She may even be trying to kill them.

Peggy and Roni meander to their spots to start the exercises. Henry has arrived and is set up between Carmen's and Peggy's mats. He greets Peggy and Roni with a big smile. "Good morning, ladies," he says in a singsong voice.

"Check out that freaking whiteboard, and you'll see it's not a good morning," Roni snaps.

Henry gives Peggy a look that conveys he thinks Roni's nuts. Roni gives him the finger, which makes Henry and Peggy laugh.

"Do you three not have enough to do back there?" Shauna yells across the gym. "Stop gabbing, and get started."

Nick, who has appointed himself the boot-camp DJ, is up on the platform, fiddling with his phone and the gym's wireless speakers. Ed Sheeran's voice blasts through the room. As usual, several class members complain about Nick's musical selection, but Peggy and Henry both sing along as they start their burpees.

"As if it's not bad enough doing these exercises, I have to listen to you two singing," Roni mutters. Without discussing it or even looking at each other, Henry and Peggy sing the next verse louder. Roni pushes her mat farther away from theirs.

By the end of the fourth round of the exercises, Peggy is too winded to speak, never mind sing. Perspiration runs down her face, arms, and legs. She pauses to wipe it off and take a long drink from her water bottle. When she puts her hands down to start the fifth round of burpees, they land in a wet spot. "Oh, gross," she says, wondering if the puddle is hers or Henry's sweat. She mops up the floor with her towel and wipes her palms on her sweatpants.

"Roni," Shauna calls.

"Finally, a break." Roni stops in the middle of a push-up and rushes to Shauna's side. She trudges back to her mat a few minutes later with a scowl. "I gained four pounds," she hisses.

"Peggy," Shauna yells.

"No..." Peggy mutters to herself. She was hoping the instructor wouldn't get to her today. Up on the platform, she removes her sneakers and notices a hole in her sock by her big toe. How did she miss that when she was getting dressed? She looks at Shauna, expecting her to be staring down at Peggy's foot, but Shauna is studying her clipboard. Without looking up, Shauna kicks at a button on the side of the scale, and the display lights up with two red zeroes. Peggy steps on it. The red digits disappear, and new numbers flash on the screen: 216. After all that work, she's only lost three stinking pounds, a half pound a week.

Sure that the number is wrong, Peggy steps off the scale, waits for the screen to clear and steps back up. Now it says she weighs 216.5. "I'm gaining weight just standing here," she says.

"Make those changes we talked about, and stick to the outside aisles of the grocery store, and you'll see a bigger loss next time," Shauna promises.

Chapter 22

The ticking of the blinker grates on Peggy's nerves, so she flicks it off. She can see the green signal ahead, but the cars in front of her don't move. She's been sitting in this line of traffic, waiting to turn right, for three light cycles. What in the world is causing the holdup? She wonders how far ahead of her Roni and Carmen are in this mess of cars. She should have walked the two blocks from the gym to Holy Grounds, but because she was so tired from boot camp, she drove.

Behind her, Peggy hears sirens. She steers her Honda to the right. A police car races by, driving the wrong direction in the opposite lane. Peggy's cell phone rings, and Roni's name flashes across the screen.

"What kind of coffee do you want?" Roni asks.

"You're already there?"

"Yeah. Carmen and I pulled over and walked when we saw the traffic. We're about to order."

Peggy really wants a pumpkin spice crème coffee, but there's no way she's drinking that thousand-calorie liquid dessert for breakfast in front of Carmen, so she tells Roni to get her a nonfat caramel macchiato, though she whispers the "nonfat" part.

Several minutes after Peggy puts down the phone, a flatbed carrying a demolished white car drives toward her. As it passes, Peggy winces, wondering what happened to the occupants of the vehicle and imagining the worst. She pictures the police knocking on a door, a mother in a kitchen, laughing with her young children before she leaves to answer it, not realizing that those few moments will be the last she is ever truly happy. When Peggy's doorbell rang years ago, she was turning on a movie for the twins so they wouldn't be underfoot while she put away the groceries. The CEO of Patrick's firm and his wife stood at the door. They both looked as if they had been crying. "I'm so sorry," he said.

"Sorry about what?" Peggy asked. There was the pitter-patter of little feet behind her, and then Grace was reaching for her hand.

The husband and wife looked at each other. Peggy hadn't invited them in, and they were standing on the landing, talking to her through the storm door. "You haven't heard," the CEO finally said. He pulled the door open and stepped inside. "There's been an accident. The plane Patrick was on..." There was no need for him to say anything else.

Now, hoping to clear her head, Peggy lowers her car window and lets a blast of cold air in. The line of traffic moves. Peggy inches forward, offering up a silent prayer that whoever was in the ruined car is okay. She reminds herself that she never saw an ambulance and convinces herself that the passengers are fine.

When Peggy enters the coffee shop, Carmen and Roni are sitting in the back. An open laptop rests on the table in front of Roni, and her fingers fly across the keyboard. Peggy sits. Carmen smiles and slides a steaming paper cup in front of her. Roni doesn't look away from her computer screen.

"What's she doing with that?" Peggy asks Carmen, who avoids eye contact and picks up her bottled water.

Peggy sips her coffee. *Phooey.* Roni must have heard her say "nonfat." *They should call it what it is—non-tasty.*

A group of laughing teenagers walks through the door. Already feeling melancholy because of her memories during the traffic jam, Peggy watches them, her heart aching for Grace and Greg. She would really like to make herself feel better right now and thinks about following the kids to the counter to order a gooey soft cookie. She can almost taste the chocolate chips melting on her tongue.

"What do you want as a user name?" Roni asks. Lost in thought, Peggy doesn't realize Roni is talking to her. Roni touches her arm. "Boot-Camp Badass? One Hot Mother?"

Peggy pulls her eyes off the teenagers, who are crowding around the counter now. "What?"

Roni turns the laptop so Peggy can see the screen. The words *IdealMate.com* run across the top of the web page.

"What's that?" Peggy plunks her coffee cup on the table and pulls the computer closer, a feeling of dread slowly washing over her. She notices a slogan near the bottom of the screen: *We know how to build relationships that last.* The coffee in her mouth tastes worse than before. She wants to spit it out, but she swallows. "What is this?"

Roni pulls the laptop back in front of her. "We're getting you a date. I'm setting up your online profile."

Peggy glances over her shoulder to make sure no one's watching them. Everyone's studying electronic devices or engrossed in their own conversations. Even though she has seen the television ads, she has a hard time believing online dating is a normal thing that real people actually do.

"Oh my God, stop!" She reaches for the laptop again, but Roni has a firm hold on it. "I would never do that."

"Get over yourself," Roni says. "It's what everyone does these days."

"I don't want to date," Peggy says. "I'm not ready."

"Peggy," Carmen says. "It's been fourteen years."

Peggy doesn't care if it's been a hundred years. She will never stop missing Patrick. Tears build in the corners of her eyes. She swallows a lump in her throat and glares at Roni. "How dare you!" She turns toward Carmen. "The two of you!" As she pushes herself away from the table, the legs of her chair scrape the floor. She jumps to her feet, and the chair flips over, crashing to the ground. "I don't care how long it's been. He was the love of my life, and he was taken from me. Gone in an instant. Dead."

The teenagers strolling toward the exit stop laughing. The man at the table next to theirs clears his throat. The barista stares at her from behind the counter, his expression kinder than usual.

"Sit back down," Roni says, reaching for Peggy's seat and turning it upright.

"Please, Peggy," Carmen adds, grabbing hold of Peggy's arm.

Peggy shakes Carmen's hand off her. "Leave me alone! The both of you." She sniffs loudly, throws back her shoulders, and storms toward the door.

A gust of wind assaults her as she steps onto the sidewalk. She yanks the hood of her sweatshirt over her head and stomps around the building. Inside her vehicle, her hand shakes as she slides the key into the ignition. *The nerve of them,* she thinks as she accelerates through the parking lot. She slams on the brakes at the end of High Street, and her tires squeal. She's about to turn left on Main but notices Roni and Carmen leaving the coffee shop, so she hangs a right so that she won't be tempted to drive over them.

Back home, Peggy lingers in a long, hot shower. Over the sound of running water, she hears her phone ringing. When she gets out, she sees five missed calls, two from Carmen and three from Roni. For the first time since she's owned the mobile device, Peggy turns it off.

Later that night, she is watching *Messages from Beyond* when her doorbell rings. It's a long continuous ring, so she knows it's Carmen. Peggy turns up the volume on the television. The ringing doesn't stop. Why won't that woman leave her alone? When the ringing finally ends, Peggy gets up to pour herself a glass of seltzer, though what she really wants is a thick chocolate milkshake to drown her

anger, and she has used all her self-restraint to keep herself from going out to buy the ingredients. A knock on the kitchen door startles
her. She turns toward it. Both Carmen and Roni are looking back at
her through the window. *Darn it.* She meant to pull the shade down
last time she was in this room.

"Come on, let us in," Roni says. The doorknob jiggles.

Peggy approaches the door. She looks directly in Roni's eyes and
pulls the shade down.

"Beyatch!" Roni screams.

From the living room, Peggy hears Lynda McGarry say, "He
passed very unexpectedly. In a tragedy."

There's pounding on the door. "So help me God, I will break this
door down. Smash the window!" Roni yells.

Peggy imagines Roni punching her fist through the glass and
reaching for the doorknob with her bloody fingers. There's a commercial on television now—that stupid gecko that Peggy would like
to squash.

Footsteps cross the deck, and Peggy hears Carmen's girlish giggle. "Oh no," Carmen calls. "She has the plant pot. You'd better open
up."

Peggy lifts the shade and peers out the window. Roni is walking
back to the door, carrying the orange ceramic planter with the wilted
daisies. "Open the door, or I will throw this through it." She hoists
the pot behind her shoulder like she's about to heave it.

Peggy rips the door open. "You're crazy!"

Roni shoves the planter at her and pushes herself inside. Carmen
tiptoes in behind her. "We're sorry, Peggy. We didn't mean to upset
you." After Peggy lowers the planter to the ground, Carmen ties her
up in a tight hug. Peggy's face gets buried in Carmen's long hair. Its
coconut scent makes her crave a Mounds bar or maybe one of those
Girl Scout cookies with caramel and coconut. *Samoas.* She hasn't had
one of those in a long time.

In the living room, a TV spokesman rambles off the possible side effects of a medication. "Are you deaf?" Roni asks, marching out of the kitchen toward the living room. "Why is that so loud?"

Peggy follows. "To drown out the excessive doorbell ringing."

"You should have opened the door the first time we rang," Roni says.

The television screen fills with Lynda McGarry's face, her eyes squeezed closed. "He wants you to know he never saw it coming. Was never in any pain." The camera focuses on a woman Peggy guesses to be a little older than she is. Lynda McGarry speaks again. "You were worried that he was afraid or was in a lot of pain. He wants me to reassure you he wasn't."

"Don't tell me you believe this crap?" Roni asks.

Peggy reaches for the clicker.

"No, don't shut it off." Carmen crosses the room and makes herself comfortable on the couch.

Peggy sits next to her, and Roni settles on the other side of Peggy. "You know she's a fake, right?" Roni asks.

"It could be real," Carmen says.

The woman on TV tells Lynda that her husband was hit by a tractor trailer while riding his bike.

"But he didn't feel any pain. Please, she's such a fraud." Roni laughs so hard that her shoulders shake.

"I don't think she is," Peggy says. "I want to go on the show. To make contact with Patrick."

Roni stops laughing. In fact, she may have stopped breathing. Peggy refuses to look at her. She keeps her eyes on the television even though she feels both women watching her. "There's so much we never got to say to each other."

Carmen reaches for Peggy's hand and squeezes it.

Roni slowly exhales. "We've all lost people we'd like to talk to again. But you can't think—"

"What do you want to say to him, Peg?" Carmen interrupts, talking over Roni.

"I don't know," Peggy says. But that's not true. She wants to tell him she's sorry, and she knows exactly what she needs to hear from him. She wants him to tell her that he's proud of her and the job she did raising their kids. He couldn't have done better himself. She wants to hear him talk about what great kids Grace and Greg are.

"Have you ever tried to get tickets?" Carmen asks.

Peggy shakes her head.

"Why not?"

Peggy's embarrassed to tell them, but maybe they'll convince her she's being ridiculous. "I don't like the way I look right now. I don't want him to see me like this."

"Oh please, he can't..." Roni stops and takes a deep breath. "What's wrong with how you look?"

"I look beat down and tired. And fat. It's one of the reasons I go to boot camp—to get in shape before he sees me."

"Oh, Peggy, you look fine," Carmen says. "But if you're unhappy with your appearance, come in to the salon, and I'll give you a makeover."

Messages from Beyond is ending. Lynda stands center stage. The camera zooms in on her bare feet and scans upward. When it reaches her face, she begins her usual pitch for viewers to call in for tickets to be part of the live studio audience. "Come see me, and one of your deceased love ones might come see you. You never know."

"Oh please," Roni says, her voice throatier than usual, as if she's trying to stifle a laugh.

Meanwhile, Carmen taps at the buttons of her Samsung Galaxy while studying the phone number scrolling across the bottom of the television screen.

DUE TO OVERWHELMING demand, not everyone who calls for tickets to *Messages from Beyond* receives them. That's what the operator told Carmen when, after dozens and dozens of tries, she finally got through. "If the tickets don't come within four to six weeks, call us back, and try again." Peggy thinks that's hogwash. She should get tickets for being such a loyal viewer. She's never missed a show and has seen most of them a few times.

Her calendar hangs on the kitchen wall. Grace made it for her last Christmas. Every page is decorated with images of the twins or George Clooney because Peggy has a mad crush on him. Grace even photoshopped Peggy's face over George's wife in a few of the pictures. Seeing them now makes Peggy smile. She counts off four weeks from today and in blue marker writes, "Messages Tix." The day next to it is marked up with red ink that says "G&G home for Thanksgiving." Well, Peggy will have two things to be grateful for on the holiday.

She's so certain that she will get the tickets that she's already made an appointment with Carmen for a haircut—or *makeover*, as Carmen called it. Peggy also has decided that she will step up her efforts in boot camp and eat a cleaner diet because she needs to look better when Lynda McGarry makes contact with Patrick. Of course, the medium won't be able to connect with the loved ones of everyone in the audience, but Peggy's certain Lynda McGarry will make contact with Patrick. She won't allow herself to think otherwise.

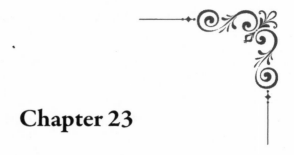

Chapter 23

Carmen's shop sits kitty-corner to Holy Grounds. *Hairo.* Peggy has driven by it zillions of times and has always wondered who would go to a salon with such a stupid name. The sign has a picture of Superman's red cape with a gold H on the back instead of an S.

As Peggy steps inside, she sees that the salon is more elegant than its ridiculous name and logo suggest. The place is quiet except for the sound of running water coming from a bamboo water slide on a tall glass reception counter. The chrome stool behind the desk sits empty, and Peggy assumes the receptionist is in the restroom. That's where she would be if she had to listen to that flowing water all day.

To the right, a man steps out of a door that Peggy didn't realize was there because it's painted red like all the walls and has no frame or handle. The man has a gray goatee but no mustache. Peggy wonders if he ran out of time shaving this morning. His cowboy boots click on the black ceramic tile floor as he makes his way toward reception. Once he is settled in his chair, he addresses Peggy. "Can I help you?"

Peggy blinks fast. She was not expecting such a deep voice from this petite man. She tells him that she's there to see Carmen.

Just then, Carmen turns the corner behind him. "Peggy," she squeals, opening her arms and rushing toward her.

For crying out loud. Why is she acting like we haven't seen each other in years when we saw each other a few hours ago at boot camp? It is actions like this that still make Peggy suspicious of Carmen's motives.

"Spencer," Carmen says to the receptionist. "This is my good friend Peggy, Grace's mother."

Good friend. Ha! Another reason for Peggy's mistrust.

"Oh yes." He nods. "I see the resemblance to Grace."

Well, that's certainly not true either, but rather than mistrust Spencer for his lie, Peggy likes him more. She wonders if the makeover Carmen gives her could miraculously make her look like her teenage daughter—or at the very least, like her teenage self. *Wouldn't that be something!*

Carmen leads Peggy around the corner to a sleek black chair facing a mirror outlined with silver light fixtures with six huge overly bright bulbs screwed into each side. The mirror reflects a magnified image, making Peggy uncomfortable. She turns away from it as Carmen wraps the Superman cape around her shoulders.

A woman with foil wrapped throughout her hair sits at the station next to Carmen's. She's reading a magazine and chewing gum. A few chairs down on the other side, a male hairdresser holds a blow-dryer to a client's head like he's holding the woman hostage.

Carmen runs her fingers through Peggy's hair. "We'll start by changing your color," she says, dipping a small paintbrush into a bowl of yellowish goop.

Peggy's muscles tighten, and a line of sweat breaks out across her chest. She hasn't been in a salon like this in years. As Carmen paints the mixture on Peggy's head, the strong scent of ammonia makes Peggy cough.

She reaches for a cinnamon disk in a jar on the counter in front of her. "What color?"

"Blue," Carmen answers. "It's all the rage."

Peggy jerks away from Carmen. "What?"

Carmen giggles. "Relax. I'm joking." She holds Peggy's head in place with one hand and paints with the other.

Peggy sighs. "You still haven't told me what color."

"Trust me."

They should give out sedatives at the hairdresser's like they do at the dentist. Hashtag Sedation Hair Styling. Maybe that will be her first tweet in the Twitter account she set up years ago to monitor Grace and Greg.

Peggy studies Carmen's long, wavy dark hair. Not a strand of gray. She notices the short layers that frame Carmen's perfectly symmetric face. "Who does your hair?"

Carmen tilts her head toward the male stylist across the aisle. "Barry."

"He does a good job."

"I'm not sure, but I think you might have just complimented me, Peg," Carmen teases.

Peggy laughs. Her muscles relax as Carmen smothers her graying roots with the goop. She doesn't feel as sweaty anymore, though her fists remain clenched beneath the apron buttoned around her neck. She uncurls her fingers and rests her hands on her knees. "Why do you put up with me? Did Grace ask you to watch out for me?"

Carmen lifts the hair surrounding Peggy's face and brushes the underneath sections. "Grace did mention she was worried about you. I told her not to. I said I'd keep an eye on you."

The woman in the chair next to Peggy blows a big bubble. It pops, and the gum sticks to her face.

"So you're nice to me because of Grace," Peggy says. Although she suspected this was the reason, her shoulders sag, and she clenches her hands again beneath the gown.

"No." Carmen meets Peggy's eyes in the mirror, and Peggy holds her stare. "I admire you. You raised two kids yourself. Without any help. While dealing with a devastating loss. Not many women could do that. You're stronger than you know, Peg."

Peggy feels like she's on the verge of tears. She looks away from the mirror. Carmen pats her shoulder. She puts the paintbrush down and sets a timer. "Can I get you a glass of water or a magazine?"

"Water, please."

As Carmen walks off, Peggy studies herself in the mirror. Covered in slimy color, her hair is slicked away from her face. Patches of yellow smear her forehead. She glances over at the woman with the tinfoil sticking out of her head. They both look ridiculous. She remembers when she was younger and didn't have to put effort into her appearance. She woke up looking good and feeling good too. When was the last time she felt that way about herself? She can't remember. But surely—she hopes—that woman is still somewhere inside of her.

A LITTLE MORE THAN two hours later, Peggy has a new hairstyle. As she checks out her reflection in the mirror, a grin appears on her face. *This gorgeous hair is mine!* Instead of dirty dishwater, her hair color is now what Carmen calls *butterscotch blond*, a mix of light brown and blond. Carmen says it's the perfect shade to go with Peggy's warm skin tones. All Peggy knows is that she looks a decade younger. Instead of a middle part, Peggy's hair now falls to the left with only a few strands of her bangs—which Carmen insists need to grow out—falling over her forehead and the rest blending into the side of her head.

As Peggy unsnaps the cape, the Superman-like logo catches her eye. *You are stronger than you know.*

"Keep that on. We're not done," Carmen says, pulling open a drawer filled with cosmetics. She reaches for a package of wipes and uses one to remove the tinted moisturizer from Peggy's face. She applies foundation with a yellow undertone instead of the pink that Peggy wears in the rare instances she uses makeup. Peggy smiles as the small lines on her face disappear. Carmen brushes on a rust bronzer and blush. Peggy resists the urge to twist in her seat to get a better look as cheekbones emerge on her doughy face.

Next, Carmen works on Peggy's eyes. She blends a terra-cotta shadow above the crease of Peggy's eyelids and applies several coats of black mascara. Peggy sits perfectly still as Carmen works her magic. It's as if the chubby flesh that swallowed her eyes is spitting them back out. Peggy never thought she'd be the type of woman who enjoyed getting a makeover, but she has to admit, she enjoys this—loves it, in fact. She can't remember the last time somebody paid so much attention to her. Carmen's not only paying attention, but she's pampering Peggy as well. And Peggy's learning so much. For instance, the way Carmen applies mascara depends on whether she is working on the upper, lower, inner, or outer lashes.

"Some lashes, we want to thicken, others, lengthen," Carmen explains.

For the finishing touch, Carmen swipes a shimmery bronze lipstick across Peggy's lips. "Ta-da!" She steps aside so that Peggy has an unobstructed view of herself in the mirror. Peggy studies her reflection, finally getting the opportunity to turn from side to side to admire Carmen's handiwork. She sees little similarity to the woman who entered this shop. The darkness that has masked her face for the last fourteen years is gone. Her skin is bright, glowing almost, just like Lynda McGarry's when she steps onto the *Messages from Beyond* set. She looks healthy, happy even. Ready to see Patrick! It's like she's looking at an old friend, one she is overjoyed to see. Peggy leans closer to the mirror. She notices a small dimple in her left cheek. She had forgotten all about that dimple, hasn't seen it for a decade or so. It appears only when her smile is not fake.

"You look gorgeous!" Carmen says.

Peggy thinks that, for once, Carmen might not be exaggerating. "Thank you."

Carmen pats Peggy's shoulder. "Spencer, come see!"

His boots click on the tile floor as Peggy shrugs out of her cape. He whistles when he arrives. "Hot damn, girl. We should have done a before and after."

Carmen's eyes widen. "We have to send a picture to Grace and Greg." She reaches for her phone, which is atop a pile of magazines.

Peggy happily poses for the picture, though she wishes she were wearing something nicer than her purple Saint Michael's College zip-up hoodie. Carmen takes several shots and emails them all to Peggy. "Look at them all when you get home, and decide which one you want to send." But Peggy has already decided she won't send any of them. Instead, she will change into a nicer shirt, take her very first selfie, and send that to her kids.

Chapter 24

Henry arrives as the class finishes burpees. He squeezes into the floor space between Carmen and Peggy and spreads his mat. Peggy sighs. She hates being crowded in this stinky room.

When he looks at Peggy, Henry's eyes widen, and the corners of his mouth turn upward. "You've done something to your hair." *No kidding,* Peggy thinks, but before she says anything, he roars, "You look grrreat." He draws out the last word in a booming voice so that he sounds like Tony the Tiger. The boot campers in the first two rows turn to see what the commotion is, but Henry doesn't take his eyes off Peggy.

"Thank you," she says, running a hand through her new locks.

Henry tilts his head and continues to stare at her with a goofy grin. "I can't believe the transformation."

"Are you saying I didn't look good before?" Peggy hates that she asked him that, but she had to say something. He makes her so uncomfortable the way he's standing there, looking at her with his mouth hanging open.

Henry chuckles. "Not at all."

Peggy doesn't believe him. After all, she put him on the spot. What was he supposed to say, and why did he laugh? *Oh boy.* She wonders why she cares. Behind Henry's back, Carmen catches Peggy's eye and winks.

"Mountain climbers," Shauna yells. The class is doing Tabata—work out hard for twenty seconds, rest for ten seconds, repeat

156

for eight rounds of each exercise. As Peggy positions herself at the top of a push-up to start the mountain climber, the music gets louder, an angry song by Pink. "Go!"

Looking down at her mat, Peggy quickly drives her right knee to her chest and back and repeats with the left. She does it over and over again for the entire twenty seconds.

By the time they reach round four, the music has changed to Katy Perry, and Peggy's pace has slowed enough so that she can hear Henry singing softly next to her. His head is down, his eyes closed, and sweat drips off his chin, soaking his mat. As the rounds continue, Peggy's movements become more lethargic, and Henry's voice gets louder. No one else seems to notice his singing, though, not even Miss Never Miss a Trick Shauna. Katy reaches the chorus, and Henry's voice booms. Peggy joins in. They sing the next lines together, and the entire class finishes the chorus. Shauna yells "Time," and Peggy and Henry collapse on their mats in a fit of laughter.

LIKE EVERY OTHER FRIDAY, Roni suggests that she, Peggy, and Carmen have coffee at Holy Grounds. As they collect their coats by the cubbies, Henry approaches them. "That was a fun class today."

"Only if you think torture is fun," Roni answers. "Nothing I hate more than mountain climbers."

Carmen smiles at Henry. "Yes, but Henry's singing made it easier to get through."

"I wasn't the only one singing," he says, taking Peggy's jacket from her and holding it open.

As Peggy slides her arm through the sleeve, Roni elbows Carmen, who looks at Peggy and raises an eyebrow. Peggy's heart races faster than it did in class. "Thank you," she mumbles to Henry.

"My pleasure," he says with the same goofy expression he had when he complimented her hair.

"So, Henry," Carmen says, zipping her jacket. "We're headed to Holy Grounds for a quick coffee. Join us."

HENRY REACHES THE ENTRANCE to Holy Grounds first. He pulls the door open and waits for Roni, Carmen, and Peggy to enter.

"Thank you, Henry," Roni and Carmen say as they file past him. Peggy says nothing. She doesn't even look at him as she walks by. She's annoyed that Carmen invited him. It's not that she doesn't like him, but the way he's been watching her and smiling makes her uncomfortable. She's not used to that.

As usual this time of the morning, a line of customers snakes its way through the shop. Peggy takes her place behind Roni and Carmen, and Henry stands behind her. He inhales deeply. "Smells delicious in here," he says.

A tall woman in a hairnet and white smock emerges from a door behind the counter, carrying a tray of blueberry muffins to the display case. Peggy's stomach growls. She licks her lips and takes a deep breath, trying to taste the muffins through their scent.

"Next," the scowling barista yells.

A woman talking on her phone steps forward. "Hold on," she says into the receiver. "House light with almond milk." She resumes talking.

"Size?" the barista asks.

"Oh, I know," the woman says into her phone. "That wasn't supposed to happen."

"What size?" the barista repeats through gritted teeth.

The woman continues her phone conversation. "He said he was—"

"Size?" he shouts, reaching over the counter for her phone.

She bats his hand. "Grande."

Several minutes later, Roni reaches the front of the line. When the barista serves her, he makes a noise that sounds like a growl. "If you're going to work in customer service, you should learn to be nice," Roni says.

Carmen steps up to the counter and smiles brightly. "Good morning, Hunter."

Hunter? Peggy didn't know that was his name, but it doesn't surprise her that he has a trendy name like that.

The barista exhales loudly, places his palms on the glass counter, and leans toward Carmen. "It is now," he says, an ear-to-ear grin replacing the scowl.

Carmen giggles. Peggy wants to puke. *Life is so much easier for attractive people.* She can't believe Roni's sitting at the table, missing this obscene flirting. *Carmen is married, for Pete's sake. She shouldn't encourage him!*

Henry chuckles, and Peggy remembers that he is standing behind her. He taps her on the shoulder. "I think Mr. Coffee has a crush on Carmen."

Mr. Coffee. Peggy laughs. Henry smiles down at her. Carmen looks back at them and winks.

Oh, for crying out loud, Peggy thinks.

HENRY PUTS HIS CUP of coffee down and takes the seat between Peggy and Carmen. His big body spills over the side of the chair, and his massive legs barely fit under the table. "Must be my lucky day that I get to have breakfast with three gorgeous women. All the other guys here are giving me dirty looks."

Carmen and Roni laugh. Peggy does not. Smarmy people get on her nerves. She hasn't looked in a mirror, but she knows she's a hot mess right now. She spent the last sixty minutes doing grueling exercises and sweating like a madwoman. She can barely stand to smell herself. She's sure her face is tomato red, and she can feel that her hair is damp with perspiration. If anyone is giving the table dirty looks, it's because all four of them look like they need a long hot shower. Well, okay, maybe Carmen doesn't.

"What's everyone doing for the weekend?" Henry asks.

"We're starting tomorrow with a nice run on the bike trail," Carmen says.

Peggy and Roni groan as Carmen explains that the three of them are training for the Thanksgiving Day 5K.

"Good for you, Peggy!" Henry exclaims, patting her on the back.

Peggy feels her face getting hot.

Across the table, Roni smirks at Henry. "What about me and Carmen? Isn't it good for us too?"

Henry's red face goes pale. "Of course."

"How about you, Henry?" Carmen asks. "What are your weekend plans?"

Henry picks up his coffee. The three women wait as he sips and swallows. "I'm seeing that Reese Witherspoon movie tomorrow night."

"Do you have a date?" Roni asks. "Because that doesn't sound like the kind of movie a guy would see on his own."

Henry looks more uncomfortable than he does holding the plank in boot camp. "I do." He addresses Peggy. "With a woman I met on Ideal-Mate-dot-com. Nothing serious."

Peggy's shoulders stiffen. Why would he think he owes her an explanation?

"So tell us about her," Roni says.

Henry glares at Roni the same way Roni glares at Shauna when the fitness guru makes the class do mountain climbers. "Her name's Denise. Quit her job as a marketing VP at some big company to start a doggy-daycare business. That's all I know."

The tightness spreads to Peggy's back. Of course, the woman he's dating loves dogs. She herself tolerates them, but she's really not a dog person. That's why the two of them would never work. One of several reasons, she's sure.

"That's insane," Roni says.

"No, it's great," Henry says. "People should follow their passions. Life's too short."

"Yes, it is," Peggy agrees.

Henry meets her eye. "I heard about what happened to your husband. I'm sorry. I lost my wife." He swallows hard. "Two years ago. Cancer."

Peggy would have never guessed Henry lost his wife. He's always so happy. "I'm sorry." For the first time, she looks at him and sees more than his hefty body and pudgy face. She imagines that the deep lines surrounding his eyes were carved by tears, and the wrinkles on his forehead and around his mouth were etched by worry as his wife got sicker. The mismatched socks must be the result of a man still not used to not having his wife to take care of him or who is overwhelmed by raising kids alone.

"Do you have children?" she asks.

Henry's blue eyes cloud over. "We had trouble conceiving. That's how they discovered the tumor. Left ovary," he says, and Carmen touches his arm. "She went into remission. Nine years. We thought we were in the clear." He swipes his cheek. "Can you excuse me for a minute?"

Peggy thinks about the day she met Henry in her backyard, how annoyed she was by the loving way he spoke to his dog. Realizing now that Wally is all he has left after his wife's death, she feels horrible. All this time, she has only thought of Henry as the fat guy in class. Unable to get comfortable, she shifts in her seat. She knows how hurtful it is when people judge her because of her size. If she wants people to stop judging her, she should be less judgmental herself.

Henry returns with a giant muffin bursting with blueberries. He places it in the center of the table. "Have some." Roni breaks off a piece. Peggy wants some, too, but somehow resists. She doesn't want to sabotage her hard work at boot camp, especially before she's even had a chance to shower and still reeks.

"Have you met a lot of women online?" Peggy asks, making an effort to be friendlier.

"A few," he says.

"Were most of them crazy?"

Henry wiggles his eyebrows. "No crazier than me."

"We're trying to convince Peggy to sign up for online dating," Roni says. "She thinks only psychos do it."

"I have no interest in dating," Peggy says quickly.

"That's too bad." Henry stares at her with a grin until she looks away.

Holy Grounds has cleared out. Besides the boot-camp friends, there is only an elderly couple left. The barista emerges from behind the counter to flick a switch on the back wall. The fireplace sparks to life.

Son of a gun. All this time, Peggy thought the fire was real. *Come on, Pegsta, think,* she imagines Patrick saying. *Have you ever seen someone put wood in it?*

Carmen's voice brings Peggy back to the table. "So, Henry, how did you know you were ready to date?"

He's quiet for a minute. "I'm not really sure I am, but Missy, my wife..." He pauses to take a bite of the muffin. "She told me she wanted me to marry again and made me promise to date."

"That's sweet," Carmen says. "She wanted you to be happy."

"I think most spouses would," Roni says.

Peggy doesn't say anything. Her hand hovers over the blueberry muffin for several seconds before she breaks off a tiny piece.

Chapter 25

When Peggy pulls into the Rite Aid parking lot, Carmen and Roni are already there, stretching by the side of the bike path. Well, Carmen is bending over, reaching for her toes, while Roni sits on a post, drinking from a mammoth coffee cup. The Thanksgiving Day race is just over a month away, and the three women have decided to ramp up the training by running three times a week—Tuesday, Thursday, and Saturday mornings. With boot camp on Monday, Wednesday, and Friday, Sunday is the only day Peggy doesn't see Carmen and Roni. It's the longest day of her week, and she usually ends up calling one or both of them.

"Catching up on your beauty sleep this morning?" Roni asks when Peggy steps out of her car.

Peggy's usually the first to arrive, but today, she's ten minutes late because she was reading an email Greg sent late last night. It included a picture of Patrick that her son found in an old yearbook. Patrick was the twins' age when it was taken. Peggy wanted to cry as she thought of Greg sitting alone in the library, sifting through old yearbooks, looking for a picture of his dad, but as always, she forced herself to stay upbeat for the twins. She wrote, *He was a good-looking son of a gun, just like you.* Honestly, though, when Peggy looked at the picture—the deep-set green eyes, long straight nose, and thick full lips—all she could see was Grace.

"Sorry," Peggy says, snapping her water belt around her waist. Carmen insisted that she get the belt, and Peggy knew that if she didn't, her friend would buy one for her. Still, she feels like an absolute poser when she wears it, as if she's pretending to be a real runner.

"Is everything okay?" Carmen asks.

"Fine." Peggy doesn't have the words to explain how Greg's email broke her heart, and even if she did, she's not used to having friends to confide in after all these years.

Roni finishes her coffee and tosses the cup into her back seat, and the three set off walking down the trail at a brisk pace. Usually, they alternate between walking and running, gradually working their way to being able to run the entire distance. Carmen, of course, would have no trouble running the whole way now if she wanted to, and on days she doesn't have to work, she sometimes continues on her own for another two or three miles after finishing with Roni and Peggy, who both think she's crazy.

Five minutes into the walk, Carmen signals that they should start running. "Already?" Roni whines.

"Yes, and we're jogging for a mile and a half. Try to keep up."

Despite her complaining, Roni stays by Carmen's side, while Peggy falls behind. Peggy stares after them, annoyed. It's not fair that she's the slowest of the three. Roni still eats whatever she wants and cheats on the boot-camp exercises, yet she's a better runner than Peggy. Peggy is determined to beat her during the 5K. For now, she keeps her eyes on the pavement so she can navigate around the fallen leaves, acorns, and twigs that litter the trail. After a few minutes, her heavy breathing drowns out the sound of footsteps and the rattling of branches. *For God's sake.* She sounds like she needs an oxygen tank.

Carmen glances back at her, probably to make sure she's not going into cardiac arrest. "Doing great, Peg."

The three women approach a young mother talking on the phone while pushing a baby stroller. As Roni peeks into the carriage, she stumbles and falls to the ground. "Shit," she cries.

Carmen and Peggy rush to Roni's side and help her to her feet, but the woman with the stroller doesn't break stride. "What happened?" Peggy asks.

Roni brushes debris from the trail off her yoga pants and glances down the path. She waits for the young mother to round a curve and disappear from their view. "I have never seen such an ugly baby. I mean, it was absolutely hideous."

"Roni!" Peggy scolds.

"No, really. Did you see it?" she asks Carmen, who shakes her head. "We have to catch up so you guys can see."

Roni sprints away while Peggy and Carmen exchange a look. "She deserved to fall," Peggy says.

"Yes. But aren't you curious?" Carmen raises an eyebrow.

The two take off after Roni. When they round the curve and the baby carriage comes into sight again, Roni is right behind it. She looks over her shoulder and beckons them to hurry. Carmen reaches the stroller before Peggy. She glances into it. "Hi, there, cutie," she says as she passes, but her voice is two octaves higher than usual.

Peggy finally catches up to the stroller. She slowly turns her head to the right, and her eyes lock with the mother's. A wave of guilt rushes over Peggy, who's been running as fast as she ever has to see if this poor baby is as ugly as Roni says. *How terrible.* Still, she wants to know. She peeks into the carriage. *Holy smokes! No wonder Roni tripped. The poor little thing!* Peggy can't stop looking at him. Eyebrows like caterpillars, nostrils bigger than his eyes, and an expression Grace would call "resting bitch face." Waiting down the trail a few yards in front of her, Carmen giggles and Roni snorts. Peggy fights an overwhelming urge to laugh. She tears her eyes off the baby to find the mother looking at her. She stops running so that the mother will get in front of her again. Instead, the young mother comes to a standstill, glaring at Peggy.

She has to say something. "I've never seen an expression like that on a baby," she says. Then because she feels bad, she lies. "He's so cute."

"She. Amelia," the mother corrects.

Roni's snort and Carmen's giggle echo down the trail. "Well, she's adorable," Peggy manages to say.

"Thanks," the mother says, not sounding grateful at all. She jerks the carriage around and stomps off in the other direction.

Peggy can't hold it back any longer. Before the stroller has disappeared around the curve, she bursts out laughing. Tears stream down her face. She bends at the waist with her hands on her knees to gather herself. It doesn't work. Her stomach hurts from laughing so much.

"Told you," Roni says.

"We're all going to be on the express bus to hell," Carmen says.

PEGGY STOPS IN FRONT of a display of Halloween candy by the cash registers. Snickers, Kit Kats, Skittles, and her absolute favorite, Milky Ways. The ridiculous holiday is a week away. Because she lives on a cul-de-sac, her street is one of the most popular for trick-or-treaters, with more than a hundred of them ringing her doorbell every year. Although she doesn't want candy in the house, she has to get something for them. She decides to go with Skittles because she doesn't like them. *Honestly, what's the point of fruit-flavored candy? Why not have the fruit instead?* She drops a few bags into her basket before stepping into line behind a twentysomething young man. He empties the contents of his shopping cart onto the belt: ground beef, frozen french fries, pizza, and ice cream.

Peggy's basket overflows with food she bought from the store's outer aisles, just as Shauna preaches—spinach, carrots, apples, oranges, string cheese, and hummus. She sighs, thinking the young man's selection looks much more appetizing than hers. He finishes emptying his carriage and slides the checkout divider to the end of his items. Peggy places her groceries on the belt but pauses when she gets to the Skittles. *Do kids even like them?* She doesn't really want to support the dreadful fruit-flavored candy makers. That would only encourage them. She imagines them taking it a step further and creating vegetable-flavored Skittles. She doesn't want to be even partially responsible for broccoli-flavored candy. She gathers up the bags of Skittles, slips past the person behind her, and swaps them for Milky Ways.

With bags of the chocolate-caramel candy bars piled high in her arms, Peggy steps back into line behind the young man, who is swiping his credit card. He studies her, first focusing on the Milky Ways and then scanning her body. His bottom lip curls downward before he turns away.

Peggy imagines him passing judgment on her. *The sweaty fat lady in the running clothes needs chocolate after a little bit of exercise. Maybe she should forget about running and focus more on giving up the chocolate.* She glares at him as he takes his bags off the carousel.

He smiles at her. "Milky Ways are my favorite too." Peggy would bet that Milky Ways are not his favorite. He only said it because she caught him staring at her, just as she told the mother on the trail who caught her gawking that her baby was cute. Well, it serves her right for laughing at the ugly baby. *Karma,* she thinks, telling herself she will be less judgmental. After all, her assumptions are often wrong. Henry's kind, smiling face pops into her mind.

Back at home after putting away the groceries, she sits at the breakfast bar and logs into her email on her laptop. She's surprised to see another message from Greg, saying he met an old priest who remembers Patrick. Greg has attached a picture from the school's newspaper, *The Defender*. In it, Patrick is standing on the stairs to the chapel, pointing to it.

Get your butt to church, Pegsta, she imagines him saying. While he never missed Mass, she rarely accompanied him. After he died, she made a point of taking the twins, but once they were old enough to go by themselves, she stopped attending. It's not that she doesn't believe in God. It's just that she doesn't think she needs to be at church to pray. *That's a piss-poor excuse.* She sees Patrick pointing at her as he says it.

"It's not!" She leaps up from the stool, trying to escape this argument that is only in her mind. As she paces around the kitchen, she thinks about Greg looking for people who knew his father. Maybe she didn't tell the kids enough about Patrick. Is this the reason for all her son's research into Patrick's life at school? And the frequent emails? Her pacing leads her to the cabinet with the Halloween candy. She convinces herself that one bite-sized Milky Way bar will not ruin her diet and rips the bag open. Later that night, when she climbs into bed, only three candy bars remain in the open bag.

Chapter 26

Peggy waits inside her SUV in the drugstore's parking lot by the entrance to the bike path. Behind her, a steady stream of cars makes its way through the Dunkin' Donuts drive-through window. She really wants coffee but knows it's not a good idea before jogging. She had a small cup before their run last week, and by the time she reached the one-mile mark, the beverage had worked its way through her system. She had to turn around and make a beeline for the donut shop's restroom. It was the fastest mile she'd run to date: eleven minutes and forty-seven seconds.

She checks the time again. Carmen and Roni should have been here fifteen minutes ago. It's not unusual for Roni to be late, but Carmen is always on time. She wishes they would hurry and get here because it's their last training run before the Thanksgiving Day race, and she wants to get it over with. In fact, she wants the entire day to fly by because tomorrow her babies will be home for Thanksgiving break. *Finally!*

A horn blares on Route 85, interrupting Peggy's thoughts. She turns in time to see Roni's silver Ford cutting off a black pickup truck. Roni flips off the driver, guns her vehicle across the parking lot, and pulls in beside Peggy's SUV.

As Peggy steps out of her car, the wind gusts, sending dirt swirling into the air. She folds her arms across her chest and jumps up and down to keep warm, wishing she had another layer on top of her long-sleeved shirt.

Roni lowers the passenger window. "Where's Carmen?" she yells over her radio, which, as always, is playing a song from decades ago.

Peggy shrugs.

"Well, get in. There's no sense freezing our asses off while we wait." Roni moves a garbage bag of empty soda and beer cans to the back seat so that Peggy can sit. "Going to recycle after our run."

"Do you record those in your food journal?" Peggy asks.

"Hell no! And if you tell Shauna, I'll kill you. I mean it."

"Baba O'Riley" comes on the radio. Peggy pictures Patrick playing air guitar and singing the lyrics. He did things like that all the time, and always to songs by the Who. She never understood his infatuation with that rock group, but hearing their music now fills her with a warmth because it reminds her of him.

Another car pulls into the lot. A man with a pit bull slides out and strolls to the trail. Peggy's phone rings. She glances down at the band strapped around her arm and sees Carmen's name flash across the screen. She scrambles to remove the phone from its case, but by the time she has it out, the ringing has stopped. Instead of waiting to see if Carmen will leave a message, Peggy calls her back. Roni lowers the radio.

"Rosalita has a stomach bug," Carmen says. "I need to stay home with Sophia this morning and find someone who can watch her when I go to work."

Peggy pictures the adorable little girl with her pudgy cheeks and mass of curly dark hair. "I'll do it."

Carmen hesitates. "Oh, Peg, I couldn't ask you to do that."

"You didn't. I volunteered." She gets a whiff of a banana and turns to see Roni peeling one. Peggy scrunches her nose. She has always hated that smell.

"You really don't mind?" Carmen asks.

The surprise in Carmen's voice insults Peggy. "Not at all. I'd love to spend the day with Sophia." She was planning to hit the mall later this morning to buy a new outfit for Thanksgiving, but she can always do that tonight. Not that she intends to get dressed up for the holiday. It's just that her clothes are a little baggy now. Peggy agrees to be at Carmen's by ten and hangs up.

"She's not coming?" Roni asks, her mouth full.

Peggy slides her phone back into the armband. "Her mother-in-law is sick, so there's no one to watch Sophia."

Roni lowers the window and drops the banana peel onto the pavement. "Do you still want to run? We could go to breakfast instead." Her voice is hopeful.

Peggy opens the passenger door. "Get your butt out of the car."

Roni steps out onto the pavement and snaps her water bottle around her waist. "Remember how delicious those blueberry pancakes were?"

"Nothing tastes as good as skinny feels." Peggy quotes a post she saw on Facebook. She's not sure if it was meant to be inspirational or comical. What she does know is that she doesn't believe it.

"You've been hanging around Carmen and Shauna too much. They're converting you."

Peggy laughs. "No chance of that."

The two women make their way down the bike path. Even without Carmen there to push them, they run fast. The houses to the right are now visible because the trees have shed their leaves. Peggy wonders how long it will be before the trail is covered with snow and ice, making it unusable. She looks up at the metal-gray sky and thinks it could even snow today.

They catch up to the man with the pit bull. As they pass, the dog growls and lunges at them, but the owner retracts the leash so that it can't reach them. Still, Peggy and Roni pick up their pace to put distance between themselves and the scary animal. Peggy slips on her headphones, and the two jog without speaking. Peggy gets lost in her music, listening to the lyrics and almost forgetting she's running. She glances over her shoulder occasionally to check on Roni. Each time, she notices that the distance between the two has increased, until finally, Roni has disappeared from view. Peggy pumps her fist. She is running faster than Roni!

A song by George Michael comes on as Peggy runs by two women walking. They smile at her, and she realizes she's singing along with it. *How about that?* When she started training, she was so busy gasping that she couldn't talk during her runs, and now she's belting out the lyrics to eighties pop music. *Exercising is paying off!* The computerized voice of her running app interrupts George Michael to announce that Peggy has reached the halfway point of her run. Her time is nineteen minutes and forty-four seconds. She pumps her fist again because she's never made it this far in less than twenty minutes. Determined to finish the three-plus miles in under forty-two minutes, her personal best, she turns around and increases her speed.

Several minutes into Peggy's return trip, Roni comes into view. She's petting the pit bull and laughing at something the owner says. Giving them a wide berth, Peggy waves as she passes them, thinking Roni's crazy. That dog could bite her face off.

Roni calls her name, but Peggy doesn't stop. If she beats her best time, she'll have more confidence when she's running with Grace on Thursday. She's been assuming that Grace will run with her, but now she wonders if Grace and Carmen will run ahead, leaving her in their dust. She pictures an impatient Grace, pacing at the finish line and whining to Carmen, *What's taking her so long?*

Peggy tries to imagine how Carmen would respond. She sees her friend putting a hand on Grace's arm and gently reprimanding her. *You should be proud of your mother. She's worked hard to get ready for this race.* Yes, Carmen would definitely stand up for her. The thought makes her smile. It is nice, after all these years, to have a friend.

Peggy's breathing turns to heavy panting. Slowing her pace, she inhales through her nostrils and blows out through her mouth. "Four hundred meters remaining," the running application whispers. To Peggy, the computerized voice sounds more supportive than usual, but maybe she's imagining it because she needs the encouragement in Carmen's absence. She lifts one heavy leg and then the other. She wants to stop and walk the remaining distance. *Don't you dare,* her inner voice warns. The application announces that three hundred meters remain. It no longer sounds encouraging. Instead, the stupid thing taunts her.

The sky spits big wet snowflakes. One lands on Peggy's forehead, and she swipes it away with the back of her hand. She'll have to check the weather when she gets home. She doesn't want the kids driving through a storm tomorrow. "Two hundred meters remaining," the application says. Peggy glances back over her shoulder. Far in the distance, Roni walks toward her with the man and his mean dog at her side. Peggy wonders what they've been talking about this entire time and laughs, thinking Roni's chatting him up because she doesn't want to run. *He started talking to me, so I had to stop and listen,* Peggy imagines her friend saying.

"One hundred meters remaining," the application announces. The snow falls harder, but there's no accumulation because the flakes melt as soon as they strike the pavement. The parking lot comes into view. In just a few more yards, Peggy can be warm and dry inside her car. She pushes on, using every last ounce of energy. "Congratulations. You have reached your goal of five kilometers. Time: forty-one minutes, thirty-eight seconds." Peggy raises her arms in celebration and slows to a walk. She strides to the intersection to give her heart rate time to come down. She's tempted to text Grace, *I'm going to crush the race on Thursday*. She almost pulls out her phone to do so, but on second thought, she decides not to jinx herself.

When she turns back for her car, Roni is standing by her own vehicle, writing on a piece of paper that she hands to the man she's been walking with. He hugs her quickly before getting into his car. Peggy stumbles. *Why is that stranger hugging Roni?* By the time she reaches her friend, he's driven off.

"I got a date," Roni beams.

"Did you know him already?" Peggy asks.

"Nope. He's cute, isn't he?"

Peggy was so busy looking at the dog that she never saw the man's face. She's almost sure he had no hair, though. She does find that attractive. "How did that happen?"

"We walked and talked, and when we got back here, he asked me to meet him for drinks."

"Just like that?" Peggy can't believe it. "You don't even know him." She opens her car door.

"That's why you go on dates, Peggy. To get to know people. You should try it sometime. With Henry."

Peggy rolls her eyes. "Don't start."

"He would be good for you."

Peggy slides behind her steering wheel. "See you tomorrow." She waits until Roni gets in her Ford. Then the two drive off in opposite directions.

Chapter 27

When Peggy arrives at the gym on Wednesday morning, she has her choice of spaces in the front row and, for once, doesn't have to park in the back of the lot. Inside, the chair behind the front desk sits empty, and no music blasts from the speakers. Instead, the sound of feet pounding a treadmill echoes through the building. The noise comes from one middle-aged man in a sweat-soaked Brady T-shirt, who is sprinting up a steep incline. He and a gray-haired woman reading on a recumbent bicycle and sometimes forgetting to peddle have the cardio machines to themselves.

Peggy makes her way to the back room where boot camp takes place. Henry is sprawled out on the floor, maneuvering his back over a foam roller. Nick and Sixty-Nine stand in a corner, chatting, while Carmen stretches on a mat a few feet in front of them.

"Where is everyone?" Peggy asks.

"People are too busy getting ready for Thanksgiving to go to the gym," Henry answers.

Peggy needs no reminder of the upcoming holiday. The twins will be home in a few hours! She has a busy day of cooking in front of her. Greg already texted to ask if she's making the cornbread stuffing, and Grace loves her candied yams. Peggy's looking forward to mashed potatoes. They are one of her favorite foods, and she hasn't had any since this class started in mid-September.

Shauna races into the room. "Sorry I'm late. Kid's got the flu or something. I was up all night with him." Shauna herself doesn't look so good. Her usually dark-brown complexion has a yellow tint. Her eyes are watery, and she's holding a crumpled-up tissue in her right hand. "Carmen, why don't you lead the class through the warm-up while I set up today's exercises."

Forty-five minutes later, Peggy's holding a sumo squat while repeatedly slamming a twelve-pound medicine ball to the gym floor. This isn't something she ever imagined herself doing at almost fifty, or ever really. Then again, she never expected to weigh more than two hundred pounds—almost two hundred twenty, if she's being honest with herself. When she was pregnant with the twins, she topped off at one hundred sixty. How in the world did this happen to her? Dumb question. She knows exactly how it happened. What she hasn't figured out is why she allowed it to happen.

How much longer is Shauna going to make me do this? Peggy's thighs burn so badly that she wouldn't be at all surprised if her sweatpants went up in flames. She glances at Henry's gallon-sized bottle of water and imagines him dousing her with it to put out the fire.

"You're halfway there," Shauna says.

Halfway? That's all? That can't be right. Peggy's legs shake. They won't be able to support her much longer, and the damn ball must be mislabeled. There's no way it's only twelve pounds. One hundred twelve seems more like it at this point. She can barely lift it over her head. That's it—she's had enough. She starts to rise out of her squat.

"Don't give in to it, Peggy," Shauna says.

Of course Shauna's watching her. Shauna's always watching her. Though truthfully, Roni would say the same thing. Peggy wonders where Roni is. She called Peggy last night to tell her about the date with the man she met on the bike path.

"He turned out to be an asshat," Roni said. Apparently he asked Roni to pay the bill.

Before Roni hung up, she told Peggy she would be at class today. She'd better not skip out on the 5K tomorrow. Peggy's nervous about it and is relying on Roni to keep her calm.

"Time," Shauna says.

Thank God! Peggy lets the ball roll out of her hands and slumps against the wall.

"Peggy," Shauna yells. "Next station. Now!"

Carmen, who has moved to Peggy's spot, pats Peggy on the back. "Almost done."

Peggy glances at the clock. There are just under ten minutes of class left, which in exercise time may as well be ten hours. She rotates to the right, where a long, heavy rope is looped around a pole. With her hands shoulder width apart, she picks up the ends and holds them in front of her hips. She alternately raises and lowers each arm in an explosive motion so that each side of the rope moves in waves across the floor. *Who the heck thinks up these crazy exercises, anyway?*

When the class has finished with the stations, Shauna tells them to line up for sitting squats. *Phooey.* Peggy hates these. As the six participants move to the back wall, Shauna explains that the first person who gives up will have to do twenty-five burpees, with the reps decreasing by five for each person who drops out after. The winner will be spared from the torturous exercise. Peggy eyes Nick, Carmen, Sixty-Nine, Henry, and the college-aged girl whose name she can never remember. She may as well start her twenty-five burpees now.

"If you don't make it to thirty seconds, it's fifty burpees," Shauna says, looking right at Peggy. "Go!" The class members squat with their backs up against the wall and hold the position. "Peggy, lower."

Peggy eyes her classmates again. Nick, Sixty-Nine, and Carmen are having a conversation and not breaking a sweat, as if they're sitting at the dinner table. The college-aged girl smiles, looking as comfortable as if she were lying on a couch. Henry looks like he might be struggling, but that's only because his eyes are closed. For all Peggy knows, he's sleeping. Why the heck isn't Roni here? Peggy could definitely beat Roni at this.

Shauna announces that thirty seconds have passed. Peggy's about to move away from the wall to get her burpees over with when Carmen stands. "Ouch. Too much squatting already today." She drops to a push-up position, jumps up and raises her arms over her head and returns to push-up form. One burpee down, twenty-four to go.

A few seconds later, Nick stands. "We could be here all day. I have to get to the office," he says before starting his twenty burpees. Well, this is Peggy's lucky day. She might be able to manage fifteen reps of the miserable exercise. Henry suddenly flees to the restroom, leaving his empty water jug behind.

"One minute," Shauna announces.

Already? Peggy looks up at the clock as if Shauna may be wrong about how much time has passed. She has never lasted this long before, always tapping out at forty-five seconds. Maybe she can win this thing and not have to do any burpees. She looks over at Sixty-Nine and the college-aged girl. They don't look like they have any intention of moving. Well, neither does Peggy. She distracts herself by thinking about her upcoming reunion with the twins. She wonders if she could convince them to play a board game. *Monopoly?*

"One minute, thirty seconds," Shauna says.

A cramp seizes Peggy's left thigh. She stands to shake it out, intending to resume the squat right after, but Shauna points at her. "Good job. Get started on your burpees. Ten of them." Her classmates are still squatting several minutes later when she finishes.

As Peggy gathers her mat and water bottle, Shauna approaches her. "Enjoy tomorrow, but don't go crazy."

"I'll do my best." Really, Peggy has no intention of dieting tomorrow. The gravy alone will be more calories than she's supposed to eat. On top of that, Grace makes the most amazing apple pie, and Peggy's planning on having a big ol' slice with a scoop or two of vanilla-bean ice cream. Anyway, she's running over three miles in the morning and figures she'll have earned the treat.

Henry reenters the room and begins his burpees. When Peggy walks by him, he stops. "Have a happy Thanksgiving."

She turns to face him. "You too."

"Oh, and good luck with the 5K. I want to hear all about it on Monday. Maybe we can grab a coffee after class."

"You, Roni, Carmen, and I can all go," Peggy says.

Henry's shoulders slump. "Sure." Behind him, the college kid and Sixty-Nine refuse to give up on the wall squat.

Carmen walks outside with Peggy. "I'll pick you and Grace up at seven thirty tomorrow. Dress warmly. It's supposed to be chilly."

As nervous as she is, Peggy grins when thinking about running with her daughter and almost wishes Carmen wouldn't be there, monopolizing Grace's attention. She wonders if Grace will notice the changes in her body. They are minor, but they are there. She knows by the way her black sweatpants no longer leave a red elastic mark around her waist.

Pulling out of the parking lot, Peggy calls Roni to find out why she missed class. "I have a stomach bug," Roni says. "I lost more weight at home in my bathroom this morning than I ever would have at boot camp."

"Thanks for that image," Peggy says, turning on the defroster and lowering her windows because they're getting steamed up from the heat coming off her body. "There were only six of us today. We had a wall squat contest at the end of class. That young college girl and..."

"Emma," Roni interrupts.

"Right," Peggy says. "Emma and Sixty-Nine were up to fourteen minutes when I left."

"Wait, who's Sixty-Nine?" Roni asks.

"The black-haired woman who's always flirting with Nick." Peggy circles around the rotary and heads up the street for Hannaford.

"Christine? Holy shit, what do you know about her that makes you call her Sixty-Nine? Spill it."

"Well, I know she has the number Sixty-Nine tattooed on her shoulder." The light in front of Peggy turns yellow, so she brings the CRV to a stop. Behind her, there's screeching of brakes. Through her rearview mirror, Peggy sees a woman with a phone pressed to her ear, the front bumper of her car almost kissing Peggy's back one.

"Oh my God, Peggy. It's yin and yang."

"What's yin and yang?"

"Christine's tattoo. It's the symbol for yin and yang." Roni laughs.

Peggy visualizes the image on Christine's arm. Well, now she feels like an idiot. She made all sorts of assumptions about that poor woman because of her tattoo, which wasn't at all what Peggy thought it was. "Well, that makes me like her a lot better."

ANTICIPATING THE TWINS' arrival, Peggy stands in the doorway, looking down the street. She's been back and forth to the front door over a dozen times in the past hour even though Grace and Greg aren't supposed to be home for another fifteen minutes. The timer buzzes, so Peggy returns to the kitchen to pull the cornbread out of the oven. She made two loaves, one for the stuffing and one for Greg to snack on tonight. Satisfied that they're done, she places the pans on trivets on the breakfast bar to cool and resumes her post by the front door.

A Subaru Outback rounds the corner. Peggy flings the storm door open and bounces out onto the landing. As the vehicle turns into her driveway, she fights the urge to race down the stairs and tear the kids from the car, because she doesn't want to embarrass them. In the front passenger seat, Greg leans toward the blond driver to hug her while Grace climbs out of the back. Before reaching for her bag,

Grace smiles and waves. Peggy decides she doesn't care if she embarrasses the kids after all. In her bare feet, she jogs down the cold flagstone of the walkway. At the same time, Greg pops out of the car and rushes toward Peggy. Soon, the three are embracing on the walkway as the driver of the station wagon backs out into the street and toots the horn.

Grace pulls away first. Peggy feels her daughter's eyes scanning her body and waits for Grace to say something about her weight loss, minor as it is. Grace points at Peggy's abdomen. Peggy smiles. Here it is, the compliment she's been waiting for.

"You really need to wear an apron when you cook. You spill stuff all over yourself," Grace says.

Peggy looks down at her clothes. A big goop of the sauce she made for the sweet potatoes drips down her St. Michael's sweatshirt, and flour from the cornbread dusts her black sweatpants.

"Some things never change," Greg says, eyeing the stain on Peggy's shirt.

THE FIRST NIGHT OF the kids' Thanksgiving Day break has not gone as Peggy imagined. They barely had time to bring their bags up to their rooms before Julian showed up and whisked them away to a homecoming party. Alone and with everything ready for tomorrow except the turkey, Peggy is curled up on the couch under a blanket, trying to fight a chill. She's even relented and turned the thermostat up to seventy-two to warm up the place, but the increased temperature has had no effect. The house still feels like an icebox. She would swear the heat isn't working, except she can hear the roar of the furnace and smell the oil burning.

She's exhausted and closes her eyes. Every muscle in her body aches. What the heck did Shauna do to them today? She hopes she feels better before tomorrow's 5K. Just as she drifts off to sleep, she's wrenched wide-awake by a sharp pain in her stomach. Before she has time to process what's happening, two more rip through her abdomen. Her throat burns, and there's a disgusting taste in her mouth. *Oh no!* She jolts upright and rushes to the bathroom, barely making it to the toilet before she throws up the soup she had for dinner. Four hours later, Greg and Grace return home to find Peggy retching in the bathroom again.

To say she wakes up in the morning feeling worse would be wrong because she can't remember ever falling asleep, but she does indeed feel worse. There's nothing left in her stomach to throw up, so she's on her knees, dry heaving over the toilet bowl. There's so much pressure in her head that she thinks it might explode. She would welcome a head explosion at this point if it would lessen the pain.

Greg taps on the bathroom door. "Mom, maybe we should call the doctor. You've been puking all night."

The last thing Peggy wants to do is talk to the insulting Dr. Richardson on Thanksgiving, or ever really. She should have never canceled her appointment with Dr. Nancy Levy, but she was able to convince Dr. Richardson's staff to call in a refill of her prescription without going to the office. "I'll be okay." *Will I? Has anyone ever vomited to death?*

When she finally emerges from the bathroom, she finds the kids in the kitchen. Greg's still wearing his pajamas and is eating a piece of cornbread while Grace, dressed in gray running tights and a light-purple sweat-wicking pullover, laces up her running shoes, an unpeeled banana resting on the breakfast bar in front of her.

"What did you do, Mom, eat some rancid food so you wouldn't have to run today?" Grace asks with a smile.

Grace has Patrick's sense of humor, and even though Peggy knows her daughter is joking, the comment infuriates her. She's worked hard to get ready for today's race. "I'm still doing the 5K," Peggy hisses, wishing she meant it.

"I don't think so, Mom," Grace says, peeling her banana.

Its pungent odor fills Peggy's nostrils, causing her to gag. She turns on her heel and races out of the room toward the bathroom. She's still in there when the doorbell rings.

"Hello!" Carmen bellows. "Are you ladies ready to earn your turkey dinner?"

"Mom's really sick," Grace says.

That's all Peggy hears before the next wave of nausea overcomes her. When she lifts her head, Carmen is standing in the bathroom entrance, even though Peggy would have sworn she shut and locked the door.

"Oh, Peggy. You caught the bug that's going around," Carmen says. "Let's get you to bed."

Look at Carmen, all radiant in her workout clothes. Grace will worship her even more. "I want to run the race," Peggy says.

"There will be plenty of others." Carmen wraps an arm around Peggy's waist and leads her up the stairs, with Greg and Grace trailing behind. "Have you had anything to drink? It's important that you don't get dehydrated."

"I can't keep anything down."

"I'll get you something for that," Carmen says.

"I should probably stay here and keep an eye on her," Grace says.

Peggy wishes it weren't so, but the idea of Grace spending time with Carmen bothers her. They might talk about her. Will Grace confide in Carmen the way she confides in her friends? Still, Peggy can't let her jealousy show. "You should go," she says.

"Yeah," Greg agrees. "I'll be here with Mom."

"I don't need a babysitter," Peggy snaps.

Grace, Carmen, and Greg all exchange meaningful looks. "What you need is rest," Carmen says.

She runs to the drugstore and returns with a package of Kaopectate and the biggest bottle of Gatorade that Peggy has ever seen. After making sure Peggy takes the medicine, Grace and Carmen leave for the 5K, and Peggy falls fast asleep.

She awakens several hours later still not feeling better but thinking she has to make dinner for the kids. She staggers downstairs, expecting to find a hungry Grace and Greg sacked out by the television, waiting for their holiday dinner.

"Greg, Grace," she calls out as she heads to the kitchen to turn on the oven. No one answers. The kitchen smells like a freshly baked apple pie, and a dirty cutting board, knife, and mixing bowl fill the sink. In the center of the breakfast bar, Peggy finds a note from the twins informing her that they are eating their Thanksgiving dinner at Carmen's, and they have brought the candied yams and cornbread stuffing with them.

Peggy crumples the paper into a ball and slams it into the trash. She supposes she should be grateful that they have someplace to go and are eating a good meal, but still, she blinks back tears. They left her alone. On Thanksgiving. Lucky Carmen, getting to spend the holiday with Peggy's kids. And why didn't Carmen get this damn stomach virus? Maybe she has some kind of weird bionic resistance. After all, the woman's mother-in-law was the first one to have it. It's all her fault Peggy's sick.

SHORTLY BEFORE EIGHT, the front door bangs open, and Greg and Grace burst into the living room, loaded down with Tupperware. "How are you feeling, Mom?" Grace asks.

"Better," Peggy answers. Her stomach still aches, her head still pounds, but now that her kids are home, at least her depression is lifting. "How was Thanksgiving with Julian and his family?" She deliberately doesn't say Carmen's name.

"We missed you," Grace says.

Well, Peggy was not expecting that, especially from her daughter. Her eyes mist over. "I couldn't believe it when I woke up and you were gone... with the food I spent all day yesterday making."

"We brought lots home for you. For when you feel good enough to eat," Greg says.

Peggy imagines feeling better tomorrow and sitting down to a midday meal of turkey, with its crisp skin drowning in gravy, mashed potatoes drenched with butter, and sweet potatoes drizzled with a brown-sugar glaze. She pushes herself up to a sitting position to get a better look at the containers the twins are holding. "What do you have there?"

Grace holds up the biggest of the containers. "A kale salad."

Peggy scrunches her nose. "Seriously?" Who eats kale on Thanksgiving? That seems ridiculous, even for Carmen. "What else?"

Greg holds up two round containers. "String beans and asparagus."

"Did you bring me any food that isn't green?" Peggy asks.

"Well, you know Carmen," Grace says. "She's all about eating clean."

"What about potatoes? Pie?" Peggy asks. "Did you bring back any of the stuff I made?"

"The only other thing we have is turkey," Grace says, heading toward the kitchen.

Greg follows his sister. "Your stuff all got eaten. Julian and Mr. Tavarez really loved it."

Of course they did. The candied yams and cornbread stuffing were apparently the only edible items on Carmen's table. Peggy hears the refrigerator door open and, a few seconds later, a drink being poured.

Grace returns to the living room and hands Peggy a large glass of Gatorade. "Mom, you hardly drank any of this. You need to stay hydrated." She sits down next to Peggy, who smiles, enjoying being taken care of by her daughter.

"It was depressing having Thanksgiving without you," Grace says.

Peggy swallows the lump in her throat. "It was no fun being sick."

"I guess the good thing about it is that it helped you stick to your diet."

Of course, her daughter would think of that. To be honest, Peggy did too. In fact, she would bet the house she has dropped two to three pounds over the past two days. Grace motions toward Peggy's head. "Your face looks thinner."

Whenever Peggy imagined Grace commenting on her weight loss, she pictured her speaking with unbridled excitement, not the nonchalant tone her daughter is using now. Peggy smiles anyway, happy Grace noticed that she has shed a few pounds.

"I'm sorry you had to miss the race. Carmen said you worked hard to get ready for it," Grace says, leaning toward Peggy to give her a hug. "I'm really proud of you, Mom." Peggy thinks this might be her best Thanksgiving ever. "If you want, we can do one together over the summer."

"I would like that very much," Peggy says.

"I'll find us a good one," Grace says. "Maybe on the Cape. We can make a day of it."

Peggy imagines a mom–daughter trip to the ocean, the two of them sitting side by side in their beach chairs, Grace sharing her dreams and secrets with her mother as the surf pounds against the shoreline in front of them.

Peggy's stomach grumbles, and she realizes she's hungry. Her headache is gone too. This is the best she's felt all day.

Still wearing his coat, Greg returns to the living room. "I'm going to Allison's. Is it okay if I take the car?"

"You just got home," Peggy says. She hasn't had a chance to talk to him since he arrived yesterday, and she was looking forward to catching up.

"Her family is expecting me. They thought I was coming for dessert."

"That's because you told Allison you were coming for dessert," Grace says.

Grace's snippy tone catches Peggy's attention because it's the one her daughter usually reserves for her. "Is everything okay between you and Allison?" Peggy asks.

Greg tosses Peggy's car keys from one hand to the other. "Why wouldn't it be?" he asks, his tone similar to the one his sister just used. He steps backward into the foyer. "Don't wait up." The front door squeaks open and slams shut.

Chapter 28

Peggy is sitting at the breakfast bar, fiddling on her laptop, when a pajama-clad Greg stumbles into the kitchen.

"I'm starving," he announces, plopping onto the stool next to hers. "Can you make me breakfast?"

"What would you like?" Peggy asks, happy to have someone to cook for.

"I was thinking French toast."

Peggy's finally feeling better today, but she hasn't eaten French toast since the incident on the first day of boot camp. She thinks about the smell of eggs and the taste of cinnamon and crinkles her nose. "How about pancakes?"

"Nah," he says. "Your French toast is the best. I've been looking forward to it for weeks."

Well, after that compliment, Peggy is willing to risk stomach upheaval. "Do you want bacon with it?"

"Absolutely." Greg's phone rings, and he answers it. "Hey, Madison." A beat later, in a much gentler tone than his usual one, he says, "Me too."

Peggy snaps her head toward him. His cheeks redden, and he pushes himself up from the stool and flees the kitchen back to his bedroom.

Madison! Me too! Peggy remembers the hickey she saw on her son's neck. Her nostrils flare. *If he wants to date this girl from school, that's all well and fine, but wasn't he out all night with Allison?*

Grace's voice behind Peggy startles her. "Julian and I are going to get a Christmas tree. Is it okay if we take your car?"

"Is there something going on between Greg and this Madison person?" Peggy asks.

Grace's eyes widen. "Whoa, I'm not getting in the middle of that."

"So something is going on?"

Grace sighs. "I didn't say that. Can we take the CRV?"

"What's wrong with Julian's car?"

"He doesn't want to get pine needles all over it." Grace looks sheepish.

"Fine, make a mess out of mine."

"I'll vacuum it."

From the hallway, there's the sound of footsteps coming down the stairs and then Greg asks, "Why don't I smell breakfast?" as he appears in the entrance to the kitchen.

Grace reaches across the counter for Peggy's car keys. "See you later."

Peggy waits for Grace to leave before addressing Greg. "Who were you talking to?"

"Madison. She wants to get an early start back to school on Sunday." He throws his arm around Peggy's shoulder. "Make me breakfast, please."

"Madison's the girl who gave you a ride. How come you didn't introduce her to me?"

Greg shrugs. "She was in a hurry to get home. You can meet her Sunday."

"How's Allison?"

"Good. She's heading back to California tomorrow."

Peggy rises from her stool and opens a cabinet, from which she pulls out a mixing bowl. "Did you two agree to date other people while at school?"

Greg rubs the back of his neck. "You don't want me dating Allison anymore? I thought you liked her."

Peggy takes two eggs from the refrigerator. "I adore her, which is one reason I want to be sure you're treating her respectfully." She cracks the eggs into the bowl and ditches the shells in the wastebasket.

"What do you mean?"

As she thinks about how to talk about this with her son, she collects the ingredients for his breakfast—the milk from the refrigerator, the vanilla extract from a cabinet, and the cinnamon from the spice rack. When she has everything she needs, she mixes it all together in a large bowl on the counter in front of him. "You and Allison are thousands of miles away from each other, and you're surrounded by beautiful girls. It wouldn't be at all surprising if you find yourself attracted to one of them. There's nothing wrong with that." She looks up from the bowl.

"Okay," Greg says.

"What would be wrong," Peggy continues, "would be to act upon that attraction without talking to Allison first."

"What?" Greg asks, rubbing the back of his neck again.

"If you want to be with other girls, you need to let Allison know that you're no longer exclusive."

"I'm not with other girls."

"Greg, you had a hickey. I saw it when we talked on the computer." She beats the ingredients together with a fork.

"I didn't!"

"You and Grace are both too young to be tied down to one person, and I encourage you both to date other people, but you need to tell Allison that's what you're doing."

"I'm not doing that." He squeezes his hands into tight fists to crack his knuckles.

Peggy winces, not just because she hates the sound of cracked knuckles but because it's what Patrick used to do when she suspected he was being untruthful. She wonders if nervous tics are genetic and tries to recall specific instances when Patrick cracked his knuckles. It happened often, she remembers, in the days before he died. *I was working late. I had dinner with a client. Is cheating genetic?* She shakes her head to clear it. *Patrick was not unfaithful. Where are these crazy thoughts coming from?*

"I know what I saw on your neck." She bends to retrieve a frying pan from the lower cabinet.

"Maybe it was a smudge or something on the screen you were looking at."

Does he really expect her to believe that? As Peggy straightens herself, she thinks about how Patrick's assistant broke down at his memorial service.

Peggy pushes the pan and mixing bowl across the countertop toward Greg. "Make your own damn breakfast."

PEGGY SPENDS A PERFECT Saturday afternoon with the kids, decorating the Christmas tree, which Grace and Julian brought home the day before. She makes chili for dinner, and after they eat, they settle in the living room to watch old holiday movies, including her and Greg's favorite, *A Christmas Story*, and Grace's pick, *Miracle on 34th Street*. Greg pays more attention to his phone than the movies, but Peggy figures that's okay because he's seen these films a bunch of times. She only gets annoyed when she asks him who he's texting, and he answers, "No one."

They all turn in at midnight, and before Peggy knows it, it's Sunday morning, and Madison is standing in her foyer, ready to drive the twins back to Vermont. The girl looks like she just rolled out of bed. Her long blond hair is pulled into a ponytail that sticks out of the hole in the back of her baseball cap. She's not wearing any make-up and is dressed in gray yoga pants and a tattered Bruins sweatshirt that Peggy immediately recognizes as her son's. Peggy thought that Greg was lying when he said nothing was going on between him and Madison, and the sight of the girl in his clothing confirms that suspicion.

Madison shakes Peggy's hand with a firm grip. "So nice to meet you, Mrs. Moriarty."

"Mmm," Peggy says. "Is that Greg's sweatshirt?"

Madison looks down at her chest as if she's forgotten what she's wearing.

"I left it in her car when she drove us home," Greg says, cracking his knuckles.

"Well, you're not getting it back," Madison says, playfully punching him on the arm.

"We should hit the road." Greg picks up his bag at the bottom of the staircase. "See you at Christmas, Ma." He kisses her cheek and pushes the screen door open. Madison waves and follows him outside.

Peggy and Grace stand at the door, watching the two of them make their way to Madison's station wagon. "That girl has nothing on Allison," Peggy says.

Grace raises one eyebrow. "She has proximity to Greg." She hugs Peggy tightly before picking up her bag. "See you in a few weeks. Keep up the good work at boot camp."

Peggy follows Grace outside and stands on the landing, waving goodbye, until the Subaru disappears down the street. Reluctantly, she returns to the empty house and wanders from room to room, picking up plates and glasses left behind by the twins. By eleven thirty, the furniture has been dusted, the floors vacuumed and swept, and the sheets have been changed. She's been cooped up inside long enough and needs to get out, so she decides to go for a walk. Before setting out, she scrolls through her phone to choose her music and finds a new playlist called Mom's Toning Tunes. She saw Grace with her phone last night, and the memory makes her smile, knowing that Grace was loading new music for her. She slips on her headphones as she enters the bike path from her backyard.

Although the sun shines brightly above her, a brisk wind chills her. She pulls the hood of her sweatshirt over her head and the sleeves of her coat over her hands. For the first few minutes of her walk, she has the trail to herself and focuses on avoiding the wet leaves scattered over the ground. Even with her headphones on, she can hear traffic on the neighboring streets. She wonders where everyone is going and wishes she could go along. Although she has only just started her walk, she already dreads returning to her empty house.

Up ahead, a dog charges around the curve toward her, its owner nowhere in sight. She silently curses the idiots who let their dogs off leash. She's certain there's a sign at the beginning of the trail prohibiting that. As the black lab gets closer, she recognizes it as Henry's. Barking, it runs straight toward her, jumping up so that two of its paws rest on her coat. She tries to push the dog off her as it licks her face.

Henry rounds the corner and races toward her. "Wally!" He grabs the dog by its collar and pulls him off Peggy. "I know. I know," he says as he snaps on the leash.

Peggy brushes the dirty paw prints off her chest. "Seriously, why don't you keep him on a leash?"

Peggy and Henry inch toward the side of the path as two bicyclists approach from behind. "I think he hates it as much as I hate ties. I don't want to do that to him."

"What does a tie have to do with a leash?" Peggy asks. She has never seen Henry dressed in anything other than gym clothes. Even now, he's wearing black wind pants and a gray sweatshirt with the Patriots logo. She imagines he has to buy his clothes in the men's big-and-tall section.

"They're both like nooses."

Wally sniffs Peggy's hand.

"I think he likes you," Henry says.

"I don't know why." Peggy pats the top of Wally's head. At least he's not as scary as a pit bull.

Henry kicks a stick on the ground. "I think he wants to walk with you. Is that okay?"

Peggy winds the cord of her earphones around her phone and slides it into her coat pocket. They continue in the direction she was heading.

"So, how was the race?" Henry asks, his big blue eyes boring into hers as he waits for her response.

Peggy turns away, self-conscious because of his intense stare. "I got the stomach bug and was too sick to run."

"You were sick on Thanksgiving? That's awful. I hope they saved you some turkey."

Peggy laughs. "Yeah, but no gravy, so..."

Henry interrupts. "You don't have to explain. I get it."

She doesn't want him to think her entire weekend was a bust. "I had a great day with my kids yesterday," she says.

At the intersection, they have to wait for the light before they can cross, and their conversation stops. Once they make it across the street, Peggy says the first thing that comes to her mind. "How's on-line dating?"

"Okay. Next weekend, I'm going to the Rockettes' Christmas show. That's something I would have never done on my own."

"You like that sort of thing?"

"I get to stare at women in skimpy little costumes showing off their legs. What's not to like?" He turns sideways and kicks one leg into the air and then the other while humming.

The sight of this extraordinarily large man trying to kick his legs into the air like a showgirl makes Peggy laugh. Even Wally barks.

Henry stops clowning around and resumes walking. "Actually, I really love shows of any kind."

So does Peggy, though it's been so long since she's been to one. Even when Patrick was alive, she never went. He claimed he couldn't sit still for that long. His excuse always ignited an argument between them because he had no trouble parking himself on the sofa for hours watching baseball or football games. Even now, her muscles stiffen as she thinks about this. She imagines herself getting all dolled up for a night out watching a musical, and when she sees herself sitting in the ornate theater, it's not Patrick sitting next to her but Henry. She shakes her head to clear it.

Wally pulls Henry toward a large boulder at the side of the trail. He watches as the dog scratches at the dirt in front of the rock. "Are you thinking of trying it?" he calls out to Peggy, who has stopped a few feet ahead of them in the middle of the trail.

"Going to the Rockettes?" As soon as she says it, she realizes her mistake. "Oh, you mean online dating. No way."

"It's not that bad."

"I'd rather date someone from the real world."

Henry cocks his head and grins, and Peggy cringes. She has no idea why she said that. She doesn't want to date, does she?

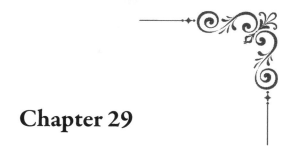

Chapter 29

A cold December wind gusts as Peggy treks to the end of the driveway to retrieve the mail. On chilly afternoons like this one, she wishes her mailbox were attached to her house. In her neighborhood, though, they all stand on posts along the side of the road so that the mailman never has to leave his truck. Maybe Peggy should become a mail carrier. That way, she could sit on her butt all day and get paid for it. She thinks about the post office's creed. Something about neither snow nor rain stopping the mail from being delivered. She doesn't enjoy driving in the elements, and she forgot about packages. She would have to leave the truck to deliver them, and some of them would be heavy. Not to mention the dogs she would have to fight off. It turns out that mail carrier is another profession she can rule out.

She opens her mailbox. It's stuffed so full that she has to yank and bend the mail to get it all out. She sorts through it, standing on the edge of her lawn while the stiff breeze rustles through everything she's holding. As usual, it's all junk—unsolicited credit card offers, advertisements for oil delivery, and newspaper flyers from retailers promoting holiday shopping specials. Christmas is only three weeks away. Peggy can't wait to spend more time with the twins, who will be home for almost a month.

She schleps back to the garage, stopping by the trash can and recycling bin to dump the mail. That's when she notices the nondescript white envelope mixed in with all the junk. It's addressed to her in loopy handwriting with a return address in Tampa. She's certain she knows what's inside, and her hands shake. *Deep breaths*, she tells herself. She thinks about ripping the envelope open here but worries she might tear its contents. Clutching the piece of mail so hard that her fingers cramp, she climbs the stairs to the house. At the top of the staircase, she pushes the button to lower the garage door. It rumbles closed as she races to the kitchen, where she uses a butter knife to slice the envelope open. Inside there is neither a letter nor explanation, just tickets to *Messages from Beyond*, three of them because Carmen thought Peggy would want to take Greg and Grace.

In fact, Peggy doesn't want the twins coming to the show because they don't believe in Lynda McGarry's gift. She imagines Grace and Greg in the audience, elbowing each other with smirks on their faces. *I can't believe people are dumb enough to believe this,* she hears Grace say. Greg would respond by humming eerie music. It's what he does when he's home and finds Peggy watching the show.

On the other hand, she doesn't want to go alone. She would love for Carmen and Roni to go with her, even if taking Roni is risky. She's as skeptical as the twins, and she's a lot louder. With Carmen's help, though, Peggy could keep Roni in line. But she can't possibly expect Carmen and Roni to go with her. It's not like she would be asking them to go out for the night, a few miles down the road. They would have to travel all the way to Florida and be gone for a few days. Why would they want to do that? They'd probably think it was strange that she would ask them and be sad that she doesn't have better friends who can accompany her. After all, she hasn't known them for more than a few months. Then again, the three of them have been spending a lot of time together, and Peggy is certain that both women care for her. After all, they came to check on her when she didn't show up for boot camp. The tickets are for February 25. Maybe Carmen and Roni would want to escape the Boston winter for a few days. That's how she can sell it to them. It's either that, or she goes alone.

Because she's so excited about going to the show, she decides to watch an episode. As she fires up her DVR, her stomach growls. All she has had to eat today is an omelet with broccoli and feta cheese and a smoothie with frozen strawberries and almond milk. She's trying not to eat a lot because boot camp is almost over, and Shauna will be weighing and measuring them again at the end of the week. Well, Peggy can't starve herself for days. That wouldn't be healthy. She pauses the show and heads to the kitchen. She finds a half gallon of Friendly's ice cream in the freezer that she didn't know was there. Greg must have bought it when he was home for Thanksgiving. Chocolate almond chip. Her favorite. Well, really any flavor ice cream is her favorite as long as it's not Ben and Jerry's. Thinking about making contact with Patrick, she slams the freezer door and pulls open the crisper drawer in the refrigerator. She takes out a carton of spinach, dumps it in a bowl, adds leftover chicken from last night's meal, and pours low-fat Italian dressing over it.

Settled back on the couch with her early dinner, Peggy hits Play on the remote. Wearing a red dress in this episode, Lynda stands center stage, welcoming the audience with her usual greeting. As it does at the start of every show, the camera focuses on her bare feet. Peggy imagines that the floor of the television studio is filthy and can't believe Lynda refuses to wear shoes or stockings. She read an article in *People* recently that said the medium regularly gets into heated arguments with her producer about the lack of shoes. The producer's afraid that when Lynda walks up and down the rows of seats, talking to audience members, someone will accidentally step on her foot and hurt her.

On the television screen, Lynda closes her eyes, and the studio darkens while she tries to connect with a spirit. Peggy can't believe that in a few short months, she'll be sitting in that studio, talking to

Patrick again. Not wanting to miss out on the opportunity to express his opinions about the twins, Patrick will come through to Lynda. Peggy is sure of that.

"I want to say this young lady died of an illness near her chest," Lynda says on the TV. "I'm seeing a cut. Maybe a surgery. Heart surgery." The camera scans the audience. People jump out of their seats, raising their hands. The camera focuses on Lynda again. She's looking at the ground, holding her hand to her chest like she's reciting the Pledge of Allegiance. She lifts her head. "Not heart disease. Cancer. Breast cancer. She had a double mastectomy."

The members of the audience who were standing slump back to their seats while new people leap up. "The name starts with a K," Lynda says, scratching her head. "The spirit is definitely that of a woman, but she says she has a message for her wife." Lynda shrugs. "She's saying something about Boston. Does this mean anything to anyone?"

The camera scans the crowd again. One woman remains standing. Lynda advances toward her. The woman tells her that her name is Gail and she lost her wife Kimberley last year to breast cancer. "How does Boston fit in?" Lynda asks.

"We got married in Massachusetts in 2004. Cambridge, not Boston."

"Close enough," Lynda says.

They're two different cities, but they are in the same state, and they do border one another, so yes, close enough, Peggy thinks.

The show breaks for a commercial, and the volume on the television surges to a deafening level. Peggy hits the mute button and finishes her tasteless salad. What she would really like to eat is a burger and fries. *No!* In just over two months, she will be with Patrick. She wants to be thinner, so she will eat a healthy diet. She gets up to put her bowl in the dishwasher and runs upstairs for her blue fleece blanket. She wraps it around herself and lies down on the sofa.

By the time she raises the volume, the show is back on, and Lynda is talking again. "This is strange. She's showing me the Pope. Mean anything to you?"

"Nope." Gail shifts her weight from leg to leg.

Lynda studies Gail through narrowed eyes. "Not the Pope. The Vatican. Scratch that. It's Big Ben. I don't know. Maybe it's the Eiffel Tower." Lynda sounds exasperated. "She can't make up her mind."

"We were supposed to take a tour of Europe," Gail says.

The audience gasps. Peggy sits bolt upright, mumbling, "Son of a gun." The blanket falls to the floor. More certain than ever that Lynda will make contact with Patrick, Peggy wishes she were going to the show tomorrow. February can't get here fast enough.

"But she got too sick…" Gail's voice trails off.

"She wants you to go." Lynda's voice is authoritative.

Gail pushes her dark hair away from her eyes. "I can't."

"Yes, you can!" Peggy says, too entranced by the show to retrieve the fleece.

"Go," Lynda says, "You're so young. You still have your whole life ahead of you."

Studying Gail's face, Peggy guesses the woman is in her midthirties, the same age Peggy was when Patrick died.

"She wants you to meet someone new and live the life you planned."

Peggy wonders if Patrick would have wanted her to meet someone new. If not for the twins, would she have tried to? Yes, she thinks she would have. The realization causes her stomach to flip. What's stopping her now? She shuts off the television and, on autopilot, heads for the kitchen, where she takes the ice cream from the freezer and a dish from the cabinet. As she's scooping her dessert out of the carton, she imagines herself stepping on the scale later that week. She carries her bowl to the sink, dumps it out, and returns the ice cream to the freezer. On her way back to the living room, she reverses direction and returns to the freezer. She removes the ice cream and buries it deep in the trash can.

Chapter 30

This is it—the last day of boot camp. Peggy made it through the twelve weeks, missing only one class. No matter what happens when Shauna measures her, Peggy's work has paid off. She feels better than she has in years—in decades even. The aches and pains that used to plague her have vanished. She no longer gets winded when she climbs the stairs to her bedroom, and she has more energy than she ever remembers. Sure, no one is whispering, "Look how skinny she is," when she walks by—in fact, most people would still characterize her as overweight—but she's thinner than when she started, and she feels better about herself.

She strides into the workout room and tosses her jacket in the coat bin. As she zigzags around the mats and weights strewn over the gym floor, she greets her classmates with an enthusiastic good morning, even addressing Sixty-Nine by her name, Christine. Carmen and Roni smile at her as she takes her spot next to them in the back row. She returns the smile, thinking she will ask them right now about going to Florida. The words are on the tip of her tongue when she reconsiders. This is neither the time nor the place. She will wait until after class when they are relaxed, sipping coffees at Holy Grounds.

"The torture ends today," Roni says, pumping her fist.

"Only for a little while," Peggy says. "The new session starts January 12."

"Only for you masochists."

"You're not signing up?"

"Not a chance."

Peggy turns to Carmen. "Are you?"

"Rosalita leaves for Brazil after the holidays and doesn't return until April, so there's no one to watch Sophia in the early morning before daycare."

Peggy knows that Carmen was able to enroll Sophia in a daycare at a neighbor's home while Rosalita is away. "Can you drop her off at daycare earlier than usual?" Peggy asks.

"She'll be there for seven hours as it is. I don't want her spending more time there." Carmen's chin quivers as she speaks, reminding Peggy that although her friend has a successful career, Carmen doesn't like being away from Sophia and prioritizes balancing her work and home life. If Peggy had known Carmen when Patrick was alive, Carmen might have helped her convince him that mothers can work while they raise their kids and that it's possible to strike the right work–life balance. Maybe then Patrick and Peggy wouldn't have been fighting when he left for San Francisco.

A loud bang in front of her pulls her from her thoughts. Henry is sprawled out on the ground, a dumbbell by his foot. "Man down," he jokes, struggling to his feet. He hobbles to the back row to the spot next to Peggy.

"Are you okay?" she asks.

"Only hurt my pride," he says, grinning at her. She used to think his smile was goofy, but she finds it adorable now, even if it still makes her nervous when he flashes it at her.

Up on the platform, Shauna blows her whistle. "Listen up," she yells. "Rotate clockwise through the stations in groups of two or three. When you get to the station at the bottom of the stairs, one person comes up for their assessment while the other does lunges."

The words are barely out of Shauna's mouth when Henry taps Peggy on the shoulder. "Will you be my partner?" Something about the way he asks takes Peggy back to dances in her middle school cafeteria, when shy boys would spend the entire afternoon working up the courage to ask girls to do the bump.

She giggles. "Sure," she says, fighting the urge to bang her hips against his. She looks over her shoulder at Roni and Carmen, who are her usual partners. Carmen winks, and Roni puckers her lips and makes kissing noises.

Mortified, Peggy turns back to Henry, who whispers, "Let's give them something to talk about." He places his hand on the small of her back while looking Roni squarely in the eye. "Excuse us. We're about to get horizontal." He guides Peggy to the push-up station, where they lie down next to each other on mats.

Forty-five minutes later, Peggy and Henry make it to the station by the stairs. They are the only two left to be measured. "Peggy, Henry," Shauna calls down from the platform. "One of you get up here."

"Ladies first," Henry says, gesturing for Peggy to go ahead of him.

"My moment of truth," she says.

"You're going to do great," he says. "You look fantastic."

Peggy knows that she does not look fantastic, but she appreciates Henry saying that.

"How are you feeling?" Shauna asks, brandishing the tape measure.

"Nervous," Peggy admits.

"Why?"

"I want the numbers to be good."

Shauna wraps the tape measure around Peggy's hips. "It's more about how you feel than the numbers."

A chill runs up Peggy's spine as Shauna's cold fingers graze her lower back. She sways back and forth.

"Stand still," Shauna commands, putting her thumb on the spot where the two sides of the tape measure meet on Peggy's hips. She leans forward to read the measurement. "Forty-nine."

Peggy doesn't know the measurements of an average woman, but she bets there are no numbers close to fifty. Clearly she still has a lot of work to do.

Shauna consults her clipboard. "That's more than two inches less than last time."

Well, that makes Peggy feel better. "The incredible shrinking woman," she says with a laugh.

"I love Lily Tomlin," Shauna says.

"You know that movie?"

"Of course."

"I didn't think you were old enough."

Shauna glances at the clipboard. "I'm your age, Peggy."

"I have at least a decade on you."

"I'll be forty-eight next month," Shauna says.

Peggy would have never guessed. "Must be all the exercise that makes you look so much younger."

"It's better than the fountain of youth," Shauna says as she wraps the tape measure around Peggy's waist.

"Don't tell me if it's not under forty-five."

"Forty-five."

Son of a gun. "I told you not to tell me."

Shauna yanks on the tape measure, pulling it tighter. "Actually, forty-four and three-quarters."

Although Peggy doesn't believe it, she feigns excitement by pumping her fist. By the time Shauna has finished with the tape measure, Peggy knows that she has lost one to three inches in every spot Shauna measured.

"Let's get your weight," Shauna says.

Peggy looks at the scale as if it's a guillotine. She does not want to climb up on it.

"Come on. I still have Henry to get to."

Peggy takes a deep breath before stepping up on the rectangular torture device. Red numbers flash across the display. When the flashing stops, the screen reads 209.

After all that hard work, Peggy still weighs more than two hundred pounds. She can't believe it.

"You lost ten pounds," Shauna says. "It's a good start, but you still have work to do. I hope you'll be back next session."

Peggy decides right then that even if Roni and Carmen don't take the class with her, she will be back. She will not allow herself to weigh more than two hundred pounds when she makes contact with Patrick. He never even weighed that much, and he was a half foot taller than Peggy.

BEFORE CLASS ENDS, Carmen announces that she's having a holiday party on Saturday night and all the boot campers are invited. "Bring your significant others."

Peggy glances over at Henry, wondering if he'll invite Denise, his online friend. She realizes that she hopes he doesn't, and that insight makes her more uncomfortable than wall squats do. She tries to distract herself from thoughts about Henry by rounding up Carmen and Roni for Holy Grounds.

"Sorry, Peggy," Carmen says, hugging her goodbye. "I need to hit the mall so I can do some Christmas shopping before work."

"I can't go today either," Roni says. "I have an eight thirty video-conference."

They both rush off before Peggy can mention the *Messages from Beyond* tickets.

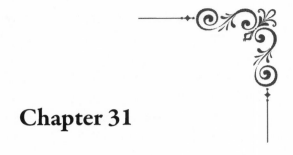

Chapter 31

Peggy and Roni stand at the edge of the lawn, gaping at the hundreds of tiny blinking red and green Christmas lights outlining Carmen's house and every tree and bush in her yard. "I'm going to have a seizure," Roni quips.

"It must drive her neighbors crazy," Peggy says.

They walk between the rows of three-foot-tall candy canes bordering the driveway and past the half dozen or so parked cars and make their way to the flagstone walkway. An inflatable snowman and snowwoman stand guard at the bottom of the landing. Peggy climbs the four stairs ahead of Roni and rings the doorbell. "Jingle Bells" blasts from a speaker under it.

When the song stops playing, someone yells, "Come in!"

Peggy opens the door and steps inside. Antonio hurries down the stairway to greet them. "Welcome," he says, hugging Peggy and then Roni. He places their jackets on top of others on a wooden coat rack to the left of the railing. "Everyone's upstairs."

Roni hands him the bottle of wine she brought, and Peggy gives him her spinach-and-artichoke dip. It's the first time she's ever made it with low-fat ingredients, and thinking about how it will go over makes her heart beat faster than burpees do.

Laughter echoes through the house as Roni and Peggy make their way to the den, where their boot-camp classmates, some with spouses or significant others, stand around a Christmas tree, chatting and drinking adult beverages. Peggy scans the room for Henry. He is talking to Emma, the college-aged girl, and appears to be by himself. Peggy does a mental high five.

Carmen weaves her way across the room, carrying two glasses of red wine. She hands one to Peggy and the other to Roni. Someone whistles, and everyone turns toward the noise. Dressed in a green shirt with a deep V-neck, fitted black pants, and black spiked heels, Shauna stands off to the side, holding up her drink. Peggy almost doesn't recognize her because it's the first time she has ever seen their fitness instructor with her hair down and wearing something other than gym attire. Shauna's street clothes make her va-va-voom figure more obvious than her yoga pants and sweatshirts. Movie-star gorgeous—that's how Peggy would describe Shauna. *If I had exercised regularly all these years, would I look half as good as that?*

"Now that everyone's here, I'd like to congratulate you for making it through twelve weeks of boot camp," Shauna says. "You all did a phenomenal job."

The guests all clink their glasses and cheer. With Christmas coming in a little more than two weeks, Peggy has so much to celebrate. In three days, the twins are coming home. She made it through twelve weeks of torturous exercise, lost ten pounds, and feels better than she's felt in a long time. Most important, she has her trip to Florida to look forward to. In just over two months, Lynda McGarry will connect her to Patrick. What more could she want?

Henry makes his way across the room toward her. He's carrying a large red plate overflowing with a mixture of appetizers, including what looks like orange meatballs, tater tots, and skewers of fresh mozzarella, tomatoes, and basil. He's wearing a long-sleeved gray golf shirt with a tiny Rudolph, light-up nose and all, pinned below the Callaway logo.

When he reaches Peggy, he grins. "Nice to see you, Peggy." Most unexpectedly, he leans toward her and kisses her cheek.

Flustered, she staggers backward, bumping Christine, who spills her drink on Nick's date. "I'm so sorry," Peggy says, fleeing to the kitchen for paper towels, but the wet woman rushes by her to get to the bathroom.

Roni's standing by the appetizers, making a plate, and Peggy joins her. "Don't be fooled by those," Roni says as Peggy loads her dish with tater tots. "It's zucchini."

Peggy pops one in her mouth. The outside is crispy like a tater tot, but the inside is definitely not potato. Well, of course Carmen wouldn't serve tater tots. The woman fed her guests kale on Thanksgiving, for crying out loud.

"Those are your best bet," Roni says, pointing to the orange meatballs, "Chicken, feta, and buffalo sauce."

Nick and Henry sidle up to the counter. Henry loads his plate with the meatballs. "Hey, big man," Nick says, slapping Henry's back. "Save some for the rest of us."

"Guys," Shauna says, joining them by the food, "just because boot camp's over doesn't mean you can eat whatever you want. You have to continue to do the work. Always."

"Killjoy," Roni says, and everyone meanders back to the den with their plates.

Peggy studies the ornaments on Carmen's tree. A ceramic yellow-and-brown snowman, with Julian's name scribbled on the bottom, hangs off a high branch. She imagines a young Julian sitting in art class, painting it. Then she sees a dark-haired little boy with a ponytail, blowing spitballs at the teacher. She knows the image can't be accurate. Julian attends a good college. He wasn't a troublemaker in school. Peggy thinks of him that way only because she's afraid he's taking Grace away from her.

Nick's date returns, her blouse wet where she tried to blot out the red wine stain. "Peggy, Roni, my wife, Amanda," Nick says.

Roni's mouth gapes. "You're married?" It is exactly what Peggy is thinking, only she didn't want to verbalize it in front of Nick's previously unmentioned spouse.

Nick nods.

Amanda is brunette and petite. She's attractive but nowhere near as beautiful as Nick. Still, there is a softness to her face and friendliness to her smile that make Peggy instantly like her.

Amanda shakes Peggy's hand. "Nick told me about how inspiring you were in class."

Peggy, inspiring? She looks at Nick, who is dunking a tortilla chip into a mound of artichoke dip on his plate. He winks at her.

Roni stares at Amanda. "How long have you been married?"

"Eleven years," Amanda answers.

"If he were my husband, I'd make him wear a ring," Roni says.

"Don't be causing trouble," Nick says. He tells his wife that Roni cheated during the mile run on the first day of class and the entire class had to pay for it by doing suicides in the gym.

As Nick speaks, Peggy notices a framed picture of Julian, Sophia, and Grace on a table in the corner of the room, where Carmen and Henry are talking. She zigzags through her chatting classmates for a closer look at the photograph. In it, Julian's arm is wrapped around Grace, who is holding Sophia.

"I love that picture," Carmen says.

Peggy does not. To her, it looks like Julian and Grace are Sophia's parents. She really hopes Grace is using birth control. "Where's Sophia tonight?"

"She's with Rosalita."

Henry leans toward Peggy to look at the picture, and Peggy explains that the older girl is her daughter, who dates Carmen's son. "That makes you two in-laws," Henry says in his usual jovial tone.

"Soon," Carmen says before turning her attention to guests on the other side of the room.

Peggy's stomach flops. *Soon?* Clearly, Carmen is joking. At least, that's what Peggy hopes.

"Your daughter is beautiful, just like her mother," Henry says.

Peggy feels her face burning up. Either Carmen turned up the heat, or she's having her first hot flash. "She looks like her father."

"I see a lot of you in her."

"If you met her in person, I doubt you would think that." Anyone who knew Patrick agrees that Grace is his spitting image while Greg takes after Peggy.

"I'd like to meet her someday," Henry says.

Peggy stares at him blankly, wondering how in the world that could possibly happen. "Maybe you'll run into her on the bike path sometime."

"I was thinking we could get together for a movie or dinner or something next week."

"You and Grace?" Of course, that's not what he means, but Peggy doesn't know how to respond and is stalling for time. She looks across the room, hoping Carmen or Roni will come to her rescue, but there is no sight of either.

Henry stands straighter. "No, me and you." His voice has none of its usual playfulness.

"I'll be busy. With the kids. Christmas break." She rushes away from him as she says it, wishing she were braver.

LATER THAT NIGHT, AFTER all the other guests have gone home, Peggy stands at Carmen's kitchen sink, washing pots and pans, while Roni dries them. Behind them at the table, Carmen wraps up the leftover food.

"What did you think of Nick's wife?" Carmen asks.

"Hated her," Roni says, but she laughs.

The two engage in a lively conversation, rehashing the party, while Peggy, lost in her own thoughts, contributes nothing. Henry left without saying goodbye to her. She watched as he hugged Carmen and Roni, wishing them happy holidays, but he didn't even look her way.

"Peggy," Roni says, grabbing the skillet Peggy's washing, "I don't think you're going to get that pan any cleaner."

Peggy squeezes more soap into the already sudsy washbasin. Tiny bubbles and orange scent float in the air.

Roni reaches for the bottle. "Earth to Peggy. It's like you've never washed dishes before."

Peggy tosses the sponge into the soapy water. "Henry asked me on a date," she blurts.

"Oh, Peggy, that's wonderful," Carmen says.

Peggy still has her back to Carmen, but she's sure that if they were facing each other, she would see tears in Carmen's eyes. She hears them in her friend's voice. Happy tears.

"I said no."

"Oh, Peg, why?"

Why, indeed.

Roni slaps Peggy with the dishtowel. "What's wrong with you?"

"I don't know," Peggy says, sinking into a chair. "I'm not ready."

"That's bullshit. It's been fourteen years."

"Roni!" Carmen says.

Roni ignores the warning. "When will you be ready?"

"I don't know," Peggy admits. "Maybe after I make contact with Patrick."

"That's never going to happen," Roni says.

"I don't know," Carmen says. "She could get the tickets for *Messages from Beyond.*"

"I got them."

"You got the tickets?" The excitement in Carmen's voice gives Peggy hope that her friend will go with her to the show. "Why didn't you tell us?" Carmen puts the last container of food into the refrigerator and sits in the chair next to Peggy's.

"They came last week."

"When are you going?"

"February 25."

"Will the twins go with you?"

Peggy swallows hard. "They'll be in school. I was hoping you and Roni would come." She looks down at the bamboo wood floor as she speaks.

"Oh, well..." Carmen begins, and Peggy knows her friend is trying to think of a way to let her down gently. "It's just that I can't leave Antonio alone with Sophia. He goes to work before her daycare opens, and Rosalita will be in Brazil."

Of course, Carmen has family obligations. It was stupid of Peggy to ask her. She turns to Roni.

"I'm probably the worst person you could think of taking. You know I think she's a con artist." Roni steps on her tiptoes and reaches upward, placing a bowl on the top shelf.

"Maybe if you see her in person, you'll become a believer."

"Doubt it." She slams the cabinet door shut.

The sadness that Peggy has felt since she turned Henry down boils over, and tears threaten to spill from her eyes. She swallows a lump in her throat before speaking again. "We should leave. It's late." Her voice cracks with emotion.

Carmen gulps audibly and a second later is wrapping Peggy in a tight embrace. She looks as heartbroken as Peggy feels. "I'm sorry, Peg. If there were any way, I would."

Peggy hates that she made Carmen feel bad. She digs deep to force a smile. "I understand."

Peggy and Roni walk down the stairs and put on their coats in silence. Carmen hugs them each goodbye and opens the door for them. Outside, Antonio turns off all the Christmas lights. Peggy treads down the empty driveway in the dark, with Roni trailing a few feet behind her, for once having nothing to say.

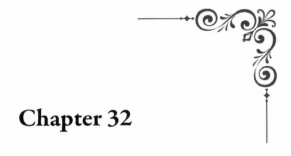

Chapter 32

Carmen calls Peggy early the next morning to apologize again for not being able to accompany her to Florida. Hearing Carmen's distress makes Peggy wish she had never asked. "It's okay," Peggy says, trying to reassure her friend.

"With Rosalita leaving, we are in a bind with Sophia's daycare. Yesterday, before the party, the neighbor who was supposed to watch her decided that she no longer wants to do daycare." Carmen sighs. "I have her on a waiting list at Curious Kids, but they say they probably won't have an opening until late February at the earliest. I don't know what we're going to do."

"I'm sorry," Peggy says.

"I just want you to understand why I can't go with you," Carmen says, sounding more upset than she did at the beginning of the call.

After she hangs up, Peggy can't stop thinking about how flustered Carmen was. She wishes there was something she could do to help. As Peggy goes about her morning, she remembers the day she took care of Sophia because Rosalita was sick. Other than the fact that Peggy caught that awful stomach bug, it was a wonderful experience, one of the best days she's had since her own kids left for college. She played Chutes and Ladders and pat-a-cake with the little girl. She remembers how Sophia snuggled on her lap and fell asleep when Peggy read to her and how Sophia hugged and kissed her goodbye and asked her to come back and play with her again.

Peggy calls Carmen back. "I would like to watch Sophia."

In the background, Peggy hears running water. It goes off, and Carmen speaks. "That's sweet of you, Peg, but—"

"No buts. I will take care of Sophia until Rosalita returns. It will give me something to do with my days."

Carmen is silent.

"So it's settled," Peggy says.

"Well, she did enjoy the day you spent together. Talked about it for weeks."

"Rosalita may have to wrestle me to get her job back." Peggy almost doesn't recognize her own voice because it's so bubbly.

PEGGY DOES NOT WANT to go to Florida by herself, but she's used to doing things alone that she'd rather do with someone else. Like raising Grace and Greg. She had no idea how she was going to manage bringing up kids on her own, but she did. Now she wants affirmation from Patrick that she did an excellent job, so she will go see Lynda McGarry even if no one will go with her. One thing she will not do alone, though, is fly. So even though the show is still months away, Peggy is at AAA, talking to a man named Don, who is mapping her route from Hudson, Massachusetts, to Tampa, Florida.

"When are you going?" Don asks, rubbing a thumb across his thick gray mustache.

The man's facial hair distracts Peggy. Because of it, she can't figure out how old he is. He has a full head of thick dark hair and a baby face, which is probably why he grew the mustache, but why in the world would it come in gray?

Don clears his throat and repeats his question.

"Late February," Peggy says.

"Well, you won't have to worry about roadwork, but the weather might slow you down."

"I'll build in extra time in case of a storm."

Don opens a desk drawer and pulls out a yellow highlighter and map of the United States. "Are you going for R-and-R?" When Peggy stares at him blankly, he clarifies. "For vacation."

"Not really."

Don watches her like he's waiting for an explanation. Mid to late thirties, Peggy decides, but she has no confidence in her estimate, remembering how wrong she was when she tried to figure out Carmen's and Shauna's ages.

"For work?" he persists.

I'm going to talk to my dead husband. Peggy wonders how Don would react if she said it out loud. Would it get him to stop with the annoying questions, or would it invite more? "To see a show."

"Is anyone going with you?"

Peggy looks at her watch and then at the map that is now spread open across his desk. "I'm going by myself."

"You might want to consider flying. That's a long trip to do solo."

"I'm driving," Peggy snaps. At the counter to Peggy's right, a light flashes as another employee takes a picture of a twentysomething woman.

"I'm going to Iceland in the spring," the young woman tells the worker. Peggy remembers learning about Iceland in high school. It's supposed to be green and lush, while Greenland is more winterish. The Vikings named them that way to confuse people. She wonders whether that's true or just something her social studies teacher Mr. Drago made up. He loved to play jokes on his students.

"You can take ninety-five most of the way." The highlighter squeaks as Don traces a route down the East Coast. Fifteen minutes later, he hands Peggy the map and a notebook with recommendations for hotels and restaurants along the way.

―――――――― ⟨∾⟩ ――――――――

AS PEGGY CUTS ACROSS the parking lot, a car blasting music pulls up next to her. She looks into the driver's-side window. Well, doesn't it figure? It's Julian. Apparently, her driveway isn't the only place he blasts his stereo.

He smiles and lowers the window. "Hey, Mrs. M."

"Is that a bun?" Peggy asks, staring at his hair.

He grins wider and turns down the music. "It's a man bun," he says in a low voice then returns to his regular tone. "Do you like it?"

Good Lord. She thought his ponytail was bad, but this—this takes ridiculous to a whole new level. "I do not."

Julian laughs. "Aww, Mrs. M, I've missed you."

Peggy thinks about this. She only caught fleeting glimpses of him in November, and she hasn't talked to him since he came over to return the ladder and change the light bulb back in September. Is it possible that she's missed him too? Well, yes, but that's because when Julian's around, Grace and Greg are also nearby. Right?

"What's all that?" Julian asks pointing to the map and booklet in Peggy's hand.

"It's a TripTik. I'm going to Florida."

"Why are you driving?"

Peggy can't believe he's asking her this. Surely, Grace has told him how Patrick died. He should realize she wants nothing to do with airplanes. "I don't like flying."

Julian squeezes his eyes shut tight. "Of course," he mumbles.

He looks so uncomfortable that she quickly changes the topic to put him at ease. "Why are you home? Are you working for your dad this weekend?"

"Yup. Trying to earn enough to get Grace a meaningful Christmas gift." He holds Peggy's eyes with his.

"What do you mean by *meaningful*?" she asks.

A car pulls up behind Julian, and the driver beeps. "We'll talk later, Mrs. M. Nice seeing you."

Before Peggy can say anything else, Julian drives off. She watches as he navigates across the plaza and parks in front of the jewelry store. Her stomach drops as she recalls Carmen telling Henry that they would be in-laws soon. Maybe she wasn't joking.

LATER THAT WEEK, PEGGY sits on her living room floor armed with scissors, tape, and wrapping paper. Bags with the kids' gifts surround her. She needs to wrap them all today because Grace and Greg will be home tomorrow, and she knows they will sneak into her room, searching for their presents. She catches them doing it every year, and it ticks her off because she likes to surprise them.

She faces the television, watching an episode of *Messages from Beyond* that she has seen twice already. In it, Lynda connects a Vietnam veteran with a soldier in his platoon killed in combat. The deceased soldier thanks the veteran for looking after his widow and kids all these years. Patrick's friends lost touch with Peggy years ago. She's to blame because she stopped returning their calls. It hurt too much to hear stories of the old days over and over again. Now, thinking of Greg scouring the campus of St. Michael's for stories about his father, she wishes she had kept in contact so that they could share their memories with him and Grace. Maybe when she gets back from Florida, she will try to reconnect with them.

A sweater for Grace is the first item Peggy wraps, and she's sure to slip the gift receipt into the box. She selects the silver paper and accentuates the package with red ribbon. She uses a fountain pen to fill out the tag, writing Grace's name in slanted penmanship and signing the gift from Santa.

As she's wrapping the next present, duck boots for Greg, her phone buzzes, but she doesn't know where it is. She searches the area surrounding her, lifting paper and moving boxes, before she finds it tucked away in a shopping bag, though she has no idea how it got there. There's a text from Carmen, inviting her to lunch today.

At first, she's excited because she has missed Carmen and Roni since boot camp ended, but then she notices Roni is not included on the message. Peggy clicks off the message and then brings it up again, hoping Roni's name will be there, but of course, it isn't. *Did Carmen leave Roni off because she wants to talk about Julian's Christmas gift to Grace?* Surely, Carmen can't think it's a good idea for her nineteen-year-old son to get engaged. Peggy's pulse quickens because she realizes that yes, Carmen could believe that. Peggy composes a response, agreeing to meet at one o'clock, and hits Send.

WHEN THE DOOR OPENS, a blast of frigid air hits Peggy. She zips her coat higher while wondering what genius designed the restaurant so that the waiting area faces the entrance. This is her first time here. She arrived less than two minutes ago and hasn't had a bite to eat yet, but she has already decided she doesn't like this place and won't be coming back, and not because of the design. The pip-squeak host with the Napoleon complex is the reason. He refuses to seat her until Carmen arrives, even though empty tables outnumber those with guests. Peggy is ten minutes early, and Carmen texted to say she'd be fifteen minutes late. Peggy spends the next half hour giving the stink eye to the host.

A large group of boisterous men stream through the door, with Carmen trailing behind them. Peggy stands when she sees her friend, and Carmen hugs her hello while apologizing for being late. After returning from seating the large group, the host leads Peggy and Carmen to the table next to them.

Peggy points to a small booth on the other side of the restaurant. "I'd like to sit over there."

The host places his hands on his hips. "We don't have wait staff for that section."

The men erupt in rowdy laughter. Peggy looks pointedly at them and back to the host. "Well, we're not sitting here."

He blinks quickly but doesn't say anything.

"We're afraid we won't be able to hear each other," Carmen explains.

"Fine." He marches across the room to the booth Peggy pointed out, and the two women follow him. When they sit, he throws the menus at them before stomping off.

Carmen leans across the table toward Peggy. "I have some exciting news."

Peggy's heart sinks, certain Carmen is about to tell her that Julian bought Grace an engagement ring. "I saw Julian," Peggy says.

"Did he tell you?"

"He hinted at it."

Carmen's mouth drops open. She looks away from Peggy, transferring her silverware off the napkin to the table and spreading the napkin across her lap. "I wanted to be the one to tell you. I thought you'd be more excited."

Excited? Peggy's shoulders rise to ear level as every muscle in her body tenses.

A mocha-skinned waitress with a large dimple denting her left cheek approaches the table, introduces herself as Beatrice, and asks if they are ready to order.

"We just sat down," Peggy barks.

"We haven't looked at the menu yet," Carmen explains in a kind voice.

"How about drinks?" Beatrice asks.

"Water is fine," Carmen says.

"Let me tell you about today's specials."

Peggy rocks back and forth while Beatrice says something about a potato soup and grilled cheese with smoked cheddar. Ordinarily, these would both intrigue her, but she can't even think about food right now. She has to convince Carmen that Julian and Grace getting engaged is a terrible idea. Peggy guesses that the waitress is only a few years older than Grace and Julian and wonders if she should solicit Beatrice's help. *Most kids that age wouldn't consider getting married before twenty-five, right?* Peggy was twenty-eight when she and Patrick tied the knot.

"I'll give you a few minutes to look at the menu," Beatrice says.

Carmen waits for her to walk away before speaking. "I know that you're nervous."

Nervous? "They're too young," Peggy snaps.

Carmen stares at her with an expression she can't read. The scent of french fries fills the air as a waiter passes by carrying a tray of food. "Who's too young?"

"Grace and Julian."

"Too young for what?"

The waitress returns with a pitcher of water and fills Carmen's glass.

"Too young to get married. They aren't even twenty." Peggy glances up at Beatrice to see if she reacts, but the waitress makes no indication that she's listening and leaves after pouring Peggy's drink.

"Of course they are," Carmen says, picking up her water and taking a sip.

"So you agree."

Carmen swallows. "Of course, but I don't understand why you're even bringing that up."

Across the room, the men break out into another fit of laughter.

"Julian's proposing at Christmas."

Carmen raises an eyebrow. "Where did you get that idea?"

"He told me he's saving for a meaningful gift." Peggy punctuates the word *meaningful* with air quotes. "I saw him going into the jewelry store. What else could it be other than a ring?"

"Ski tickets," Carmen says. "He's getting her a season's pass to Smuggler's Notch and a ski charm for her bracelet."

"Are you sure?" Peggy wants to leap across the table and hug Carmen.

"I wrapped the gift myself."

All the tension leaves Peggy's body. Her shoulders drop to their normal height. "So what's your exciting news?"

Carmen reaches for Peggy's hand. "Julian's agreed to commute to school from home for a few days in February so he can help with Sophia in the mornings."

Peggy stares blankly, not sure why she should be excited about this.

"It means I can come with you to Florida, but we're flying." Carmen squeezes Peggy's hand before letting go.

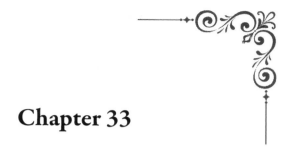

Chapter 33

Peggy checks her Fitbit for her step count—4,234. The kids gave her the fitness tracker for Christmas. In the two weeks she has been wearing it, she has reached her goal of seven thousand steps every day. Usually, she walks with Roni and Carmen, but both complained that it is too cold today and bowed out, so instead, Greg accompanies her. While Peggy is bundled up in a ski coat, hat, and gloves, Greg wears an unzipped sweatshirt and nothing covering his hands. Peggy argued with him about his inappropriate cold-weather attire before they left the house, but she couldn't convince him to put on a jacket. She always thought of Grace as her stubborn child, but Greg is giving his sister a run for her money these days.

Tomorrow, the twins will leave for Vermont to begin their second semester. Their three-week break has passed in a chaotic blur. Most days, Greg and his friends were camped out in the living room playing video games, binge-watching television shows, and wolfing down food Peggy cooked for them. He went out with Madison on New Year's Eve but didn't spend any time with Allison. When Peggy asked him about Allison, he cracked his knuckles and said they broke up because of the distance between them. Grace and Julian, on the other hand, are still going strong. Grace spent her break snuggling with him on the sofa or playing loud music alone in her room. Frankly, Peggy can't wait to have the house to herself again. She's tired of picking up after the two of them, and she needs some peace and quiet. It reminds her of the way she felt before Patrick died, when the twins were small and all she wanted was to be alone for a few minutes. She never thought she would feel that way again, but she has come to enjoy having time for herself.

Feeling guilty for thinking this way, she peeks over at Greg. His shoulders are tense, his ears and nose glow red, and his hands are crammed into his jeans pockets. "We should head back," she says. "You must be freezing."

"I'm fine, Ma." A plume of steam escapes his mouth as he exhales.

She checks her step count again. It's still two thousand under her goal, so she really doesn't want to stop walking. In the few weeks she's owned the fitness device, she has become a slave to it, sometimes pacing around her bed in circles so she can reach her goal before going to sleep. "Are you sure?" she asks.

Greg relaxes his shoulders and pulls his hands out of his pockets. "This is nothing compared to Vermont."

Peggy has heard all about the brutal winter weather at school from Grace and suspects her daughter is exaggerating to make an argument for spending spring break in a tropical climate. Any day now, Peggy expects Grace to ask to go to Cancún in March. Peggy won't want to say yes—not because she doesn't want Grace to have a fun vacation but because she doesn't want her kids getting on an airplane, ever. She blinks hard, knowing she has to get over this fear.

"How do you like St. Mike's?" she asks Greg.

"Love it."

His response warms Peggy's heart. All she wants is for her kids to be happy. "Have you found any more pictures of your father or met anyone else who knew him?"

"Just the old priest. He was Dad's philosophy professor."

"What did he tell you?"

Greg shoves his hands into his sweatshirt's pockets. "Nothing much. Dad was a good student but a wise guy."

Peggy laughs. "That he was." She's quiet for a minute. "You know, if there's ever anything you want to know about him, you can ask me."

They have reached the section of the bike trail that winds under the road above it. Greg looks away from Peggy and at the mural of a soccer game painted on the tunnel wall. "Do you think I'm like Dad?"

"You have some of the qualities I loved most about him. His kindness. His intelligence. His..." Peggy stops talking as they exit the tunnel and turn the curve. A large man wearing a red-and-black lumberjack coat and a black aviator hat with faux fur around the edges is coming toward them, an unleashed black lab by his side. "Oh no," she mumbles. She hasn't seen Henry since Carmen's party and doesn't want to face him now. She grabs Greg's arm. "We should turn around."

Greg follows his mother's gaze down the trail, where Wally bolts from Henry's side and charges toward them. "Easy, big fellow," Greg says as the dog leaps up on him.

"Wally, get down," Henry shouts, rumbling toward them.

"He's okay," Greg says, petting the dog's head.

Henry reaches them. He looks at Peggy with his usual goofy grin. Peggy's relieved to see it because she thought he was still mad at her for turning him down at Carmen's party.

"Happy new year, Peggy," he says.

"You too." Peggy feels Greg's eyes studying her as she talks to Henry.

"Did you enjoy the holidays?" Henry asks.

"I did." She reaches for Greg. "We should head back."

Greg pushes Wally off him and extends a hand toward Henry. "I'm Greg. Peggy's son."

"Henry. Your mom and I were in boot camp together." He pats his enormous belly. "Your mom obviously had more success than I did. She looks great, doesn't she?"

Greg steps backward, putting more space between himself and Henry. "She looks like Mom."

"Well, moms can look good too," Henry says. "And yours does."

Greg makes a face that reminds Peggy of his expression when he eats broccoli. "I thought boot camp was only for women," he says to Peggy.

"It's also for men confident in their masculinity," Henry says, looking at Peggy again with his enormous smile, which is causing her to sweat even on this frigid day.

Wally has wandered off to the side of the trail and is scratching at the frozen ground. Peggy wishes he'd dig a hole big enough for her to climb in. "We should get going," she says to Greg, reaching for his arm again.

"See ya," Henry says.

As Peggy and Greg walk off in the direction they came from, she looks back over her shoulder. Henry hasn't moved. He's standing in the middle of the trail, watching her. He waves.

"Will I see you next week when boot camp starts again?" Peggy calls back to him.

"Haven't decided yet," Henry says, which makes Peggy's heart sink. He salutes her before turning and walking away.

After advancing several yards without speaking, Greg checks behind him. "That fat dude likes you."

"He's actually a nice man." Her tone is harsher than she intended.

"So you like him." Greg's eyes widen.

"He asked me out," Peggy says.

"You're going on a date with him?"

"I said no."

"Thank God," Greg mutters.

Peggy comes to an abrupt stop. "Why don't you like him?"

"I think you can do better, Ma."

"You're underestimating Henry." Peggy stalks off, certain that Greg's comment about Henry has to do with the man's size. Thinking about her son's pettiness, she balls her hands into tight fists inside her gloves. Soon there are several feet separating her from Greg. When he calls out after her, she quickens her pace. Although she has a hard time admitting this to herself, she knows people judge her because of her size too. She knows Grace does, but she didn't think Greg did. She pulls at her jacket, which suddenly feels too tight, and starts to jog, trying to outrun her thoughts. When she reaches her neighborhood, she scrambles off the path, through the bushes, and into her yard.

Greg catches up with her at the porch door. "Is Henry anything like Dad?"

Her hand freezes on the doorknob. *Henry, like Patrick?* "Not at all." She turns to face her son. His cheeks are bright red, and his nose is running. "But your dad made me laugh, and so does Henry."

Greg stares at her with his big eyes, looking like a little boy and making it impossible to stay angry with him, especially when he kisses her cheek.

Peggy smells coffee as she steps into the kitchen, where Grace sits at the breakfast bar, typing into her computer, with a steaming mug beside her. Peggy breathes in the delicious aroma and pours her own cup, hoping it will warm her.

Behind her, Greg slams the door. "Mom has a boyfriend."

Grace's hands freeze on the keyboard. Her head snaps up. "Really?"

"Yeah. I just met him. He's huge."

"Greg," Peggy chides, "what does his size have to do with anything?"

"I was about to say he goes to boot camp with you. Jeez, Ma."
He sniffs loudly before leaving the kitchen, sulking in that way Peggy
hates. She bites her lip to keep from saying anything and turns to remove all of her outer winter layers.

"We've been home for three weeks. Why are we just finding out
about this now?" Grace asks.

"There's nothing to find out. He's a friend. That's all."

"What's his name?"

Peggy ignores Grace, but from the bathroom, Greg yells, "Henry.
He asked Mom out." He makes a horn-like noise, and Peggy knows
from the sound that he is blowing his nose. Patrick used to make the
same sound.

"Where's he taking you?" Grace is smiling, and her eyes shine.

"He's not. I said no."

"Why? You said he's your friend, so you must like him."

"She doesn't like him that way," Greg says, returning to the
kitchen. He opens the refrigerator, pulls out a carton of milk, and
raises it to his mouth.

"Don't you dare." Peggy opens a cabinet and hands him a glass.

"You need to give him a chance," Grace says. "Tell him you
changed your mind."

Can I do that? What would I say?

"She doesn't want to go out with him. Leave her alone." Greg
guzzles down his drink and heads for the living room, leaving the
dirty glass on the counter.

"I don't think your brother would be okay with me dating." Peggy reaches for Greg's cup, rinses it, and places it in the dishwasher.

"That's because he's afraid if you get a life, you'll be too busy to
clean up after him, or you'll stop cooking for him and all his friends."

Peggy sits on the stool next to her daughter, who lowers the cover
of her laptop, piquing Peggy's curiosity. She wants to ask Grace what

she was looking at but decides against it. "I'm too old to start dating again."

"You're not *that* old," Grace says. "Seriously, Mom, don't you ever get..." Grace pauses.

Peggy looks away, certain her daughter is about to ask her if she ever gets horny. She stands, intending to flee.

"Lonely?" Grace finishes.

Peggy exhales and sinks back into her seat. Of course Grace wouldn't ask that. That's something Roni would ask. "How could I when I have you and Greg?"

"But you must miss Dad."

Peggy answers without thinking. "Every day." It's an honest response, but as soon as the words are out, she wishes she hadn't said them. She has worked hard over the years to hide her pain from the twins. As Peggy reaches for her coffee, she feels Grace's hand on her back, rubbing it. The gesture brings tears to Peggy's eyes.

"Mom, you've spent the last eighteen years looking after me and Greg. It's time to take care of yourself. We want you to be happy, and if that means dating that guy from your gym class, or someone else, you should."

Peggy leans toward Grace and kisses her cheek. "I'm happy taking care of my kids."

"No, there has to be more to your life than that," Grace says, avoiding Peggy's eyes. "Sometimes I feel like you, the real you, died on that plane with Dad."

Peggy flinches. She herself has felt exactly that way so many times through the years. *How does Grace know?* "My life is looking after you and your brother. It's what I want to do and what your father would have wanted."

"Greg and I are old enough to look after ourselves. It's time for you to take care of yourself. You're allowed to have fun, Mom. Go out with that guy."

"I'll think about it," Peggy says.

Grace drums her fingers on the counter. "Don't overthink it. Just do it."

Peggy wonders why her daughter is so insistent. *Why does it matter to her if I date?* The only answer she can come up with is because Grace wants her to be happy. Peggy beams and reaches toward Grace, pulling her into a tight embrace. "I will think about it," she repeats, but this time, she means it.

As Peggy stands, Grace reaches for her again and says, "There's something I want to show you." She lifts the cover of her laptop so that Peggy can see the screen. The Assumption College website comes up. "I'm thinking of transferring."

Peggy was not expecting that. She tries to remember if Grace ever said anything about being unhappy at St. Michael's. "Why?"

Grace shrugs. "I don't like Vermont. It's too cold."

Peggy reads the webpage. "The school you're looking at is in Worcester?"

"Yup."

It can't be coincidental that Julian's school is in the same city. "You want to be near Julian."

"I'd be close to you too." Grace grins.

Peggy knows full well that Grace isn't thinking of transferring to be near her, but she still imagines herself driving to Worcester to take Grace shopping or to lunch, and Grace could come home once a week to do her laundry. How wonderful would that be?

"Maybe I'd even live here and commute," Grace says.

Live here? "Oh no, Grace, that's not a good idea." Peggy can't believe she just said that, since it is exactly what she prayed for all last year—that the kids wouldn't go away to college.

"Well, Julian and I could always get a place together."

"Grace, if you are serious about leaving St. Michael's, you shouldn't pick a new school based on where Julian is. If he's the right one, it will work out."

Grace closes her laptop. She slumps in her stool, and her voice softens. "I thought you'd be happy about me being closer."

"Of course I'd love it if you were here, but part of the college experience is living away at school with your friends."

"Are you telling me I can't transfer?"

Yes! It's on the tip of Peggy's tongue, but then she reflects on the calm way Grace asked the question and the conversation they just had about Henry, and she reminds herself that Grace is no longer a little girl who needs to be told what to do. She's a young woman capable of making her own decisions. All Peggy can hope for now is that she raised her kids in such a way that they are capable of making good choices.

"I don't think it's a good idea, but ultimately, it's your decision." Peggy sips her coffee. She's not using creamer anymore and still isn't used to the bitter taste. She doesn't think she ever will be. "If you're serious about wanting to leave Vermont, research schools, and find one that will be a good fit. If Assumption is the best, then by all means, transfer there."

"Do you think Dad would be disappointed if I left his college?"

Peggy studies the black liquid in her cup, trying to remember how Greg and Grace picked Patrick's alma mater. It was their idea originally. They met a recruiter from St. Michael's at a college fair and decided they wanted to go there. Before they applied, Peggy took them to see the college. When they were touring the campus, she told the twins how proud Patrick would be to see them at his school. Did her words inadvertently sway Grace's decision?

"He'd want you to be happy. Just like I do. And he'd also want to be sure you're leaving for the right reason."

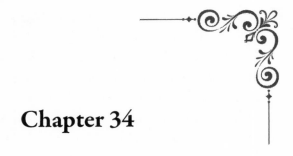

Chapter 34

Peggy hits the snooze button three times before dragging herself out of bed at half past six on Monday morning. She hasn't been up this early since boot camp ended over a month ago. It's still dark outside. All she wants to do is crawl back under the covers, but she forces herself to get dressed in her workout clothes because she doesn't want to miss the first day of the new session. Fifteen minutes later, she pulls into the gym's parking lot. Carmen's vehicle is parked in the next row, and the sight of it makes Peggy smile. Today is the first day she will be taking care of Sophia. Antonio will work a later shift to be home with Sophia in the early mornings, and Peggy will stay in the afternoons until Carmen gets home from work. It worked out perfectly, and Peggy's happy that for once, she is able to do something to help her friend, not to mention that she gets to spend the day with a four-year-old.

Without even thinking about it, Peggy searches for Henry's green Mini, and her heart sinks when she can't find it. She won't have someone to sing with. Yes, that's the reason she's disappointed. The only reason. She pushes her car door open, and a bell dings, letting her know she left the headlights on. She yawns as she switches them off.

An SUV squeals into the parking lot. Peggy stares at it, thinking it's Roni, but Roni didn't sign up for boot camp again. The vehicle comes to a screeching stop next to Peggy, and the window comes down. "I can't believe I let freaking Carmen talk me into this again,"

Roni yells over the song that's blasting from her radio. "I'm going to kill her."

Peggy smiles. Boot camp wouldn't have been the same without Roni. A sporty red Lexus turns into the aisle and can't get past Roni's SUV. After waiting a few seconds, the driver beeps her horn. Roni glares at the woman through her rear windshield. The two women stare at each other, and the Lexus driver blares the horn again. Roni gives the woman the finger.

"I'll meet you inside," Peggy says, rushing to get away from this scene before it escalates.

In the gym, Shauna stands by the entrance to the workout room with a clipboard, greeting class members as they arrive. Maybe it's Peggy's imagination, but Shauna seems to be giving her the once-over, as if checking to see if she gained weight over the holidays. Well, she probably did but not that much. Still, Peggy knows she's being ridiculous. There's no way the instructor can see through Peggy's bulky winter jacket. Shauna, of course, looks like her usual fit self. She's wearing gray yoga pants with a peach tank top that shows off her toned arms. Honestly, Michelangelo couldn't sculpt arms more perfect than Shauna's.

"Good to have you back, Peggy," Shauna says, smiling.

"Good to be back," Peggy says. She plans to work hard and eat a clean diet over the next few weeks before her trip to Florida.

Carmen waves to Peggy from the back of the room. There's an older man whom Peggy doesn't recognize standing next to her in Henry's usual spot. "This is Tom," Carmen says. He has thin gray hair and a well-lined face. Peggy guesses that he's in his sixties and wonders if he'll have a hard time doing the exercises.

Roni enters the gym with the woman from the Lexus trailing a few steps behind. The two are bickering. Peggy thanks her lucky stars she missed whatever happened in the parking lot. The Lexus driver stops to talk to Shauna. Now that the woman is out of her car, Peggy can see that she is about the same size as Peggy and Roni but a few years younger. Done talking to Shauna, the woman turns. She looks in Peggy's direction and waves. Caught staring, Peggy feels like an idiot and gives a small wave back.

"Do you know Andrea?" Carmen asks, waving at the woman.

Peggy realizes the woman's greeting was intended for Carmen and feels like a bigger idiot. "No," she says.

"She's one of my clients. Recently divorced. Getting ready to enter the dating world again."

At the mention of the word *dating*, Peggy feels her back stiffen. She weaves her way through her classmates to the front of the room and grabs a foam roller. When she returns to her spot, Roni is there, spreading her mat beside Peggy's. A few rows in front of them, Andrea sets up her station, occasionally glancing back over her shoulder to glare at Roni.

"What happened outside?" Peggy asks.

"I don't know what her problem is," Roni says, eyeing Tom. "Who's the old dude?"

"The old dude still has his hearing," Tom says, introducing himself.

"Pay no attention to her," Carmen says, patting Tom on the back.

Peggy shakes her head at Roni. "You haven't even been here five minutes, and you've already offended the two new people."

"I don't like new people," Roni says, looking around the room and smiling goofily when Nick acknowledges her with a wink.

By now, Shauna is on the platform, giving her welcome speech. "It doesn't matter how hard you work here if you don't do the work in the kitchen," the fitness guru says. Although Peggy knows exactly what the trainer means, she envisions herself doing jumping jacks and push-ups by her breakfast bar.

Toward the end of Shauna's talk, Henry rushes through the door, dumps his coat in a cubby, and heads to the back row with his mat.

Peggy's heart soars when she sees him, and he flashes that special grin of his at her. It disappears quickly, though, and confusion washes over his face. "You didn't save my spot?" he asks, looking at Tom. Peggy's throat constricts. She should have told Tom to move, but she didn't know Henry would be here.

"Henry, there's space up here," Shauna yells, pointing to a section of the floor next to Andrea.

Henry stares at Tom and clears his throat. "Excuse me," he says. Tom stares straight ahead without acknowledging him. *So much for the old guy's hearing.*

"Henry, let's go," Shauna bellows.

Henry sighs and drags himself to the front row, next to Andrea, who smiles at him, touching his arm as she introduces herself. Peggy decides right then that she doesn't like the new people either.

DISPLAYING THE AIRLINE'S website, Carmen's iPad sits in front of her on the table. Peggy positions her chair so she can see the screen. She also has a clear view of a tray of giant chocolate chip cookies in the display case. She wishes she could have a bite of one to see if they taste as good as they smell. Their aroma has been driving her crazy since she walked into Holy Grounds twenty minutes ago.

"How about this one?" Carmen points to a flight leaving Boston at 2:15 p.m. on Monday, February 23, and arriving in Tampa at 5:37 p.m. "We can take the 6:20 flight home on Thursday night."

"Fine with me," Peggy says, though really, it isn't. She doesn't want to fly, but Carmen doesn't have the time to drive to Florida.

Carmen reaches into her bag for her wallet and pulls out a credit card. "I'll book it, and you can pay me later."

Roni has been quiet since they sat. Now she speaks. "Oh, hell. Get me one too."

"You want to come with us to see Lynda McGarry?" Peggy thinks Roni would be happier doing burpees than attending *Messages from Beyond*.

Roni empties a packet of sugar into her coffee. "Well, I can't let you two go alone. You'll believe everything she says. Someone has to be there to poke holes in it."

Behind their table, a bell rings, indicating someone has entered the coffee shop. A blast of cold air chills Peggy's back. She hears Henry's goofy laugh and peeks over her shoulder. He's standing behind her with someone who looks like the new woman in boot camp, but Peggy's not sure because she's no longer dressed in sweatpants, sweat-wicking T-shirt, and sneakers. Instead, she's wearing short brown boots, a long brown skirt, and a coral cashmere sweater under a long tan wool coat that's unbuttoned.

"Hi, ladies," Henry says in a chipper voice. He steps between Peggy's and Roni's chairs. "Did you meet Andrea in class?" He places his hand on Andrea's lower back and pushes her forward.

"Met her in the parking lot," Roni growls.

Andrea makes a show of tossing her wavy auburn hair behind her shoulder. At the gym, it was tied into a severe ponytail, and having it down makes her look softer, pretty almost. "Carmen and I know each other. She does a fantastic job on my hair." Andrea smiles at Peggy. "We haven't met."

"Peggy Moriarty." She feels Henry looking at her but refuses to meet his eye and pushes her chair away from him.

"You're welcome to join us," Carmen says, pointing to empty chairs.

Please, no.

Henry notices the website displayed on Carmen's tablet. "Are you ladies planning a trip?"

"We're going to Florida to see *Messages from Beyond*," Carmen answers.

Henry turns sideways to address Peggy. "Isn't that the program where the woman talks to dead people?" He sounds excited.

For the first time since he arrived, Peggy looks at him, trying to ignore the way his eyes crinkle at the corners as he stares back. "Yes, she passes on messages from the deceased to their loved ones."

Henry flashes that adorable grin he seems to save just for her. "Maybe she'll have a message from your husband."

"I hope so," she says, turning away from his intense stare.

Andrea places a possessive hand on Henry's forearm. Roni raises an eyebrow and kicks Peggy under the table. "Oh, that woman is a fake," Andrea says. "I've read articles that say she researches the audience members. That's why it takes so long for people to get tickets."

The door opens, and Peggy gets blasted with cold air again.

"I've seen articles where people swear she's the real deal," Roni says.

Peggy bites down on her lip to suppress a smile. She can't believe how convincing Roni sounds. The fondness she feels for her friend swells.

After a few seconds of awkward silence, Henry and Andrea say goodbye and stroll to the counter. Peggy keeps her eyes trained on them as they order their coffee, her stomach churning as Andrea laughs at something Henry says.

"Day one, and she's already going hard after Henry," Roni says. "Showering before coffee? We've never done that."

"That's because the bathroom at the gym is disgusting," Peggy says.

Roni and Peggy continue to discuss the condition of the restroom while Carmen taps away at her iPad, booking their flight to Florida.

———— ❦ ————

LATER THAT MORNING, Peggy rings Carmen's doorbell, ready to begin her first day with Sophia.

"Is it already ten thirty?" Carmen asks when she answers the door. She's wearing a red fleece bathrobe, her wet hair is piled high on top of her head, and her eyes have a wild look. "I've been playing with Sophia and lost track of time."

Peggy follows Carmen to the living room and freezes in the entranceway, taken aback by the mess. Cheerios crushed into the rug outline a path to the sofa, which is buried under enormous piles of unfolded clothing. Below it, two overflowing laundry baskets spill their contents onto the dirty floor. Bowls with milky bottoms and cups half filled with juice teeter on the edge of the dusty coffee table.

"Sorry about the mess. Rosalita usually helps me with all this. I meant to get to the laundry last night but was too tired, and Sophia wanted to play this morning." Carmen is slouching. Peggy notices dark circles under her eyes.

In the center of the room, Sophia sits in front of the Candy Land board game. "Your turn, Mommy."

"I'll play with you," Peggy says, "so Mommy can get ready for work."

"No, no," Carmen says. "I always have time for my baby."

As Carmen continues the game with Sophia, Peggy collects the dirty dishes.

"You don't have to do that," Carmen says. "Honestly, I'll do it tonight when I get home. If it bothers you, take Sophia to your house."

Peggy ignores her and brings the dishes to the kitchen, where dirty plates, pots, and pans fill the sink. Peggy stares at the disarray, baffled, but then she breaks out in a grin. Even Carmen can't do everything.

Peggy remembers when the twins were toddlers. Her house, too, was often a catastrophe. Patrick helped when he could, but the mess never bothered him. "The house looks lived in. It's how it should be," he said.

Peggy had other thoughts. The mess made her feel like she was failing as a mother and housewife. After all, she was home all day. Shouldn't she be able to find time to clean?

Carmen and Sophia patter into the kitchen. "Oh, Peggy, you don't have to clean. It's enough that you're here to watch Sophia," Carmen says.

Peggy hands a dishtowel and small pan to Sophia. "Do you want to be my helper and dry this?"

Sophia nods enthusiastically, and Carmen races upstairs to get dressed. By the time Carmen is ready to leave, Peggy and Sophia are sitting on the couch doing laundry. Peggy folds towels while Sophia searches through a massive pile of socks.

The little girl pulls out two black socks, one with a blue Nike swoosh at the top and the other with a green. "I found a match."

"Close," Peggy says, pointing to the Nike logo. "But what color is this?"

"Blue," Sophia answers.

"And this?" Peggy points to the other sock.

"Gween."

Peggy and Carmen both laugh at Sophia's mispronunciation. "They have to be the same color to be a match," Peggy explains.

"Thank you, Peg. I'm a bit frazzled without Rosalita," Carmen says. Right now, though, she looks anything but frazzled. She's standing straight, and the circles under her eyes have disappeared. Her hair is dry and styled, and she's dressed in sleek black pants and a lavender blouse. Once again, she looks like a woman who has it all together. Peggy stares at her friend, realizing that the perfect look is a uniform Carmen wears when she's out in public.

Chapter 35

Once again, Peggy has horribly misjudged someone's age. Tom, the old guy who stole Henry's spot, really isn't all that old. She was also wrong about his fitness level. He might be more fit than anyone else in the class. She knows this because three weeks ago, on his birthday, Shauna had the entire class sing happy birthday and made him do fifty-five push-ups, one for each year of his life. He tore through them one after another without breaking a sweat.

"He's like the Energizer Bunny," Roni quipped, licking her lips. "He keeps going and going." The look in her eyes was the same one Greg used to have when he came home late after a hockey game, starving.

Since that day, Roni has taken a liking to "the old geezer," which is what she calls him even though he is only a few years older than she is. His nickname for her is Mouth. The two have even gone out for drinks several times. After one of their nights out, they both missed class the next day. When Peggy asked Roni why, her friend smirked.

"Don't you worry—Tom gave me enough of a workout," Roni said. Peggy held up a hand, not wanting to hear any more.

Since then, every time Shauna tells the class to work in pairs, Roni chooses Tom, leaving Peggy with Carmen, which is fine with Peggy. What's not fine is that Henry and Andrea are usually partners. Sometimes Peggy finds herself staring at them, wondering if they are having nighttime workouts together as well. Then she gives herself a mental slap because why does she care? She doesn't! She is only in boot camp to get fit for her trip to Florida where, through Lynda Mc-Garry, she'll speak with Patrick.

Today, the class is working out in teams of two, tossing ten-pound medicine balls back and forth over their heads. From where she's standing, Peggy has a clear view of Andrea's birdlike face and Henry's broad back. Each time Andrea catches the ball, she giggles at something Henry says, and his shoulders shake, letting Peggy know he, too, is laughing. Each time Peggy sees this, she fires her ball back to Carmen with increasing force. Carmen, in return, steps backward to get farther away. Finally, she runs out of space, colliding with Roni, who somehow knows exactly what's going on.

"Easy, Peggy," Roni says. "You're going to kill Carmen. Next time, partner with your archrival over there, and hurl the death ball at her head."

Yes, that is exactly what Peggy would like to do. Maybe she should whip the ball at Andrea now and catch her off guard. With the ball poised over her head, she glances in Andrea's direction again. But Andrea has disappeared.

Henry's standing by himself, looking at Peggy. He points to his chest and then at Peggy. "May I join you?" he mouths. He doesn't wait for an answer before coming over.

"Where did Peggy's nemesis go?" Roni asks, causing Peggy to cringe. Henry will think she's jealous.

Is she jealous? Of course she's not. She just doesn't believe a sweaty boot camp is the place for flirting. Andrea should be focusing on working out.

Henry looks at Roni blankly, so she clarifies. "Andrea."

"She has to be at work early today."

Peggy, Carmen, and Henry form a small circle and toss the ball around it. By now, Peggy's fatigued arms shake as she holds them above her head and tosses the ball to Carmen. How much longer is Shauna going to make them do this? After the ball makes three loops,

Peggy can't take it anymore, so she excuses herself to go to the restroom. She takes her time meandering upstairs. As she pushes open the door to the women's room, she hears the shower. It goes off when she's in the stall. She makes her way to the sinks, turning the corner and coming face-to-face with a buck-naked Andrea.

Peggy freezes, staring at Andrea's chest with her mouth gaping. Why is this woman parading around the restroom nude? Peggy realizes she's looking at Andrea's nipples and drops her eyes to the ground.

"What time is it? Has class ended?" Andrea asks.

Peggy does not want to raise her head. "No, I just needed..." She stops talking. It's too awkward having a conversation with someone who isn't wearing clothes. She walks past Andrea to wash her hands.

"I'm really enjoying this class," Andrea says. "I'm so glad Carmen told me about it."

"Yes, it's great," Peggy says. Without thinking about it, she glances in the big mirror over the sink so that she can see Andrea as she speaks. *Oh boy*. She shouldn't have done that. Andrea is bending over, putting moisturizer on her feet, so what Peggy sees is Andrea's ass, cellulite and all, sticking up in the air.

"The morning workout keeps me energized all day," Andrea says as she steps into her underwear.

"It's a great way to start the day," Peggy agrees. She realizes that if it were her changing, she'd cover herself up with a towel, not just because she's modest but also because she's ashamed of her body with all its rolls and cellulite. Andrea's body is no better than Peggy's. In fact, Peggy might even argue that it is worse. Yet here Andrea is, parading around the locker room in her birthday suit without a care in the world about who sees her. Clearly, she is not embarrassed by her appearance. Peggy has to admit, she respects that—envies it, even, in her own small way.

Chapter 36

In the days leading up to Peggy's trip to Florida, she's so nervous that she can't eat. She has no idea if she's lost weight, but Shauna, Nick, and Carmen all comment that she looks good. She's not sure she agrees. The night before she leaves for Tampa, she stands in front of the full-length mirror in Grace's room, the only one in the house, and studies herself in the bluish-green top she purchased to wear to the show. The medium-sized shirt stretches tightly across her abdomen, calling attention to a fat roll in her gut. *Darn.* She should have listened to the saleswoman and bought the large, but she swears the shirt didn't look this bad in the dressing room. *Did it shrink on the way home?*

Peggy turns and looks over her shoulder at her backside in the mirror. The tan pants aren't doing her butt any favors. What was the point of working her ass off in boot camp if she still looks like the Stay Puft Marshmallow Man's wife?

Well, clearly you didn't work your ass off, Pegsta, she hears Patrick say.

She slides the slacks down and studies the backs of her thighs. What she sees is cellulite. She slams the closet door and stomps out of Grace's room and back to her own. She rummages through her drawers, trying to find something else to wear, but nothing inspires her. She would go back to the mall, but it's already closed. It serves her right for waiting till the last minute to pack, but she wanted to lose as many pounds as possible before picking out the outfit she would wear for her reunion with Patrick.

Somewhere under the jumble of clothes scattered over her bed, her phone rings. She scrambles across the room and forges through the piles until she finds it.

"Are you ready to go?" Carmen asks, her voice giddy with excitement.

"I have nothing to wear to the show."

There's a swooshing noise on the line, and Peggy imagines all the enthusiasm being sucked out of Carmen. She wishes she weren't such a killjoy.

"You must have something," Carmen says.

"Nothing that looks good on me."

"What about the outfit you wore when we went to dinner last week? The black pants and green sweater."

"I'll be too hot."

"Nonsense," Carmen says. "The studio will be air conditioned."

Peggy shuffles through the clothes strewn over the comforter and picks up the sweater. It's not as heavy as she thought, and she does love the way it looks on her. "I guess that's my only option at this point." Before she has finished the sentence, she wishes she could swallow it and rephrase it in a more peppy-Carmen-like way.

"You'll look gorgeous. How could you not?" Carmen says.

Peggy knows that's not true. She looks like a dowdy middle-aged mother, like most women her age. She glances toward her bureau at the framed pictures the twins gave her before they left for school and hears Grace saying, *Dad wouldn't even recognize you.* That may be true, but since Peggy's been attending boot camp, she feels like her old self, and isn't that what matters? She thinks of Andrea parading around the gym locker room in the buff. Clearly, the woman is proud of her body. So why is Peggy so obsessed about what her dead husband thinks about her body? She knows she shouldn't be.

"Of course, I'll look gorgeous with you there to do my makeup and hair." As the words spill out, she realizes they're true.

"Even without my help, you'd look gorgeous," Carmen says. She tells Peggy she's not going to boot camp tomorrow because she wants to spend the morning with Antonio and Sophia. "I'll see you when Roni comes to get us."

Now that Peggy knows what she's wearing to the show, packing is easy. She finishes the task and cleans her room in under an hour. After lugging her suitcase downstairs and putting it by the front door, she settles on the couch to call Grace and Greg. Grace doesn't answer, so Peggy leaves a message telling her daughter that she loves her, something she wishes she had said to Patrick before he left for the airport on that fateful day.

Greg answers on the first ring. Peggy can tell that he's eating by the way he mumbles hello. They talk for a few minutes about his classes, and he asks her if she's excited to go to Florida.

"I am," she answers.

Greg hums the opening music to *The Twilight Zone*. Then, in a serious tone, he says, "Tell Dad I say hey," and Peggy feels a twinge in her heart as she hangs up.

SHORTLY BEFORE SIX the next morning, Peggy awakes to the sound of a motor running. It's so loud that she expects a vehicle to come crashing through her bedroom wall. A few seconds later, gears grind, followed by heavy scraping and a thunderous boom. She forces herself out of bed, stumbles to the window, and pushes aside the curtains. As she looks outside, she bites down on her lip and mutters to herself, watching a black pickup truck plow what looks like a mountain of snow off her driveway into an Everest-sized pile to the right of the garage.

It was not supposed to snow today. She knows because she watched the news last night and heard the good-for-nothing meteorologist talk about how they were dodging a bullet with a monstrous storm going out to sea and missing them. "Morning clouds will give way to blue skies by lunchtime." Those were his exact words less than seven hours ago, and now it's snowing to beat the band.

Her cell phone buzzes with a text from Shauna, announcing that boot camp is canceled due to the storm. Peggy wonders if the airport is closed and hustles downstairs to turn on the news. A young female reporter dressed like an Eskimo, her faux-fur-lined hood pulled tightly over her head, stands by a seawall, the ocean raging behind her, snow whipping in her face, and the wind gusting so loudly it blocks out everything she says. The news station cuts back to the anchors sitting comfortably behind the desk in the warm studio. "Better her than us, right, Sara?" says the bespectacled male.

"I hope there's a big mug of hot cocoa waiting for her inside the news van," the female anchor, Sara, says as cancellations scroll across the bottom of the screen. "Logan Airport is still open, but most flights in and out have been canceled, so check with your airlines if you're scheduled to fly today."

Peggy sends a message to Carmen and Roni: *Do you think we'll be able to fly?* She doesn't know whether to hope her flight is canceled or not. On one hand, she doesn't want to fly in blizzard-like conditions, but she also doesn't want to miss her opportunity to hear from Patrick.

Not looking good, Roni answers, and Carmen adds a sad-face emoticon.

On the television, a pregnant meteorologist explains why the forecast was so wrong. She points to the map and says the snow will continue falling until early Tuesday evening. "When all is said and done, we'll be counting the accumulation in feet and not inches."

Peggy's throat tightens. If it doesn't stop snowing until tomorrow night, she won't get to Florida in time for Wednesday's show. *Of all the times for a nor'easter.* The storm just has to be blowing in when Peggy's supposed to fly for the first time in over fifteen years. Just her stinking luck.

She picks up her phone and scrolls through her contacts until she reaches Roni's name.

"Hello," Roni says, her voice groggy.

"I thought you were up. You texted."

"I went back to bed."

"It's supposed to snow until tomorrow night."

Roni yawns. Peggy pictures her sitting up and stretching. "What time is the show on Wednesday."

"Ten."

"Find out what time the earliest flight leaving Boston gets into Tampa."

"Okay," Peggy says. "I'll check."

"Don't call me back. I'll call you when I'm up."

At the breakfast bar, Peggy fires up her laptop and searches for flights to Tampa. Through the window of the kitchen door, she sees the falling snow whipping in circles in the powerful gusts. Trees sway back and forth. *Just perfect.* She turns her attention back to her computer screen. Her heart races in anticipation as she sees that there's a flight leaving Boston at 5:00 a.m. That should get them to Tampa by eight, she thinks, but she lets out a heavy sigh when she sees the arrival time is 9:45 a.m. Apparently, the plane stops in Philadelphia. *Dang.* An hour later, she slams her computer shut. No flights will get them to Florida before nine forty-five, and that won't give them enough time to make it out of the airport and across town before ten o'clock. She wouldn't mind being a few minutes late for the show, but the tickets clearly state that there is no late admittance.

Peggy gets up to make herself a cup of tea and stares out the window as she waits for the water to boil. The snow piling up on the deck reaches all the way to the halfway point of the four-foot railing, and the flakes are falling faster than when she woke up. She briefly wonders if this storm is Patrick's way of telling her that he doesn't want to talk to her. Her lower back tightens. She inhales deeply and slowly lets it out, reminding herself that Patrick always wanted to talk. She was the one who ignored him on the day of his death. The kettle whistles, and at the same time, her phone rings. She turns the burner off before answering.

"Just got a text from the airline," Roni says. "Our flight is officially canceled. Any luck finding something for Wednesday morning?"

"Nope."

Roni doesn't say anything, but Peggy hears typing. It stops, and Roni speaks. "I booked us on the last flight out tomorrow night. It leaves at seven thirty and will get us to Tampa just before eleven. Maybe the snow will stop in time."

Outside, there's a loud crash. The kitchen light flicks off, the refrigerator stops humming, and the illuminated clock on the oven no longer glows with the time. "Aw, shit," Roni says. "Power just went out."

"Here too."

"May as well go back to sleep. Talk to you tomorrow."

Peggy paces around the kitchen. After a few minutes, she sits at the counter in front of her laptop again. She tries to navigate to a weather site, but an error message pops up telling her she has no Internet connection. *Duh!* Laughing at herself, she moves to the living room, sprawls out on the couch, and watches the snow come down, burying her dreams of flying to Florida to see Lynda McGarry and make contact with her dead husband.

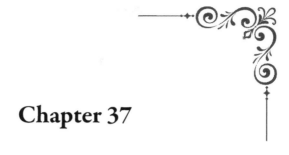

Chapter 37

The snow tapers off late Tuesday morning. By midafternoon, the roads have all been cleared, and at dinnertime, Peggy, Roni, and Carmen are standing in the security line at Logan Airport. Since Peggy entered the terminal, the contents of her stomach have been swirling like the inside of a snow globe that has been shaken. Everything about this place reminds her of what happened to Patrick. She taps the toe of her boot on the floor as she wonders whether the pilot got enough sleep last night, if the plane will strike a bird, or if a mechanical glitch will bring it down. Engine failure caused Patrick's plane to crash.

"Relax, Peggy," Roni says.

She does need to relax. Every single one of her muscles is tense. An announcement blasts over the PA system, warning passengers not to leave their bags unattended and to tell security if they see an unattended bag. Peggy sighs. The strap of her duffel bag digs into her shoulder, so she slips it off and places it on the floor, nudging it along with her foot as she moves forward.

A woman standing outside the queue leans over the ropes and hugs a man near the front of the line. "I love you," she says.

"I'll call you when I land," the man says, pulling away.

Tell her you love her, Peggy thinks. *You might not get another chance.*

The man steps toward the TSA agent without saying another word.

Peggy's stomach churns as she remembers how she refused to say goodbye to Patrick that morning. Lost in her thoughts, she stumbles over her carry-on and knocks down one of the rope-barrier poles. A TSA agent cranes his neck to see what all the commotion is.

"Breathe," Carmen says, wrapping her arm around Peggy's waist and keeping it there until they make it to the front of the line. Peggy's hands shake as she gives the TSA agent her license and boarding pass. She accidentally kicks the podium he's standing behind as he studies her ID. Finally, he scribbles something on her ticket before handing it back.

Peggy turns, expecting to see Carmen, but Carmen and Roni have both been directed to a different line. The man behind her steps on the back of her boot as he reaches around her for a bin. In front of her, people pull laptops from their bags and take off their coats. Without removing anything from her bag, she places it on the belt and slips out of her jacket. She bends to remove her boots but struggles to pull them off. The man behind her sighs loudly. She wishes he would back off. He's standing so close she can smell coffee on his breath. A TSA agent tells her to move to the side and directs people around her.

She finally yanks her boots off and makes her way through the metal detector. On the other side, she watches the man who didn't say "I love you" put his shoes on. She wants to tell him to call or text the woman, but by the time she collects her belongings from the conveyor belt, she has lost sight of him.

WHEN PEGGY, RONI, AND Carmen make it to their gate, they learn their flight has been delayed ninety minutes. Roni insists they go to the bar across from the gate, where she orders a round of Dark 'n Stormy cocktails. "They go with the weather," she says.

Peggy excuses herself to go to the restroom and returns to find that the beverages have been delivered. Based on the strong alcoholic taste, she wouldn't be at all surprised if, while she was gone, Roni asked the bartender to be heavy-handed with the rum. The drink goes down smoothly, and Peggy feels her muscles relax. By the middle of the second round, her lips have loosened up as well.

"I can't believe what good friends you've been to me," she says, and the three clink their glasses. She turns to Carmen. "I didn't like you when we first met."

"I know," Carmen says with a smile. "I'm glad I won you over."

Peggy leans toward Carmen and hugs her. "I'm so happy you're coming with me." She pulls away from Carmen and slouches toward Roni for another embrace. "You too. I might not have gone on my own."

Across the hallway from the bar, an airline employee at the gate uses a microphone to announce that the plane has been delayed an additional ninety minutes. Roni orders another round, and Carmen excuses herself to use the restroom. Peggy and Roni sit quietly at the table, watching passengers rush down the hallway, pulling small suitcases behind them.

When the drinks have been delivered and Carmen is back at the table, Roni asks Peggy, "What do you expect to happen at the show?"

Peggy sits up straighter. "I want Patrick to tell me that I've done a good job with Greg and Grace." She takes another sip of her drink. "I always suspected he thought I didn't love them enough or wasn't a good mother because I sometimes needed a break from parenting and wanted to spend time away from them."

"Nonsense," Carmen says. "Spending time away from your children helps you be a better, more present parent during the time you spend together."

Peggy often voiced similar thoughts to Patrick, but he couldn't be swayed. "It was something we fought about a lot. We were fighting about it when he died." She looks down at the table. "I didn't even kiss him goodbye when he left."

Peggy balls her hand into a tight fist as she remembers Patrick's alarm clock buzzing the morning of his trip. She lay in bed, pretending to be sleeping, as he showered and dressed. Ordinarily, she would have gotten up and made coffee and toast for him, but she was too angry from the hurtful insinuations he had made the night before when he'd asked, "What kind of mother wants to be way from her young children for a week?"

She smelled the piney scent of his soap and felt the mattress sink as he sat next to her on the bed. "I'm leaving now," he said.

Her back was to him, and she didn't move.

"I know you're awake. I can tell by your breathing."

Still, she didn't move.

He sighed, and she felt the warmth of his hand on her shoulder and the brush of his lips on her cheek. "I love you," he said. "I'll call you tonight."

She listened as his car started and backed out of the driveway, and she fell asleep again, not knowing that those past few minutes were the last she would ever spend with her husband.

Carmen reaches across the table for Peggy's hand. "I'm sure he knew you loved him, and tomorrow, you'll get the chance to clear the air."

Roni rolls her eyes. "There are gonna be a lot of people in that audience. Chances are Lynda McQuacky, or whatever her name is, won't pick you, and even if she does, she's making stuff up, not talking to ghosts."

Carmen and Peggy both glare at her. "Why are you so skeptical?" Carmen asks.

Roni smirks. "People aren't who they seem to be. It's a lesson I learned from my husband."

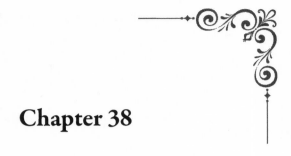

Chapter 38

Peggy can't believe she's really here, in the studio where *Messages from Beyond* is filmed. She wonders if she's dreaming. She doesn't remember waking up this morning. Then again, she can't be sure she ever made it to bed last night. All she knows is that because of all the flight delays, she, Roni, and Carmen didn't make it to their hotel until after four in the morning. The next thing she knew, they were scrambling around the room, getting ready to leave for the show, and now they're here.

Peggy turns, expecting to see someone behind her, but the seats in the next row remain empty. Ever since walking into the building, she has felt someone looking over her shoulder. She hopes it's Patrick and imagines him taking in Roni and Carmen, wondering who they are. As she studies the hundreds of people making their way to their seats, she wonders if Patrick will have to fight his way through a mob of ghosts crowding Lynda McGarry to make contact with their loved ones. She thinks back to the night she first met him in that crowded pub, how all the customers except him had to claw their way to the bar. She nods, certain Patrick will make his way to the medium.

"Look at all these people," Roni says, pointing to a steady stream of men and women pouring through the entrance. "I can't believe they all believe in this crap."

Peggy glares at her and considers asking Carmen to trade seats so that she doesn't have to listen to Roni's skeptical comments through-out the entire show. She would definitely do it if not for the burly

256

man sitting next to Carmen, whose enormous arm spills over the armrest into her seat.

Ushers are now rushing the audience members to their seats. Carmen says something that Peggy can't hear over the din. "Are you nervous?" Carmen asks again, louder.

"Excited," Peggy answers. "I've been waiting to talk to Patrick for a long time."

"Well, don't get your hopes up," Roni says. She, Carmen, and Peggy all smile at two elderly women who pass by them on the way to their seats. There is a lot of space between each row, and Peggy wonders if the studio was designed that way so no one will step on Lynda's bare feet.

Peggy checks her watch. The show should have started already. Several minutes later, when the entire audience is finally seated, a man appears center stage. He introduces himself as Jason and says he needs to go over three rules before Lynda comes out. The number one rule is not to touch Lynda. "You'd be surprised at how many people we have to ask to leave because they grab at her." The second rule prohibits use of cell phones or any electronic devices, including all recording devices. "The electrical currents interfere with Lynda's ability to reach the other side."

"Oh, please." Roni snickers.

The man continues with the final rule. "Be careful not to step on Lynda's feet."

He disappears from the stage, and the lights dim. Peggy's heart pounds. Two neon signs mounted to the walls on each side of the stage flash the word CLAP. Applause slowly breaks out in the room. Seconds later, Lynda McGarry emerges from behind the teal curtain and walks to a black X taped on the stage floor. She raises and lowers her hands, palms up, until the clapping becomes thunderous.

"Even the applause is orchestrated," Roni whispers.

Peggy wonders how uncomfortable she'd be sharing half her seat with the big man's arm. Carmen looks comfortable, but then again, Carmen is half her size.

"Thank you," Lynda says. "I'm so glad that you came to see me. I hope that one of your deceased loved ones will come to see you."

Peggy can't take her eyes off Lynda, whose face is grotesquely tanned and extremely wrinkled, things Peggy has never noticed about the medium in all the television episodes she has watched.

Lynda points to her shoeless, sockless feet. "If you watch the show, you know I don't wear shoes. I feel I make a better connection when they're bare. So if I come into your row, please be careful not to step on them." She goes on to recite the same spiel she gives at the beginning of every show. "Spirits don't speak like people do. They make noises or show symbols that need to be interpreted."

Peggy hears jiggling to her left and turns to see Roni shaking Junior Mints out of a large box. *How is she eating at a time like this?* Roni offers the candy to Peggy, but Peggy shakes her head and turns her attention back to Lynda.

"We're going to turn the lights all the way down," Lynda says. "I'm going to close my eyes, and I ask that you all be quiet while I connect with those from beyond."

The room turns dark and silent. A chill runs down Peggy's spine as she gets the sensation of someone looking over her shoulder again. She conjures up an image of Patrick and holds on to it while pleading with him not to stand her up. The room remains dark, with time passing as slowly as it does when Peggy's at the gym, holding a plank or squat. She smells peppermint and chocolate. Behind her, someone sniffs. A few rows in front of her, a cell phone buzzes. Finally, the lights click back on. Lynda's expression is much more somber than before the room went dark. "There are a lot of them coming through, all fighting for attention." She covers her ears with her hands.

"They're not usually this loud, and there aren't usually so many of them."

Lynda closes her eyes and rubs her temples. Roni chuckles. "She's already making excuses for when she gets it wrong," she says. Peggy jabs her with her elbow.

With the spotlight on her, Lynda descends the steps leading down from the stage. "A male presence is the strongest," she says. Carmen reaches for Peggy's hand as Lynda makes her way up the center aisle toward them. Peggy takes a deep breath as the medium gets closer. Lynda steps into their row. Carmen's grip on Peggy's hand tightens, and Peggy sits up straighter. Lynda jerks backward, momentarily losing her balance as she falls into the center aisle, and continues toward the back of the room.

Peggy lets out the breath she's been holding, and Carmen releases her hand. "What the hell was that?" Roni asks.

Though there is no way Lynda could have heard Roni's question, she answers it. "They're pulling me in all different directions." She walks all the way to the rear of the studio and enters the last row.

Peggy mutters to herself. When she's watching on television, Lynda always makes contact with a loved one of someone sitting in the first ten rows. Now that Peggy's at the show, sitting in the fifth row, Lynda's talking to spirits in the last row. Just her luck.

Lynda stops in front of a young man who looks to be about the same age as the twins. "He's older than you. A father figure."

"My father," the kid says.

"What's your name?" Lynda asks.

"Chris."

"Your father's name starts with a J," Lynda says. "Joe, John, Jim."

The young man shakes his head.

"The J sound is very strong," Lynda says.

A woman a few seats down from the young man raises her hand. "My father was Jerry."

"He's pointing to his hand, which is usually spirit's way of telling me they took their own life," Lynda says, working her way toward the woman. "You understand?"

"My father died of lung cancer," the woman says.

Lynda stops moving. "Well, then it's not your father," she snaps.

Roni laughs, and Peggy elbows her again. "I'm sorry, but this is a disaster," Roni whispers. "She hasn't gotten anything right."

"It takes a while. She needs to connect," Peggy hisses.

The young man Lynda originally spoke to raises his hand. "My dad committed suicide."

Lynda walks back toward him. "What was your father's name?"

"George."

"That's a J-sounding name. You need to pay attention to what I'm saying." She wrings her hands. "They're all shouting at me. This is so much harder than usual." She covers her face and looks down at the floor.

In all the shows she has watched, Peggy has never seen Lynda behave this way and wonders why the medium is so cranky today.

"Okay, he's making a motion like he's dribbling a basketball. Mean anything to you?"

The spotlight shines on the young man. He flinches. Roni leans toward Peggy. "Duh, he's wearing a LeBron James shirt."

"I was supposed to be at practice." Tears stream down the kid's face.

"You found him."

The boy, who is sobbing now, nods. "I wasn't feeling good, so I came home."

Lynda wraps her arm around the boy's shoulder. Finally, Peggy recognizes the compassionate woman she watches on television. "He's so sorry and wants you to know it didn't have anything to do with you. You couldn't have saved him."

"If I had gotten home a few minutes earlier..." the boy says.

You wouldn't have been able to stop him, Peggy thinks, certain Lynda will say it. After all, she's seen enough shows to predict Lynda's reaction.

"You wouldn't have been able to stop him," Lynda says.

Next to Peggy, Carmen fiddles through her purse. She pulls out tissues and offers them to Peggy and Roni. Peggy takes one, but Roni rolls her eyes and whispers, "Come on. You can't be crying over this."

"How are you not?" Carmen asks. Peggy, who sometimes wonders if Roni was born without tear ducts, can't believe that Carmen's surprised by Roni's lack of emotion.

Lynda walks down the center aisle toward them again. She passes their row but then backtracks. "Okay, I have a very aggressive woman pulling me in here."

Peggy sighs. *Where the heck are you, Patrick?*

Lynda slowly makes her way down the row, passing Carmen and stopping between Peggy and Roni. "She's showing me that she stands over you, which means she's older than you." As she speaks, she looks at Roni, who has gone pale. Peggy wants to tell Lynda not to waste her time with Roni. It's so unfair.

"Did you lose your mother?" the medium asks.

Roni nods. *Damn you, Patrick,* Peggy thinks, but she's also intrigued by what Lynda is saying to Roni. Peggy didn't know Roni lost her mom.

"This is what she's showing me." Lynda presses the palms of her hands together and holds them up to the side of her head. "Usually, it means the spirit passed peacefully."

Roni, who is now beet red, shouts, "If by peacefully, you mean after the cancer and chemo ravaged her body for months on end!"

Lynda remains calm. "This woman did not die of cancer."

The medium's eyes lock with Peggy. A wave of guilt rolls over Peggy. She slouches in her seat. For months, years really, she's only ever dreamed about making contact with Patrick, never even thinking of her mother, who passed of an aneurysm in her sleep shortly before Peggy met Patrick.

"There's a younger man with her now, and she's pushing him forward."

Peggy gasps. Patrick and her mother are together. Her mother is making him speak. This is so like her mother.

"This means something to you?" Lynda asks.

"Yes," Peggy whispers. Carmen rubs her back.

"He's trying to tell me his name. Matthew, Richard, Matt, Rick."

"Patrick," Peggy whispers. This time, Roni elbows her.

"Patrick," Lynda says.

"Oh my," Carmen cries.

Lynda grabs Peggy's arm, pulling her to her feet. "What's your name?"

Peggy's legs wobble, and her hands tremble. "Peggy." She clasps them together to stop them from shaking and rests them on her stomach.

"The man is showing me he's on your level. That means the same generation. Is it your brother?"

The bright spotlight hits Peggy in the face. She steps forward, trying to get out of the glare, and in the process, she loses her balance, and her shoe lands on Lynda's foot. "Ouch," Lynda cries, pressing her lips together and closing her eyes. It happens so quickly Peggy can barely register the gasp of the audience and the hot flush of her own face. Lynda takes a deep breath and hops on one foot down the aisle, out into the main row. A woman and man appear from backstage, rushing to her.

Tears fill Peggy's eyes. Devastated, she sinks to her seat and hangs her head. Patrick was here. With Lynda. In the same room. Now Peggy will never know what he thinks. A muffled sob escapes her lips.

Carmen reaches for her hand.

"It's stupid that she doesn't wear shoes," Roni says.

The man and woman help Lynda up the stage stairs, the house lights brighten, and the man who reviewed the rules at the beginning of the show reappears. "They're tending to Lynda backstage. If she's able, she'll be back." He looks in Peggy's direction. "In fifteen years, you're the first to step on her feet."

"We should go," Peggy whispers.

Carmen stands.

"No," Roni says. "You didn't kill her. You stepped on her foot. It's not that big of a deal. She'll be fine."

Peggy hopes that Roni is right, but even if Lynda does return, she probably won't come near Peggy again. Several minutes later, the lights dim, and Lynda appears from behind the curtain. Applause breaks out. The spotlight shines on Lynda's face and trails her body, landing on her feet. The left one is wrapped in an Ace bandage even though Peggy would have sworn she stepped on Lynda's right foot.

"I'm in a bit of pain, but I will power through because the show must go on," she says to more applause. Lynda limps down the stairway and heads back up the middle aisle, turning into Peggy's row.

"Your brother really wants to talk to you. Please stand, but be careful where you step." Lynda leaves plenty of room for Peggy.

Peggy gets to her feet. "I don't have a brother. It's my husband."

Lynda nods. "He's showing me impact. He died in a car crash?" she asks.

Peggy doesn't want to risk angering Lynda, but she has to correct her. "Plane crash."

"Plane crash, car crash. Close enough," Lynda says.

It's not really close at all.

"Does March 10 mean anything? Is it a birthday, an anniversary?"

"Nothing I can think of," Peggy says

"How about the number 310?"

Peggy shakes her head.

"He's showing me that number, and that usually means a date."

Peggy tries to think of something important that happened in March but comes up empty.

"Do owls mean anything to you?" Lynda asks.

Peggy shakes her head.

"He's making a noise like an owl. Hooo, hooo."

The audience laughs at Lynda's impersonation. Peggy stares blankly, not thinking it's funny. *All this time, and Patrick is showing numbers that mean nothing and hooting? He would never! He didn't even like birds, for crying out loud.*

"He wouldn't do that," she stammers.

"Well, I don't have the best connection," Lynda points to her bandaged foot. "Did you see an owl together? Do you have an owl poster?"

"No!" Peggy spits.

Lynda shrugs. "Sometimes the things I say don't make sense here, but later, they will. He's definitely hooting—hoo, hoo." She starts to walk away but stops. "Your mother is patting you on the back. That means exactly what you would think it does. She's proud of you."

Peggy's eyes fill with tears.

"Your husband too."

Oh, how Peggy wants to believe that. That's why she came here—so that Patrick could tell her he's proud of her, of the job she did raising their kids. She steps closer to Lynda. "How do you know that? Please. What did he say?"

"He's patting you on the back too. He's still hooting like an owl, but he's patting you on the back."

Chapter 39

How could Patrick not mention the kids? How could her mother not comment on her beautiful grandchildren? That's what Peggy wants to know.

Roni has a simple explanation. "Because Patrick and your mother can't talk. They're dead. Lynda McGarry is a fraud."

After seeing the so-called medium in person, Peggy agrees with Roni. She clenches her teeth as she thinks about her morning at the show. "What was that crap with the hooting?" Peggy asks. "What could it mean?"

"Maybe you'll see an owl on March 10," Carmen says.

Not likely. She's never seen an owl, and even if she sees one on March 10, what kind of message would that be? It certainly wouldn't be the message that she wanted—that Grace and Greg are fine and she did a good job raising them.

She picks up her glass and drains the rest of her cocktail. She started the afternoon drinking margaritas, but at some point, Carmen convinced her to switch to rum and Diet Coke because it has fewer calories. "Less than a hundred," Carmen claimed. Peggy's lost count of how many she has had but knows she's been in this bar for hours.

After the show, they went shopping. They returned to the hotel late in the afternoon and tried to nap by the pool. As soon as they were sprawled out in their chaise lounges, though, it started to rain, so they moved inside to the bar, where they have been ever since.

When they first sat down, they had the place to themselves. It's seven thirty now, and there are a few other customers scattered throughout the restaurant. Peggy feels underdressed in her shorts and T-shirt at this time of night. Roni's dressed similarly to Peggy and seems perfectly comfortable in her attire. Carmen's clothing is more appropriate. She's wearing a dress, and no one can tell she has a bathing suit on under it. They just finished dinner. Peggy and Roni split an order of potato skins and ordered burgers and fries. Carmen, of course, had a salad. Peggy doesn't feel bad about what she ate. She deserved a treat. Her dream of hearing from Patrick again is over. She will never know if he thinks she did a good job with Grace and Greg.

Her belly is full, and she's exhausted. She wants to go to bed. Really, she wants to go home and forget she ever took this disastrous trip or wasted so much time watching Lynda McGarry. "I'm calling it a night." She removes her napkin from her lap and places it on the table.

"You can't," Roni says. "It's too early. I just ordered dessert. I can't eat it by myself, and Carmen won't help."

As if on cue, the waitress drops off an enormous piece of key lime pie with three forks.

"We'll take another round too," Roni says. When the drinks come, Roni proposes a toast. "May Lynda McGarry get revealed for the fraud that she is."

Peggy toasts with her. After a few minutes, she says, "I didn't know about your mother. I'm sorry."

"How long ago did she pass?" Carmen asks.

Tears form in the corners of Roni's eyes. She blinks hard, and they are gone. "A long time ago, when I was twelve."

"Oh, Roni," Peggy says while Carmen reaches across the table and takes Roni's hand.

Roni sighs. "For a second, when Lynda approached, I thought maybe she was for real, but she's a fake." She pulls her hand from Carmen's and looks at Peggy. "I'm glad you stepped on her foot. I wish you had stomped on it."

"I know I stepped on her right foot, so why was the left bandaged?" Peggy asks.

Roni's lips curl downward. "She wasn't hurt. She was acting. That's what she does."

Peggy pictures Lynda hobbling around the studio and decides the so-called medium was laying it on thick. Still, it might be Peggy's fault that Lynda made up the message from Patrick. "Do you think if I hadn't stepped on her foot, she would have been able to connect?" she asks, pushing the pie away from her toward Roni.

"No!" Roni says.

Carmen leans toward Peggy. "I know you wanted Patrick to tell you that you've done a good job raising the kids, but you don't need him to tell you that, Peg. Anyone who knows Grace and Greg knows they're good kids, and that's because of you."

Peggy wonders if that's true. Greg cheated on his girlfriend, and Grace is eighteen years old and planning to shack up with her boyfriend. "Do you really think they're good kids?"

Carmen places a reassuring hand over Peggy's. "I'm certain they're great kids."

Peggy blinks back tears. "Thank you."

Carmen's phone rings. She pulls it from her bag. "It's Antonio," she announces and excuses herself from the table.

A man at the bar watches Carmen as she makes her way across the room and out the door. The way he looks at Carmen makes Peggy envious. Maybe the envy is the result of all the drinks she's had, or maybe it's because she realizes she will never talk to Patrick again, not in this life anyway.

"I wish someone would look at me that way again," she says.

Roni glances at the man and then at Peggy. "Someone does. Henry."

"He doesn't."

"He does," Roni insists.

There's a vent in the ceiling blowing directly down on Peggy. She wraps her arms around herself, wishing she had a sweater.

"And you look at him the same way, whether you know it or not."

"I don't!"

Roni leans across the table toward Peggy. "You act like a crazy jealous lover when you see Andrea flirting with him, but you spurn all his advances. You'd better hurry up and decide what you want before it's too late."

"I do not act like a jealous lover," Peggy protests, stumbling over the last word. She eyes Carmen, who has returned to the table and is typing something into her phone. "And he doesn't make advances toward me. He's just friendly."

"Oh no," Carmen says. "Henry is definitely sweet on you. It's why he asked you out."

Peggy buries her face in her hands. Maybe he was interested, but she blew it when she shot him down at Carmen's party. "I wish I had said yes," she admits.

"Then ask him out, or tell him you reconsidered," Roni says.

"I can't!"

"Why not?" Carmen asks.

"If he's really interested, he'll try again."

"So you're just going to wait to see if he asks you out again?" Roni asks.

Peggy addresses Carmen. "What would you do?"

"I would call him," Roni answers.

"I would talk to him," Carmen says.

"Call him," Roni says.

Peggy thinks about how she's spent the last fourteen years waiting for a sign from Patrick that never came and never will come. What if Henry never asks her out again? Chances are he won't. She needs to take charge of her life. She needs to be Peggy again, not just the twins' mom. "I'll ask when we get back."

"No time like the present," Carmen says. "Call him."

Call him? From Florida? Peggy can't do that. "I don't have his number."

Roni pulls her phone from her bag and scrolls through it. "It's the 714 number that replied to Shauna's group text from Monday."

Peggy picks up her drink and moves it in circles so that the ice clangs against the glass.

"You have nothing to lose," Roni persists.

Peggy takes a long drink before reaching into her purse for her phone. If she doesn't do it now, she may never. She looks to Carmen, who nods, and scrolls to Shauna's message. "I'm not going to call him. I'll text."

Carmen claps.

"What should I say?"

"Tell him you want to have sex with him," Roni says. Peggy glares at her.

"Invite him to dinner," Carmen suggests.

Peggy taps away at the keyboard with her index finger. Several minutes pass, and she's still typing.

"You writing a book?" Roni asks.

Peggy glances up. "Just telling him the truth." She takes a deep breath and hits Send.

A second later, Carmen's phone vibrates, and Roni's pings. They both read something on their screens. "Shit," Roni says.

"What?" Peggy asks.

Carmen fidgets with her silverware. Roni turns her phone so that Peggy can see the screen. "You texted the whole class."

No, no, no. "I couldn't have done that."

"Sorry, Peg," Carmen says.

The blower above Peggy clicks off. She feels her cheeks heat up as Roni reads the text Peggy sent to her entire boot-camp class. "Henry, sorry I wasn't ready when you asked, but I'm ready now and would like to go on a date with you. Would you like to get dinner some-time? Peggy."

"Well, it could be worse," Carmen says. "You could have told him you wanted to sleep with him."

Chapter 40

Peggy checks the time. It's 6:55 p.m. Any minute now, Henry will be pulling into her driveway to take her out on their first date. Should she close the blinds, turn off the lights, and pretend she's not home? She'll tell him she thought he meant next Friday. Of course, he wouldn't believe her. Their entire boot-camp class knows they're going out tonight. This morning, Emma, the college girl who has never said anything to Peggy other than "Great job" or "Way to go," made a point of sitting next to her during wall squats. Peggy felt the girl giving her sideways glances during the entire exercise. Finally, Emma tapped her on the shoulder. "You and Henry make an adorable couple. I can't wait to hear all about your date."

Peggy had no idea how to respond, so she said nothing. Does the girl expect her to text updates to the entire class as the evening progresses? Well, maybe she does, considering that Peggy texted everyone to ask Henry out, and he replied, in group text, *Hell Yes!*

The only one who didn't seem happy about Peggy's date was Andrea, who glared at Peggy and Henry throughout the entire class. Even Shauna offered advice about tonight. "Henry, Peggy," she called out over the microphone at the end of class. "No dessert tonight."

At the coat bins when they were leaving, Nick slapped Henry on the back. "Have fun tonight!"

Peggy's not entirely sure, but she thinks Nick may have thrust his hips as he spoke. That's what has her scared. Does Henry expect her to sleep with him? Do people do that on first dates now? She doesn't care. She's not going to. No way. Not tonight. Her eye twitches as she thinks about it.

The doorbell rings, but Peggy doesn't move from the couch. How did she get herself into this? Is there any way she can back out now?

You've got this, Peg, she imagines Carmen saying. It's what she always says to Peggy during a particularly hard exercise.

After a minute or two, there's a knock on the door. "Peggy?" Henry's voice booms.

She takes a deep breath before heading to the foyer. When she answers the door, he beams at her. His friendly face and enormous smile put her at ease. She exhales as she lets him in.

"You look grrreat," he says in that Tony the Tiger way of his. She stressed for days, thinking about what she would wear tonight, but then Carmen told her that no matter how she was dressed, Henry would think she looked beautiful. The important thing was for Peggy to wear something that gave her confidence. She chose simple black pants and a mauve blouse.

"You look nice too." His khaki trousers are wrinkle free with crisp pleats. She imagines him ironing before he came to pick her up, and the image, right or wrong, endears him to her a little more.

He reaches into the pocket of his peacoat and pulls out Godiva chocolates, the four-piece box. "I got you this, but don't tell Shauna."

She laughs and asks him if he would like a drink.

"I don't want to be late for our reservation," he says.

Peggy grabs her coat. When Henry steps forward to help her with it, she smells wintergreen and wonders if he just ate a Life Saver. The thought makes her picture Patrick when they first started dating. She remembers him reaching for a peppermint one in the center console of his car as he drove across Chicago at the end of a date, bringing her home. She wonders what he would think of her going out with Henry. Would he be mad?

She sees him shaking his head. *Why would I be mad, Pegsta? I want you to be happy.* Yes, he would want her to be happy, she realizes. *You gotta admit, though, I was way better looking than this guy. Not even close.*

"Ready?" Henry asks, pulling the door open.

She notices him limping down the walkway. "Did you hurt yourself?"

"Pulled something in class this morning. Surprised you can't smell the Bengay."

"I thought it was a new type of aftershave," she jokes, oddly relieved that he's not popping Life Savers like Patrick used to.

Henry hobbles around the car to the passenger side and holds the door open for her. Peggy ducks into the seat. As she waits for Henry to get in, she inspects the interior of the Mini. It's even smaller inside than it looks on the outside. The biggest thing in the car is the speedometer, which is in the center of the dashboard. Henry opens his door and jams himself into the driver's seat. The top of his belly rubs against the bottom of the steering wheel. He fires up the ignition without saying anything and backs out of her driveway.

"Don't you think you'd be more comfortable in a larger car?" Peggy asks.

"Definitely." He pauses, chewing the inside of his cheek. "I won it from a radio station that Missy listened to a lot at the end. She had me program the contest line into her phone, and she'd call in at every opportunity. Said we were going to win it." He yields to a car in the rotary. "A few days after she died, I got the call that we won. Figured it was a sign from her."

Peggy stares out the window at the filthy exhaust-stained snowbanks they pass. She's done hoping for signs or messages from Patrick. "I don't believe in that."

"But you just went to Florida to see that medium." He stops at a red light. Peggy doesn't want to think about that fraud Lynda Mc-

Garry. The only sound in the vehicle is the humming of the engine. The light turns green, and Henry eases the car forward.

"In person, it was easy to tell she's a fake," Peggy says, her neck stiffening as she remembers Lynda hooting like an owl.

"I don't think she can speak to the dead," Henry says. "But she does offer people comfort at a time when they need it most. There's something to be said for that."

HE TAKES HER TO A TRENDY wood grill and bar in a neighboring town. The hostess leads them through a packed dining room to a dark corner table in the back. Peggy puts on her glasses to read her menu while Henry uses the flashlight app on his phone to illuminate his. Peggy giggles at the absurdity of this.

They split a bottle of wine and linger over their meals, wood-grilled salmon for Peggy and jambalaya pasta for Henry. She tells him about her childhood in the Midwest and explains how she ended up in New England. He entertains her with impressions of their boot-camp classmates, including a dead-on imitation of Roni whining that the exercises are too hard. Peggy is too busy laughing to notice whether the food tastes good. They ignore Shauna's advice and split a crème brûlée for dessert.

"So, what made you change your mind about going out with me?" Henry asks over coffee.

"I didn't change my mind. I got over my fear."

"You were afraid of me?" Henry points to himself.

"I was afraid of being me and not being the twins' mom," she says.

Henry scratches his chin. "I've never been a father, but I would think to be a good parent, it's important to have a life separate from the kids as well, or you'll burn out." He shrugs as if he's embarrassed. "But what do I know?"

"You know a lot," Peggy says, remembering how she always tried to convince Patrick of exactly what Henry just said.

On the drive back to Peggy's, they are quieter than they have been all night. He walks her to the door, and they stand on her stoop in the biting cold. Her heart races faster than it ever does at boot camp.

"I hope we can do this again," he says. "Lots of times."

"Me too." Peggy's hand shakes as she pulls her keys from her purse.

He touches her cheek, his fingers warm on her face. They lean toward each other. He kisses her softly on the mouth. It's not a long kiss, it's not a passionate kiss, but it is a kiss that lets her know he cares about her and is willing to go as fast or as slow as she wants.

Through the window next to the door, she watches him bounding back to his car. She floats upstairs to her bedroom. By the time she climbs into bed, he has already texted, and they have made plans to see each other again the very next night.

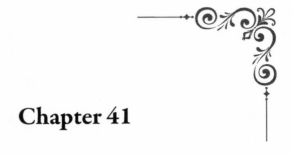

Chapter 41

Two months after their trip to Florida, Peggy, Roni, and Carmen are camped out in Peggy's living room, watching the *Messages from Beyond* episode they attended. Peggy has boycotted the show since the debacle at the studio, and seeing Lynda again stirs up mixed emotions. She wishes it weren't so, but still, more than anything, she wants to know that Patrick thinks she did a good job with the twins, and she's angry at Lynda for not delivering that message. She's also embarrassed by her faith in Lynda. The woman is an actress, not a medium who can connect with spirits. Why didn't Peggy see that before, and why does a piece of her hope that she's wrong and Lynda is for real?

"Why didn't you invite Henry tonight?" Roni asks.

Peggy has been seeing Henry two to three times a week, and they sometimes do things with Roni and Carmen. She thought about asking him to join them but decided against it because tonight is about Patrick.

"It's girls' night," Carmen answers. "Peggy can see Henry tomorrow."

In fact, Peggy is seeing him tomorrow. He's taking her to a show in Boston.

She turns her attention to the television. As the camera scrolls down to Lynda's bare feet, Peggy shifts uncomfortably in her chair, remembering the feel of Lynda's toes under her shoe. Will the fans be angry at her for stepping on Lynda's foot? What if the video goes viral? She imagines her Facebook page filled with hateful messages.

"Do you think after seeing me on the show, people will be able to find me online?" she asks.

"Are you expecting Hollywood to come calling?" Roni asks, reaching toward the container of two-bite brownies on the coffee table.

"Why did you bring those?" Peggy asks. "Shauna's weighing us on Friday."

Roni shrugs. "They're two bites. How much damage can they do?"

"Probably about three pounds' worth, considering you're going to eat all of them before the night is over," Carmen says.

Lynda McGarry has climbed down from the stage and is now talking to the boy whose father committed suicide. The three friends watch with confused expressions. "What happened to the part where she snaps at the kid and the lady at the end of the row?" Carmen asks.

"It's the magic of editing," Roni answers.

Magic indeed. Lynda appears affable and patient. If Peggy hadn't been there in person, she would never know how rude Lynda had been. "Do you think that happens every show, and they cut it out?"

"Absolutely!" Roni says.

If Peggy had known that, she would have thought differently of the medium before she went to the show. Maybe she wouldn't have become so invested in the program, so sure that it would be the thing to help her.

The program breaks for commercial. Peggy stands and paces the living room. Her segment with Lynda is up next. During the past two months, she has gone over every word Lynda said to her time and time again. While holding planks or squats during class, she has distracted herself by replaying Lynda's message in her mind. On March 10, she walked the bike path, even though it was still partially covered with snow, hoping to see an owl. She didn't. Still, she clings to the hope that tonight, she will decode a message from Patrick. She would never admit this to Roni or Carmen, but part of the reason she's watching this evening is to see if she hears anything she missed the first time.

The commercial ends. Peggy returns to her seat, ready to see herself on television.

Roni stuffs another brownie in her mouth. "I hope I don't look fat. They say TV adds five pounds."

"Ten pounds," Carmen corrects. Peggy's not surprised Carmen knows that.

Lynda's face fills the screen. "I'm making contact with a young child, a girl."

"What's going on?" Carmen asks.

Peggy scoots to the edge of her chair and squints at the screen.

"They cut us out," Roni announces.

"Why would they do that?" Carmen asks.

Peggy knows exactly why they did it. They cut her out because Lynda did not make contact with Patrick and couldn't even fake that she had. She cited a number that Peggy could make no sense of and hooted like an owl, for crying out loud. Peggy clenches her teeth as she thinks about Lynda saying, "Hoo, hoo." In all the episodes that she has watched—and until two months ago, she had watched every one—she has never seen Lynda make bird noises or animal sounds. Now she imagines that Lynda has an entire repertoire that gets gutted from the episodes.

"Maybe they're showing things out of order," Carmen suggests.

"I don't think so," Peggy says.

"They edit out the parts that reveal her for the fraud that she is," Roni says.

They watch the show to the end. Henry and the twins text during the episode, asking when Peggy will appear. At one point, she sees herself in the audience, but the part of the show when Lynda spoke to her doesn't air. "It's like the entire trip to Florida didn't happen," she tells Roni and Carmen as they leave.

"Not true," Carmen says. "You would have never asked Henry to dinner if we hadn't been in Florida."

Well, there's that.

ALONE IN THE HOUSE, Peggy sits in her dark living room in silence. *I tried, Patrick. I really tried to talk to you.*

She imagines him nodding. *I know you did, Pegsta. And if I could, I would tell you our kids are amazing.*

She pops one of the remaining two-bite brownies in her mouth, wondering if he really would say that. She decides that yes, he would because Grace and Greg are amazing. She doesn't know if they are that way because of her efforts or despite them. All she knows is that she did the best she could, and Patrick would know that too. If he had lived, they would have done their best together. Sure, they wouldn't have always been on the same page, but they would have worked out their differences. They always did because they loved each other.

Peggy glances at the darkened television, wondering why she thought she needed Lynda McGarry to connect with Patrick when she has been able to hear his voice all along.

ANOTHER SESSION OF boot camp is coming to an end. Peggy's goal at the start of the session was to get her weight below two hundred pounds. Six weeks ago, she was five and a half pounds away from that number, but today, she's nervous that she won't reach her goal. She even worries that she gained weight. Henry's to blame. Well, not really, but dating is hard on her waistline. All their dates involve food. He takes her to trendy restaurants, she cooks for him, and now that the weather is nice, he grills steaks and burgers for her. Last weekend, she spent the night at his place for the first time. On Sunday morning, he made her his famous chocolate chip pancakes. He'd been bragging about them for weeks, telling her how he couldn't wait to cook breakfast for her. They turned out to be as good as he'd promised, but thinking back now, they most certainly weren't her favorite part of the sleepover!

She does her squats, watching him climb the stairs to the platform to be weighed. As he steps on the scale, he says something to Shauna that causes the instructor to bend over in a fit of laughter. Peggy loves the way he puts everyone around him at ease, and she hopes he'll have the same effect on the twins. Last month, Carmen arranged another FaceTime conversation with Greg and Grace, and Peggy told them she was dating someone.

"I'm so excited for you," Grace squealed.

"It's not that big dude from the bike path, is it?" Greg asked.

"His name is Henry," Peggy said, wondering why Greg, and so many others, described people by their sizes.

Grace shot her brother a look, and he mumbled that he was happy for Peggy and looking forward to getting to know the guy. A second later, he told Peggy he met a kid whose dad graduated from St. Mike's the same year as Patrick and knew him well. "He's coming up next month, and we're having lunch."

Peggy felt a pang in her heart and promised herself that over the summer, she would share more memories of Patrick with the kids and call one of his friends.

"Peggy," Shauna calls across the room, pulling her from her thoughts. "You're up."

"This is going to be ugly," Peggy says to Roni and Carmen, who have transitioned from squats to lunges.

"You look fantastic," Carmen says. "You'll do great."

"Who cares?" Roni grunts as she lowers her left knee to the floor. "You're in a relationship. You're supposed to be fat and happy."

Relationship? The word makes Peggy shiver. It sounds so serious. She and Henry are dating, taking it day to day. No pressure.

"Go get 'em, Peggy," Henry says as she passes him on the gym floor.

"How did you do?" she asks.

"I'm down eight and a half pounds." He lifts his arms in a power pose.

Peggy thinks about the steaks, lobster macaroni and cheese, and ice cream sundaes he's been eating and wonders how he lost so much weight. She decides Shauna's scale must be broken and is excited to step on it. "Good for you," she says.

Shauna greets her at the top of the platform. "How do you think you did this session?"

"I worked hard in class, but we... we went out to dinner a lot." *We.* Peggy almost tripped over the word, but yes, she is part of a *we*, no matter how slow she and Henry are taking it.

"Even when you're at a restaurant, you need to make good choices," Shauna says, pointing to the scale. "You can't out-exercise a bad diet."

Peggy takes a deep breath and steps on the scale. She looks down at the flashing red number. It starts with a two. *Son of a gun!* She doesn't even bother to read the rest of it. Her classmates, who are doing walking lunges around the perimeter of the gym floor, pass by the raised platform. Carmen gives her a thumbs-up.

"Two hundred one," Shauna announces when everyone else is out of earshot.

"Completely disappointing," Peggy says.

"Roni, get that back knee down lower!" Shauna yells. Her head snaps back toward Peggy. "Disappointing?"

"I wanted that first number to change."

Shauna glances down at her clipboard. "Patience, Peggy. You're doing great. You've lost almost twenty pounds since starting boot camp."

"Whatever," Peggy says. She sounds exactly like Grace, but twenty pounds in seven months is not impressive.

Shauna points to the bottom of the stairs, where there is a rack of medicine balls. "I want you to get that red-and-black ball and carry it up and down the stairs to the second floor five times and then repeat the same amount of reps without the ball."

Peggy stares at the trainer. She'd rather do the lunges.

"Just do it." Shauna calls Emma's name, indicating her discussion with Peggy is over.

Peggy grabs the ball and heads into the other room. The ball is heavy in her arms, and after two flights, she pauses to rest. The fourth time up, she bends to catch her breath at the top before carefully descending. The fifth time up, she's panting heavily, and the ball feels like lead in her arms. At the bottom, she lets it drop to the floor and pushes it into a corner with her foot so that it's out of the way. She waits to catch her breath before starting her second set. This time, she doesn't need to stop to rest, and she isn't panting as hard.

When she finishes, she returns to the exercise room, where the class is lying on their backs with their arms at their sides, palms down on their mats, raising their outstretched legs to a forty-five degree angle and lowering them to an inch above the floor before lifting them again. On the platform, Shauna looks up from her clipboard. "So," she calls down to Peggy, "did you notice a difference?"

"Of course. It was much harder with the ball."

"That ball weighs twenty pounds," Shauna says. "Before you started coming to boot camp, you carried that weight around with you every step you took."

Thinking about that, Peggy feels better about her weight loss.

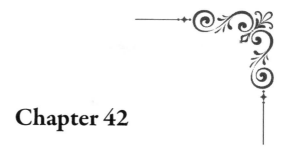

Chapter 42

After waiting in line at the pharmacy for almost fifteen minutes, it's finally Peggy's turn. She steps up to the register and gives her name, address, and birth date. The clerk searches the M bin for Peggy's blood pressure medication, reading the names on all the bags until he gets to the end. "What did you say your last name is?"

"Moriarty." Peggy spells it for him.

He rifles through the same bin again and checks a few others before returning to the counter. "I don't have a prescription for you."

Peggy sighs. Her medication is on automatic refill, and she always picks it up on the ninth of the month. "How long will it take you to fill it?" she asks.

The clerk checks the computer. The man behind Peggy mutters. After several seconds, the clerk looks away from the screen and back at Peggy. "You're out of refills."

"Call my doctor," Peggy instructs. The man behind her steps forward, bumping her arm. "Excuse me," she says.

"We did," the clerk explains. "She wants to talk to you."

"Why?" Peggy asks.

The clerk shrugs. The man behind Peggy mumbles, "Are you kidding me?"

It's the same thing Peggy's thinking—though, honestly, she knows exactly why Dr. Richardson wants to talk to her. It's because Peggy canceled her last appointment.

She walks out of the store, pulling up her jeans, which keep slipping below her waist. She dreads speaking to Dr. Richardson, who she is sure will make her come in for an exam and insult her again about being overweight. She sits in her SUV, digs up the doctor's number in her contacts, and calls. When the receptionist answers, Peggy explains that she needs a refill. After she gives her information, she can hear the receptionist typing.

"Oh, dear," the receptionist says. "There's a note saying not to call in a refill until after the doctor speaks to you."

Son of a gun, Peggy thinks. "I'm at the drugstore now, and I'm out of pills."

Peggy is put on hold so that the receptionist can check with Dr. Richardson. The receptionist returns to the phone several minutes later. "She'll call you back in ten minutes."

As Peggy waits for the doctor to return her call, she sees someone who looks like Julian cutting across the parking lot. She'd swear it's him, except that he has a buzz cut. She lowers her window and calls his name.

"Mrs. M," he shouts, jogging over to her car.

"What happened?" Peggy asks, staring at his hair.

He runs his palm over his scalp. "Supporting a guy at school who's going through chemo."

"I'm sorry for your friend," Peggy says, impressed that he would sacrifice his beloved locks to support a classmate. "You look handsome with it short like that." And he really does.

"Are you flirting with me, Mrs. M? Am I going to have to tell Grace?"

Peggy laughs. "Have you spoken to her recently?"

"An hour ago. I guess you know she's not transferring."

Peggy did know that. Grace called her earlier in the week to say now that she is skiing so much, she is enjoying Vermont a lot more. "Well, that's probably for the best."

Julian shrugs. "I guess."

Peggy's phone rings. She looks down at it and sees Dr. Richardson's name. "Julian, if you and Grace are meant to be, it will work out in the end."

He nods. "I miss her, you know."

"Me too," Peggy says before pressing the answer button on her phone.

"See you soon," Julian says, reaching through the open window to squeeze her shoulder before walking toward the store.

"Mrs. Moriarty," the doctor begins.

Peggy's grip tightens on the phone. "Peggy," she corrects.

"You were supposed to come in over a year ago to have your blood pressure checked. We agreed we'd monitor it carefully before deciding if we need to adjust your medication."

"I'm out of pills," Peggy says, watching as two cars in the rotary nearly miss colliding. *Honest to God, who thought replacing the simple intersection with this collision circle was a good idea?*

"It would be irresponsible of me to prescribe more medicine without seeing you first. Do I have to remind you that blood pressure is a silent killer?"

"That's why I want you to call in a prescription—so it won't kill me," Peggy says.

"I'll call in seven days' worth, Mrs. Moriarty. Within those seven days, I expect to see you here in my office." She transfers Peggy back to the receptionist to make an appointment.

SITTING IN THE DOCTOR'S waiting room, Peggy flips through the periodicals on the table next to her. *Health and Nutrition, Clean Eating, Prevention, Vegetarian Times,* and *Your Health Now* are the only choices. *For crying out loud, what about* People *or* Us? Even *Newsweek* or *Time* would be acceptable. Rather than read these preachy magazines that will give her hundreds of reasons to worry, she takes out her phone and scrolls through Instagram, stopping on a picture of Carmen and Julian with his new short hair. She has to admit, she misjudged him. She was sure he would break Grace's heart, but it's obvious to Peggy now that he really cares for her daughter and that he's a good kid with strong family values and parents who are bringing him up right. *Grace could do a lot worse.*

Peggy hears her name called and stands. A nurse introduces herself as Lisa and leads Peggy through a door and down a long hallway to the last room on the left, where a neatly folded hospital gown lies on the exam table.

"Everything off but your underwear," Lisa says, pointing to the gown. "Opening in the front."

"She's just checking my blood pressure. I don't need to change," Peggy explains, dropping her purse on the counter next to the exam table.

Lisa shrugs. "Let me get your weight, then."

Peggy looks at the scale as if it might attack her. "I'm only here for my blood pressure," she repeats.

"I have to weigh you," Lisa insists.

Peggy folds her arms across her chest. "No, you don't." She's not going to have that young, fit doctor read a number on the chart and then look at her as if she were a child molester and not an overweight woman. She doesn't want to go through that again. She just wants her meds.

"I really need to weigh you," Lisa says.

"No, you don't." Peggy sits in one of the two chairs.

Lisa scribbles something on Peggy's chart. "The doctor will be right in to see you." She slams the door on her way out.

While Peggy waits for Dr. Richardson, she reads the posters on the walls, one about a flu shot, another about the importance of colonoscopies, and another about skin cancer with pictures of moles.

The posters are new, and she wonders if Dr. Richardson is trying to scare her patients to death. When the practice belonged to Dr. Sheridan, there were beautiful watercolor paintings that helped Peggy relax. She especially loved one of the sun setting over the ocean with brilliant shades of red and orange.

The patient in the next room sneezes three times. "God bless you," Peggy hollers. Footsteps in the hallway stop outside Peggy's room, and there's a metallic rattling. A few seconds later, she hears a heavy sigh, followed by a knock on the door. She wants to say, "Go away!" Instead, she says nothing. Dr. Richardson enters anyway.

"Mrs. Moriarty," the doctor says. Her long brown hair is pulled back in a tight ponytail, making her look as young as Grace and Greg. She taps Peggy's chart with her index finger. "You refused to be weighed." She looks over her glasses at Peggy.

"I need my prescription refilled," Peggy says. "That's why I'm here. Not to be weighed."

The doctor takes a deep breath in and slowly exhales. She's standing so close that Peggy can smell the coffee on her breath. "Please, take off your shoes and step on the scale."

The two women stare at each other for several seconds without speaking. "Weight impacts blood pressure," the doctor finally says.

"Two hundred one," Peggy says. "My trainer weighed me last week."

"You're working with a trainer?" The tone of Dr. Richardson's voice suggests Peggy just told her Jillian Michaels stops by her house every day for a morning workout and healthy breakfast.

"Yes. I take a boot-camp class at my gym." Peggy's phone whistles with a text message. She could have sworn she muted it.

"I'd like to weigh you myself."

Peggy's phone whistles again. She looks toward her purse, debating whether she should reach inside it and silence the device.

"Please, Mrs. Moriarty, I have other patients."

Peggy realizes Dr. Richardson won't let this go. *What the heck?* She already told her how much she weighs. She stands, steps out of her shoes and onto the scale, expecting alarms to sound or an electronic voice to scream a warning: "Fat person on the scale! Fat person on the scale!"

Instead, her phone whistles again. Who is texting her?

"It's 199.5," the doctor says.

Grinning, Peggy looks down at the number and pumps her fist. She knew all along that Shauna's scale was wrong. She weighs less than two hundred pounds. *Woo-hoo!*

"How many days a week do you work out?"

"Three," Peggy answers, sliding her shoes on.

"Good for you, Mrs. Moriarty," Dr. Richardson says. "Losing fifteen pounds is hard to do." Peggy notices that the young doctor does indeed know how to smile.

"It's a twenty-pound weight loss," Peggy boasts. "I was two hundred nineteen when I started boot camp."

"Even better," the doctor says. "Keep doing what you're doing."

"I'm just getting started." Peggy smiles because she means it. With every pound she loses, she feels better about herself. Exercise has changed more than her body—it has also changed her attitude, making her happier. She has no intention of stopping anytime soon.

The doctor leads her to the exam table. As Peggy rolls up her sleeve so that the doctor can take her blood pressure, there's a knock on the door. A nurse enters. "You're needed down the hall."

"I'll be right back," the doctor says.

While Peggy is waiting, her phone whistles again. Leaning to her left, she reaches into her purse and pulls it out. There are six texts from Greg. She reads the first. *Had lunch with Austin and his dad today, the guy who knew Dad. He brought a photo album with him.*

The next five messages are pictures of Patrick. He's in his hockey uniform in the first. In the second, he's throwing a snowball. Peggy looks at the third. Patrick's standing in front of a doorway in a dorm, a beer in his hand and his eyes glassy. As she scrolls to the next picture, something about the third catches her eye, so she goes back to it. The door he's standing in front of has a number, 310. A chill runs down Peggy's spine as she remembers Lynda McGarry asking if that number meant anything to her. She didn't put it together at the time, but Greg lives in room 310 in Joyce Hall, the same dorm room that Patrick lived in when he was a freshman at St. Michael's. *Son of a gun!*

Using her thumb and index finger, Peggy makes the picture bigger. There's a poster on the door. She expands the photo as big as it can possibly go and sees that the poster has an image of four men napping with a British flag draped over them. In big letters above the sleeping men are the words, "THE WHO," and in smaller letters, it says, "starring in." She hears Lynda McGarry hooting like an owl. Her heart pounds, and her hands sweat.

Below the image, in a cursive script, there's more writing: "The Kids Are Alright." Peggy's hand shakes so much that the phone slips out and crashes to the floor.

The door to the exam room swings open. Dr. Richardson steps inside and comes to an abrupt stop. "Are you okay, Mrs. Moriarty? You look like you've seen a ghost."

Peggy jumps off the table to retrieve her phone. "I didn't see one, but I heard from one."

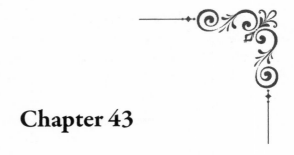

Chapter 43

As Peggy and Roni bite into their burgers, Carmen and Grace stare at them across the picnic table. "What do you think?" Grace asks.

Peggy notices that her daughter's cheek twitches as she asks the question, which is a sure sign that Grace is trying not to laugh. Peggy wonders what's so hilarious about a hamburger. Come to think of it though, the burger does taste funny. It's spicy, which is probably because Henry dressed it with chipotle mayonnaise when he made it. *But why is it mushy? Is it undercooked?*

Maybe Peggy should have asked Greg to do the grilling instead of Henry. Then again, Henry brought his own grill tools with him, so how could she not have let him cook? She glances over at him and watches him turn the meat with his heavy-duty stainless-steel spatula, which he has named Flip. Antonio and Tom stand in a cloud of smoke beside him, laughing at something he says.

"Well?" Grace persists.

"It's the best burger I ever tasted," Roni says.

Grace elbows Carmen, who giggles. Peggy wonders what the two of them are up to. "What do you think, Peg?" Carmen asks.

Grace stares at her mother while sipping from a red plastic cup, which Peggy knows is filled with the sangria Antonio made, even if Grace thinks she doesn't know.

"It's good," Peggy says, swatting at a mosquito that is circling her head.

Grace can no longer control herself. Her drink comes out her nose as she laughs.

"Should I tell them, or should you?" Carmen asks.

"You do the honors," Grace instructs.

"It's a black-bean burger."

Roni spits her partially chewed food into her napkin. "Gross!" she yells.

Peggy agrees. She knew there was something weird about it. She can't believe they tricked her into trying it. Well, she's not going to have another bite. That's for sure. She drops the half-eaten sandwich onto her paper plate.

"Come on," Carmen says. "You both just said you liked it."

"That's before we knew it was made out of beans," Roni protests.

"So because it's healthy, you don't like it?" Grace asks.

Roni looks over her shoulder and shouts toward the men. "Can someone over there bring me a real hamburger?"

Peggy stands. "I'll get it." On her way to the grill, she drops what's left of her black-bean patty into the trash. Sure, she's made many healthy dietary changes over the last ten months, but she's not messing with her burger. No sirree. That's un-American.

As she cuts across the deck, Henry beams at her. They've been dating for almost six months now, and he still looks at her with the same smitten expression he did when they were getting to know each other in the early days of boot camp. She doesn't think she will ever grow tired of it.

"The veggie burgers were Carmen's and Grace's idea. I had nothing to do with them." He uses the back of his hand to wipe away the sweat dripping down his forehead.

Peggy laughs. "I didn't think you did."

He transfers chicken, steak tips, and hamburgers from the barbecue to a plate and hands it to Peggy. As she carries it back to the table, Wally charges up the steps of the porch with Greg, Julian, and

Sophia trailing behind him. Sophia is riding on Julian's shoulders, holding the dog's unclipped leash. Peggy watched Greg clip it onto Wally's collar before they left for their walk, and she imagines the dog whimpering until someone removed it. Julian, she would guess, is the culprit because he, like Henry, is softhearted.

Peggy's not sure how it happened, but she's become Wally's regular dog walker. She takes him on long strolls down the bike path on days when Henry is at work. Never once has she been tempted to take off his leash. She thinks the dog respects her for this.

Barking, Wally bounds toward the men. Henry takes a steak tip off the grill and tosses it to him. The dog snatches it with his mouth before it hits the ground. Henry rewards him with more. It's no wonder that Wally is getting fat. Maybe Peggy will ask Shauna to have a "bring your dog to boot camp" day. She imagines Wally scampering around the gym with a dumbbell in his mouth. He'd probably outperform them all.

Sophia approaches Peggy and raises her arms. Peggy bends down and scoops her up. Even though Rosalita is back in town, Peggy insists on continuing to take care of Sophia two days a week. She has grown quite attached to the little girl and looks forward to the time they spend together.

Henry finishes cooking, and everyone sits down at the table. By the time they all are done eating, the sun is setting, taking daylight with it, so Peggy steps inside to turn on the outside lights. On her way back to the deck, she stands by the door to take in the scene in her backyard. Henry, Tom, and Antonio are sitting with Roni and Carmen, engaged in a lively discussion. Wally is lying under the table, chewing on a napkin he no doubt stole from someone's lap, and Grace, Julian, Sophia, and Greg are laughing, playing cornhole on the lawn below the deck. A warmth spreads across Peggy's chest that has nothing to do with the evening's heat. As the sun sinks below the horizon, the sky turns bright pink, and maybe Peggy's imagining it, but in the distance, an owl hoots.

You done good, Pegsta, she hears Patrick say.

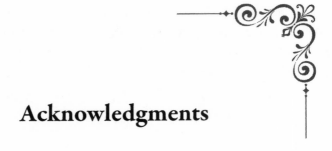

Acknowledgments

A heartfelt thank you to everyone who reads my novels, and especially to those who take the time to write reviews. Your support means everything to me.

When I was coming up with story ideas for this book, my mind kept circling back to something I loved doing: going to boot camp. The only idea I had for the novel was a character who attends an exercise class at her local gym. Somehow the story developed from there. So, thank you to my 5:45 a.m. friends for all the laughs and good times that inspired this novel.

My story picked up steam while I attended Novel in Progress workshops at Grub Street led by Steven Beeber. I completed it in a workshop taught by Annie Hartnett. I'd still be struggling with plot issues without Annie's and Steven's wisdom and guidance. Thank you also to the writers in these and my other Grub Street workshops for their insightful feedback and enthusiasm for this story.

As always, my writing group at the Hudson Library was with me from the first draft to the last. Thanks for all your comments and encouragement and for always pushing me to be my best.

Thanks, Dad, for suggesting more Henry. Mom, sorry Peggy isn't Italian, but she and her mom do make a mean lasagna, and that was for you. Sue, no, Peggy is not even loosely based on you.

Lauren Hughes, editor extraordinaire, the book is stronger today because of your feedback. Thank you for the kind and encouraging way you critiqued.

Thank you, Susan Timmerman and Julie Peterson, who cheerfully listen to me obsess about my characters, plot, and all things publishing and always offer sound advice.

Jay Clifton, Thank you for my website, but more importantly, thank you for being the incredible person you are and pushing me out of my comfort zone.

Lynn McNamee, thank you so much for taking a chance on this novel. Being a part of Red Adept has been a wonderful experience. Jessica Anderegg and Sarah Carleton, I learned so much from your edit/redlines, and my book is much better because of them.

Love you, Steve. Thanks for ALL you do that gives me time to write and for your understanding when I'm locked away in my office. There will be a quiz on this book, so read up. ☺

Thanks to everyone at Liza Royce Agency who worked on this story and helped to find it a home. Liza, I could write an entire novel, a series even, filled with all the reasons I'm grateful to and admire you. I can't imagine that there is another agent who has as much enthusiasm, compassion, determination, and energy. I told you before, I love the books I've written, but the thing I'm happiest I wrote is my query to you.

About the Author

Diane Barnes has been a marketing and corporate communication writer in the health care industry for over a decade. When she's not writing, she's at the gym, running or playing tennis, trying to burn off the ridiculous amounts of chocolate and ice cream she eats.

She and her husband, Steven, live in Massachusetts but dream of moving to Turks and Caicos, at least for the winter months. She hopes you enjoy reading her books as much as she enjoyed writing them.

Read more at https://www.dianembarnes.com/.

About the Publisher

Dear Reader,

We hope you enjoyed this book. Please consider leaving a review on your favorite book site.

Visit https://RedAdeptPublishing.com to see our entire catalogue.

Don't forget to subscribe to our monthly newsletter to be notified of future releases and special sales.

Made in the USA
Middletown, DE
28 March 2020